Josiah Falls

ISBN: 978-1-939091-03-1 (pbk)
ISBN: 978-1-939091-04-8 (ebook)

www.moonlight-literature.com

For my wife

Josiah Falls

Michael Taylor

Prologue

When I look back on my younger days, most of those first years are no more than bits and glimpses of places and faces that have long since lost the names that went with them, and I suppose that is true of most people, but sometimes there is a moment in life that sticks with you forever. I don't think about that particular moment all of the time; sometimes years pass, and I wonder if it's still there in the back of my mind at all. Then I think about it, and it all comes back to me just like it was never gone…almost like I never even left Josiah Falls. Long ago people and places come back to life, and I am a boy again.

For me, that frozen moment in time was the spring and summer of 1950. It wasn't the heat or the humidity that makes me remember so many things, because the steamy weather always came early to little Josiah Falls, Mississippi. Partly, I think it was the new friend that I made that spring, but mostly I remember it for all the things that happened in that small space of time that changed so many lives forever. I knew my little piece of the story at the time, and over the next many years I found out even more about what happened from the people involved. Now, more than sixty years later, I think I know just about everything that did happen and why it happened just the way it did.

Folklore of the region attributes the name of Josiah Falls to a half French and half English fur trapper by the name of Josiah LeBoef. Legend says that Josiah was traveling to New Orleans in 1805 when he lost his way in the dark and wandered onto a finger of the Mississippi River in his canoe. There was no moon that night, and in the darkness he went over the falls. Josiah survived his adventure, eventually traveling on to New Orleans as he planned, but the local Indians were so amused that they called the place Josiah's Falls from that time on. The name stuck, but eventually it became known simply as Josiah Falls.

When asked where Josiah Falls was located, most folks would have said that it was just off US 61, the old Blues

Josiah Falls

Highway, about a stone's throw from the Mississippi River, but it was a little farther than that. In my day, I was a pretty good ballplayer with a good arm, but I couldn't have hit the Mississippi from there; it was a full day's walk to the Mississippi if it was a mile. Today, Josiah Falls is nothing more than a little speck of a town with a history that few people recall anymore. The new interstate highway system drew most of the traffic away from the US highways and county roads, and eventually the biggest share of the people was drawn away as well. The falls are still there, of course...not as tall or majestic as I recall as a boy, and the drop that seemed like an eternity is really no more than twenty feet and possibly not even that; the woods that I used to roam with my friend, Willie Horton, have been logged almost completely since then, but now and again I still traveled there in my mind...just like it was that summer and nothing has changed at all. I have just one more visit to make there, but to see it the way it was, all I have to do is close my eyes and remember.

Josiah Falls

Chapter One

"Hey, you boys!" called a stern voice that I knew very well. I recognized the deep booming voice of Claxton Delaney right away. "You stop that fightin' right now." The new boy in town punched me in the right arm again. "I mean...like RIGHT NOW!" He was serious, and I knew it even if the other boy didn't.

"We ain't really fightin', mister," said the new boy. He was a tall boy with sandy hair and freckles wearing a white T-shirt and cutoff blue jean shorts. "He won't even hit back...acts like he ain't got no backbone a'tall."

"Well," Claxton said as he took off his wire-rimmed glasses and cleaned them with a handkerchief from his white dress shirt pocket. "Son, I happen to know that this boy's daddy don't hold with fightin'...if he was to fight, his daddy would whup him good." I noticed Minister Washburne standing nearby listening. I thought he might come over and give us a talking to as well, but he was hanging back and letting Claxton handle it. He was different that way from the ministers who had been there before him, and I think people respected that. I know I did.

"That right? Your daddy would whup you?" said the new boy scratching his head as he looked at me curiously.

"I reckon it is," I said as I rubbed my sore arm. "He could hit a might harder than you do. Can't say I like either one very much."

"Shux," said the new boy. "I can't rightly fight with you if'n you can't fight back...just ain't right." He dropped his fist and opened his hand.

"How 'bout you boys find something else to do," suggested Claxton with a smile. "What's your name, son?"

"Willie," said the boy. "Willie Horton. We just moved here from Natchez last week. Left as soon as school was out there."

"Didn't think I'd seen you before," said Claxton with a broadening smile that almost always meant something more was coming. "Do you play ball, Willie?"

"Sure I do," said Willie. "But I ain't got no glove. Didn't think I'd need it here in this little burg, so I left it with my friend, Bobby, back in Natchez."

"Just so happens Nathan's baseball team is a boy short this year," Claxton smiled. "Think you could handle second base?"

"Reckon I could if I had a glove," said Willie with a shrug of his shoulders.

"Nathan," said Claxton, "why don't you go by your house and have Bertie scare up that old mitt of yours. Then you boys go off and have a catch…maybe run by the other boys and get up a game."

"Yes, sir," I said. "Beats fightin' anyway. Come on Willie." We hadn't yet walked away when Minister Washburne came over to Claxton.

"So, his daddy would whup him a good one, eh?" said Washburne with a grin. He was a young man, just thirty years old, but he looked older than his years. It was a hot enough day, but he was dressed in black and still wearing his little white collar. He even wore it when he umpired one of our baseball games the summer before. He claimed that it kept anyone from arguing with him.

"That's what I've always told him," said Claxton with only a trace of a smile. "Spare the rod and spoil the boy. Says so in the Good Book." I had heard that one a few times.

"It does at that," said Washburne. "But, I don't think the rod's been worn out on that boy."

"'Bout a year ago," Claxton began with a glance at me, "he was one for trouble all the time. Came home from school with a note 'bout once a week. Had to do something…looks like it took just one promise. Leastwise he believes his daddy would." It was funny sometimes how grownups would talk about you like you weren't even there. I guess they figured that kids didn't pay any attention to them.

"Belief can be a powerful thing," said Washburne.

"It can. It can move mountains sometimes," Claxton gave him a clap on the shoulder. At six feet five, he towered over the five foot six Washburne by almost a foot. "So, you keepin' a close eye on the church these days?"

"Nothing special," said Washburne with a glance down the street. "Think I need to?"

"Couldn't hurt," said Claxton. "Two churches burned in the last week."

"I guess I don't figure it's coming this way," said Washburne. "Seems like they were singled out if you know what I mean." Everyone did know even though he didn't say it right out.

"I do," said Claxton, and he also knew. The two churches were black churches. There had been some racial tensions around the region lately, though nothing much in town, but some tempers had flared and there had been some words spoken in the heat of the moment that Claxton imagined some people would like to have had back, but the two churches had been burned to the ground, and people were nervous. That kind of trouble had a tendency to spread, and once it started it was hard to stop.

"Well, maybe nothing more will come of it," said Washburne. "I'll pray on that for sure."

"Amen to that," Claxton nodded. "On a more personal note…speakin' as your doctor…you and the missus doin' better these days?" The fact that the Washburnes were hoping to start a family was not exactly the town secret, but in three years there had been no success, and Washburne had approached Claxton more or less discreetly to inquire about things he might try.

"Maybe," said Washburne with a frown. "I'm takin' those supplements regular. I'm just not sure they're doing much, but I'm trying to be hopeful."

"Takes time to build up," said Claxton encouragingly. "From what I read, just give it some time to get in your system. Just have a little faith." Washburne smiled at that last, and Claxton joined him.

"And a pound of patience to go with that ounce of faith," Washburne sighed. "Might make for a good sermon this Sunday. I'm learnin' something about that these days…might be good for the missus, too. Can't overestimate the virtue of patience."

"Good things do sometimes come to those who wait," said Claxton still trying to be encouraging.

"I think sometimes God just needs to try our faith a bit," said Washburne. "It keeps us humble."

"Anytime you need to talk 'bout it," said Claxton with a look of concern. There was something more he would have said if there hadn't been anyone else around, so maybe he hadn't forgotten that Willie and I were still close by after all. Claxton had known Addie Washburne since she was a child, and he always said that she could be hell to live with when she didn't get her way. She wanted a baby in the worst way, and not a lot of people were unaware of that fact.

"I appreciate that," said Washburne. He checked his watch. "Guess I'm due at the church. Addie's coming by with Odessa wanting to talk about something. Guess I'll find out soon enough what that's all about."

"Good luck with that," said Claxton. Washburne sighed and went on his way. It was easy to tell that Claxton didn't envy him, and neither did anybody else. Addie and Odessa had been closer than sisters for just about their whole lives. Either one could be hard to deal with; together, they were just about more than one man wanted to handle at one time and would try the patience of a saint. Evan Washburne was just a minister. Claxton figured that he was probably overmatched, and so did I. He had been sorely tempted to tell him that he was probably going to get some very good news from his wife for a change. Just a day ago, he had confirmed that Addie was finally pregnant, but she had made him promise that he would let her tell Evan in her own good time. I had heard about it from Bertie before Claxton had told her too keep it quiet. He said that Addie had seemed happy, surprised, and upset all at the same time, a fairly common reaction from the dozen or more women he had given the news to over the years. He thought Evan should know, but he had promised to keep quiet in the end, and he told me to do the same. Claxton had long since stopped trying to figure out the female of the species and had written it off as a lost cause for better men than he to pursue. We watched Minister Washburne heading for the steps of the Baptist Church of God; Claxton, like just about everone in town, thought Evan was a good man at heart, and we all wished him the best. Claxton made a motion for us to go on and find something to do, and he turned and headed towards his small office across the street.

Aside from his quiet legal practice, Claxton also filled in as best he could as the town doctor. Claxton had been reluctant to take on the job, but the two doctors who periodically traveled into town each month were getting up in the years, and they had finally convinced him to do it. Claxton didn't talk much about his time in the army, but the few times he did I had been listening. He had spent three years working in field hospitals in Italy, France, and Germany during World War II. At first he had been working as an orderly and a lot of times assisting the surgeons, but one day the casualties had come in too quickly for the doctors to treat and he had been called in to help the surgeons by performing surgery on his own after handling the triage outside almost entirely by himself. It turned out that he had a knack for the work. Before the day was out, he had operated on a dozen men while the two surgeons on either side coached him on what to do. Two men died on his table that day, but ten more lived that would have died while waiting for one of the other doctors to work on them. Over the course of the next eighteen months, he became a full-time surgeon and also began learning a lot about general medicine since the doctors treated many of the local people in the region as well. As a lawyer, he had developed a capacity for reading huge amounts of information and taking it all in, and that helped him enormously when he started to pour over all the medical journals and texts that the other doctors and surgeons supplied him. The colonel in charge of the mobile field hospital supporting the Third Army was not disturbed by the fact that he was practicing medicine without a license, but the general in command of all the medical facilities in Europe was not so pleased to find out that an orderly with the rank of sergeant had performed more than two thousand surgical procedures without one and not so much as a single day of medical school. That minor oversight was corrected in May of 1945 when he was granted a degree in medicine by the United States Army and promoted to the permanent rank of Captain. His discharge came through five months later and he returned to civilian life in Jackson, Mississippi.

But, the transition back to his legal practice was not easy. He told me once that he was a different man after the war...quieter and more thoughtful about things. Claxton had gone off to the war when I was little, so I really didn't remember much of him from before. I was five when he got back home, and after a few months of half-hearted effort in his law practice, Claxton decided that he wanted to move back to his hometown of Josiah Falls and settle down in what he called 'a smaller place with smaller worries'. But, that hadn't set well with my mother, Anita. She liked life in the city and had no taste for rural country life and didn't care much who heard about it. I heard them arguing a lot about it, but the jist of it was that after his long absence she was no longer the wife he knew any more than he was the husband she knew. She had gotten used to making her own decisions and her own way in life. It was never spoken aloud, but Claxton thought that she had also enjoyed a few other things while he had been gone. She finally agreed to the move, but after a few weeks in Josiah Falls, she packed her bags and left for New Orleans to start over, leaving us behind and very little else. Claxton received the divorce papers a few months later. He signed and returned them the same afternoon. At first, she wrote letters every few months addressed to me, but after the first year, those started to come just on my birthday and at Christmas. This past year, even those letters had stopped coming. If Claxton even noticed it, he didn't say anything about it at the time, and we never talked about it except one time later. Claxton had asked me if I wanted to see my mother sometime. If I did, he would try to arrange it. I told him that it really didn't matter to me either way, and Claxton had dropped it there. He supposed that I had a sore spot against her for leaving. She walked out on us without so much as a goodbye and didn't seem to miss us one bit. Claxton said at the time that he figured that a certain amount of resentment was natural, so if I felt that way he understood. I heard him more than once wonder if staying in Jackson might have made things turn out differently, but when he considered that he always came back to the same conclusion. They were simply different people after the war. They had each moved on, and then there was no going back to what they had been before. I was all right with that.

Chapter Two

"Wanna go to the falls?" I asked Willie while we were playing catch. He was wiping the sweat off his forehead. It was only late May, but it already felt like the middle of summer.

"I don't know," Willie shook his head slowly. "Is it far? I'd have to let my ma know."

"It ain't far," I lied. It was the better part of three miles walk, but it was through the woods and it was cooler there than anywhere else around. "We can swim when we get there."

"Sure would like that," Willie said thoughtfully. "Think we would be back by supper? My ma hates it when I come in late for it." I looked up at the sun. I guessed that it was after one o'clock already. It would be two by the time we got there. I did the math in my head and figured that we might have two hours to spend there.

"Sure," I said with a big smile. I knew we *could* make it there and back, but I also knew from my many other trips there that it wasn't likely. It would be fun and cool, and the two hours would stretch into three maybe even four. But I wanted to go, and I skipped telling my new friend about that almost certain probability and hoped he wouldn't get into too much trouble for being late getting home.

We walked from the makeshift baseball field on the edge of town to the nearby woods that seemed to start right where the field ended. I had walked through these woods hundreds of times over the last few summers and figured that I knew them pretty well. There were four good trails that were worn through them, and another couple that were harder to travel except early in the spring and late in the fall. Only two of the trails led directly to the falls, and I thought today we needed to take the quickest one, which by chance was also my favorite.

"This one here is the straightest one to the falls," I explained as we took a handful of steps into the trees. "Up yonder a piece is another one that branches off to the right and comes down under the falls."

"How 'bout that one over there?" Willie asked as we walked on a bit further. He had a good eye. I had been in the woods fifty times before I'd seen that one myself.

"Winds around mostly," I answered. "But it runs into two more trails that will take you all the way to the Mississippi once you cross the shallows. I'd have to ask Claxton, my daddy, about going that far." My daddy was an odd guy sometimes. In public, I either called him daddy or sir, but when it was just the two of us, or maybe just Bertie with us, it was always 'Claxton' like we were no more than fishing buddies or something. When I asked him about it, he just said that he wanted us to be friends when I grew up. There was something dark in his eyes when he said that, and I wondered if he was really thinking about something else. Claxton did that sometimes. He would be talking to you, but somehow you knew that there was another voice going on inside his head having a talk with him that you couldn't hear. Then he'd smile and come back from where he'd been. There were times I thought that voice was wearing on him, but he never admitted it if it did.

About the river…I already knew the answer I'd get to that. It was a good day's walk to the Mississippi for a grown man in a hurry. We would have to camp to make that trip and would be gone for a few days at least. Claxton had promised to take me this summer sometime, and I was looking forward to that, so I wasn't about to do anything that would make him change his mind.

"Thought you said it wasn't far," said Willie after about forty-five minutes.

"It ain't," I smiled back, "just a little farther up here. You just ain't got your hikin' legs yet. You'll be glad you come along when you see it." And, I was sure about that. Josiah Falls didn't have a lot to see, but the falls near the edge of the woods were really something. About ten minutes later, I stopped.

"Listen," I told him. "You hear it?" I listened myself and heard that dull roar.

"That it?" he asked with a little excitement. I nodded. Willie tried to look through the trees, but they were way to thick already at this time of year to see more than a little stretch. That suited me just fine for what I had in mind.

"We're almost there," I told him. I could see him looking around and taking in the landmarks. The trail had been going slightly uphill for the last half an hour, and there were some large boulders beginning to take the place of the now thinning trees. We walked up the last stretch of the trail and it opened up into a clearing beside a gentle running stream.

"Is that all?" said Willie in clear disappointment with a hand on one hip. He looked out at the shallow stream. There was a little dip where the water fell down over some small stones and splashed before continuing on. "Shux...I could *wade* through that."

"This is just the top," I laughed. Claxton had brought me up here this way the first time I had been here, and I had thought the very same thing. Claxton said that it was just his 'flair for the dramatic'. I hadn't had a clue what he had meant back then, but I did now. "Let's go on in." Willie started to take his shoes off.

"Best leave 'em on," I told him. "Lot of rocks...'sides they'll dry on the way back." I stepped out into the sun-warmed water, but it still felt cool in the midst of the scorching hot day. "Come on." Willie followed me in after a moment's thought. We waded out towards the middle and carefully climbed down the short three-foot drop into the lower part of the stream. There had been a lot of rain up north lately, so the water was deeper and faster than usual at this time of year, and I knew that would make this a lot more fun. I began wading downstream and pretty soon the water was just past waist deep on me. Willie was a few inches taller, so it had yet to reach his belt buckle.

"Willie, can you swim?" I asked suddenly as it occurred to me that could be a very important thing to know in the next few minutes. I hadn't thought to ask before. I didn't know *anyone* that couldn't swim and just figured that everyone around the Mississippi could.

"A little, I reckon," said Willie. "Aw...but this ain't nothing to be scared of." Willie plunged on ahead into the stream ahead of me and the water immediately began to deepen. "Hey! The bottom just up an' disappeared!" Willie bobbed up and down twice and came up with a sputter as the current began to take him. I dived into the water to try and catch up. Swimming hard I caught up to him a minute later and grabbed onto his shoulder. He was staying on top of the water okay, but he was going to need to change position shortly.

"Get your legs up in front of you," I said as I demonstrated, "kind of float on your back a little." With an effort, Willie managed to get his lower body in front of him and lay up on the now swiftly flowing water.

"What's that?" he asked over the growing roar of water ahead.

"Josiah Falls," I laughed. "It's right up there a little bit." We sailed on down the stream even faster, and I knew the trees in the distance would suddenly appear up out of the water just like you were going to flow right into them.

"Holy..." Willie screamed. His eyes were wide with fright, and he knew for certain that his new friend was totally insane. We hit the top of the falls a few seconds later and floated off into the empty, mist-filled air.

"Hold your breath!" I screamed back. We plunged downward and hit feet first going deep under the surface of the water. I still had a grip on Willie's shirt just in case he needed help, but when we hit bottom, he pushed up with both legs just fine, and I could see right then that he was going to be okay. I pulled with both hands and kicked. That was always the long part...the way back up. I broke the surface and took in a breath of air as I paddled around and looked for Willie. He came up a few feet away, took a choking breath, and blinked in amazement.

"You''re plum crazy, Nathan!" he yelled. At first I thought he was mad. "Can we do that again?" There was a huge grin on his face.

"Sure!" I yelled back. "Come on, we can get out over there." I pointed to the near left bank. We swam over to the side, gradually got into shallower water where we could stand up, and waded the last few feet up onto the black mud bank.

"I thought we were gonna die!" he laughed as we climbed up to the grass.

"I was screaming like a little girl the first time Claxton took me over the falls," I said. I recalled how he had held onto me only at the last second, pretending that he had no idea what was coming up ahead. Claxton had braved the falls like that as a kid a thousand times, but he had not given away a thing on his face to tell me that. We climbed up the last of the bank and managed to get back to more or less level ground.

"Shorter if we go up by those rocks over there," I said as I pointed to the outcropping of stones by the side of the falls. There was a trail up above the rocks that had seen a lot of use over the years, and it was a fairly easy climb at a sloping angle leading around the falls. We reached the rocks and started to climb up. I always liked the way the mist from the falls covered the rocks. If you just came down here and sat on the rocks, you would be soaking wet in a few minutes just like you were walking in a rainstorm. In all, the drop off the falls was probably no more than fifteen to twenty feet, but it always seemed like it was a hundred. As we were reaching the top of the trail, Willie was still going on about the splashdown in the water, but I heard something else off in the trees. I grabbed his arm to get his attention.

"Sounds like somebody's out here," I whispered. I wasn't really afraid of getting into trouble for being out here, but you never could tell with grownups. I didn't think Claxton would light into me for being out here without telling him, but I stopped and tried to listen just the same in case it was somebody that might try to make trouble for us. There was one voice and then another joined in. I couldn't make out what they were saying, but the voices were raised, and there was no mistaking that this had the makings of an angry gettogether. The echoes made it impossible to tell much more than that. I thought at least one of the voices belonged to a man, but I couldn't really tell for certain about it and could not have sworn to either.

"Maybe we need to get clear of here," said Willie. He was feeling the same instinct for avoiding trouble that I was. I nodded and pointed off to the right where we could pick up the lower trail and head back through the woods.

We worked our way in that direction and slipped into the trees leaving the dispute behind us and to the left. I whispered to Willie that this trail would lead us back to where we came in. It just wouldn't have the steady climb upwards that the other part of the trail had. A few minutes later, the voices were behind us, and we relaxed a little bit.

"Think we might come out here next Saturday?" Willie asked.

"There's a game at eight o'clock," I said as I remembered the season was going to start then. It was awful early to be out of bed on a Saturday in the summertime, but I knew we would be glad we weren't playing in the heat of the middle of the day. "You gonna play?"

"I don't reckon my folks would mind," he said with a shrug. "Can I use your mitt?"

"You can have it if you want," I told him. "I got a new one last summer."

"Thanks," Willie began, "maybe we can play some…" A sharp crack cut through the air from behind us. It echoed for almost half a minute. "What was that?"

"Rifle shot," I said almost immediately. I felt that little cold touch of fear rise up in my chest, and then remembered Claxton saying once that if you heard the shot you're probably not dead. "Not supposed to be any hunting around here." The town had placed the woods around the falls as off-limits to hunting years ago after an accidental shooting, and there were signs posted everywhere now. There were still a few night hunters who sneaked in to go after a deer or two, but this was midday. "Maybe we need to get on." We started walking a little faster, but my mind was on that rifle shot. There was only one shot, and Claxton had always told me that it usually took two or three for you to figure the distance and direction, but I had a bad feeling that this rifle shot had come from very near the falls where those voices had been. I heard a noise behind us along the trail. By the sound, it seemed that someone was running...and running fast.

"Run!" I whispered, and we began running as fast as we could. I could hear the water squishing in our shoes as we ran along with the soft thump of our feet hitting the worn path. We ran as hard as we could for more than ten minutes and then slowed to catch our breaths. There was still someone or something coming from behind us, so we started running again, but not as hard since we were getting closer to town now. We reached the clearing of the baseball field several minutes later and picked up our mitts. I didn't feel good about us stopping there, so we kept on until we reached town.

"Should we tell someone about what we heard back there?" Willie asked.

"I don't know," I shook my head. "I don't want any trouble. Your folks don't even know you were out there today. I'd hate it if they said you couldn't come back again just 'cause somebody was shootin' out there." Willie nodded. I thought it was just bad luck. We could go out there every day for the next ten years and never hear another shot. "Let's just dry out." We took off our shoes and went around behind the general store where there was plenty of sun and out of sight of most anyone who might be walking around this time of day. Despite my best intentions otherwise, Willie was probably going to be home on time for supper after all. I imagined that it was probably for the best.

"Anybody asks," I said, "we were playing ball out at the field today."

"Don't like lying," said Willie ruefully. "Always seems to catch up to ya'."

"Ain't exactly lying," I said slowly. "We *were* playing ball out there. Just thought we might not mention the falls if nobody asks." And I didn't think anyone would ask since no one had seen us.

"Okay," Willie said after a moment. "Don't reckon anybody'd be hurt by that."

We sat out behind the general store for almost an hour just letting our clothes dry out. It had been a fun day, but it was coming to a close. Willie said goodbye and headed to his house down Maynard Street, and I headed to my own house on Poplar. I pushed open the front screen door and made sure I closed it all the way.

"Get that door closed," I heard Bertie call from the kitchen. "Don't want no…"

"Don't' want no flies after your pies," I called back with a deep sigh. "I know. Door's closed good and tight."

"And make goodn' sure those shoes is clean…don't be trackin' up my clean floors with no mud from that field," she went on.

"Ain't even wearin' my shoes," I laughed back at her. "Wiped my feet on the matt, too."

"Well, that's good," she sighed from the kitchen. "Now go on and clean up the rest of yourself. Supper be ready in just a bit."

"Yes ma'am, Bertie," I said into the kitchen as I passed by and headed up the stairs. I tossed my glove into my open closet, and dropped my shoes in front. I sniffed of my clothes. They smelled mysteriously like they had been dipped in the river. I hadn't thought to tell Willie to get his into the wash before anyone else wondered what the smell might be. I reminded myself that Willie was sharp. Probably he figured that out on his own. All in all, I had had a full day. I started the day off with a fight, found a new friend, played some ball, went over the falls, and even got shot at maybe. It was quite a start to the first day of summer vacation. I couldn't wait to find out what might happen tomorrow.

Chapter Three

"How'd you and Willie make out today, son?" asked Claxton as he pulled up his chair to the table. His plate was already filled, and he began to eat right away.

"Played some ball," I said casually. I wasn't very good at lying. I never could get away with one with Claxton, but Bertie rescued me this time.

"All this eatin' and jawin' 'bout boys and ball playing," she said as she sat down at her chair. "Ain't heard nothin' 'bout my cornbread that I done worked on all afternoon."

"Bertie...you are absolutely right," said Claxton. "I have once again taken your delicious home cooking for granted when everyone knows it's the envy of the entire world."

"Oh, now you do go on," the old woman waved at him with one hand. "Ain't the envy of the *whole* world...just them parts that is civilized enough to know better." We all laughed at that, but the truth was that Bertie *was* widely sought out for her recipes, and had been approached more than once to write a cookbook by the local women's club.

"Ought to reconsider writin' down all those recipes in that cookbook," Claxton smiled as if he was reading my mind. "Nobody else in these parts is eatin' this good...just ain't right an' Christian not sharin' it with the world."

"Now, mister Claxton," Bertie said, "takin' care of you men is 'bout all I got time for. Maybe in my old age. I see 'bout it then."

"How many years you feelin' right now?" Claxton asked her. Bertie's age ranged between fifty-five and seventy-five, and I wasn't really sure if she even knew exactly what it was.

"'Spect I feel 'bout sixty-five today," she said with a chuckle after a moment's thought. "Was about sixty 'till I done them stairs a few times."

I finished eating quickly, excused myself and headed upstairs. I looked out over the backs of the houses towards the field and at the woods beyond and wondered just what might have happened out there today. It gave me a cold feeling in my stomach that lasted until I went to bed that night. Claxton looked in on me as he always did before he turned out the light in the hallway. He didn't say anything, but I could feel his eyes on me until he closed the door. About three times, I talked myself into getting up and telling him what I'd heard today, and three times I decided that I really didn't know anything for sure. I half convinced myself that somebody else must have heard that shot and dropped by the sheriff's office to report it, but I knew as well as anyone that a shot down in those woods wouldn't travel all that far beyond the canyon and the falls, and Willie and I hadn't seen anyone else out there. But we had heard. I made up my mind that the only way I could put my mind at rest would be to go back out there and look around.

I waited until the house was totally quiet. The radio in the den downstairs had been off for more than an hour when I got up, got myself dressed, and slipped out the window onto the little bit of roof that sloped down from the window to the edge of the house. The big maple on the side of the yard was taller than the house, and one big limb reached most of the way to the house. I jumped out about a foot and caught the big branch with both hands. Swinging one leg up and over it, I climbed over to the trunk and then down the branches staying close to the trunk all the way to the ground. I had done this quite a number of times before, so it was nothing new, but it was the first time I had done it after midnight. I had what passed for a plan in mind that included getting the lantern from the garage along with a few matches, but it didn't extend much further than that.

Josiah Falls was a quiet place during the day. After midnight, it was as quiet as a churchyard cemetery. I kept an eye out for anyone or anything that might be around, but mostly I was just trying to stay clear of anybody's dog that might start barking if I got too close. When I was thinking about going out into the woods from the relative safety of my own bed, it had seemed like a lot easier thing to do. Now that I was out in the dark with nothing but the crickets chirping and a few locusts buzzing, I was starting to wonder how hard it might be to climb back *up* that tree and get back onto the roof. That was something I had not thought of when I jumped *from* the roof, but I was thinking mightily upon it right then. I was also thinking that I wished I had some company.

With nothing more than a faint hope, I took a turn down Maynard Street wondering if somebody else I knew might also be awake this night. Finding Willie's house wasn't going to be too hard. Maynard Street only had six houses on it, and only one of them had been for sale until last week. I walked down to the middle house on the left and stopped in the front yard. This had been Preston Stoneman's house until they moved away at Christmas. Preston hadn't been a close friend, but I had been inside the house once or twice and figured that Willie's bedroom would be either on the back corner or in the middle of the back of the house. The big room was on the left corner, and Willie's parents would be there. The only question now was corner or middle. Probably it didn't even matter, I told myself, because everyone would be asleep. Still, I held out a small ray of hope and crept around the side of the house. I turned the corner of the house and walked past the first window, it was open halfway as was the window in the middle. Willie had told me that he had a little brother. The last thing I needed was to get some little kid screaming. Caught between looking in one window or the other, I finally decided to do neither and leave.

"Whatcha doin'?" came a voice from the corner window just as I passed by. How I didn't scream, I don't exactly know, but somehow I didn't. It was Willie.

"'Bout scared me to death," I whispered through the window. He pushed the window open a little wider.

"Scared?" said Willie. "You were lookin' for me weren't you?"

"Didn't expect you to be *watchin'* at the window," I said as my heart started to slow back down. "Didn't think you'd be *awake,* either."

"Couldn't sleep," Willie shook his head. "Been sittin' here thinkin' 'bout it all night. You goin' out there tonight?"

"I was 'till I 'bout died a minute ago," I smiled at him. If him talking through a window was going to scare me, I was having serious second thoughts now. "Maybe we can go out there tomorrow."

"I've got church first thing," said Willie. "Then a family dinner. Don't 'spect I'll get away till after midday."

"I reckon I'll see you at church at that," I said. I'd lost track of the day with thinking about all of this. "Got to be tonight then."

"Hold on a minute..." said Willie. He disappeared from the window. I heard some things being moved around in his room.

"Don't have all night," I whispered. I looked up at the sky as the clouds and haze from the day were clearing. The moonlight was bright that night, and I hoped that would help. A few minutes passed. Then Willie was back at the window. He stepped through and dropped down to the ground. He didn't make a lot of noise, but it was so quiet that we both looked around. When we didn't hear anything we started walking away from the house and towards the field. His house was only a street over from the field, so it didn't take us long to get there, and a few minutes later we were in the woods.

"Could still go back if you want," I offered. If he had said 'okay' I would have turned around on the spot, but he just shook his head and kept walking. One thing I had noticed about Willie in the three-quarters of a day I had known him was that when he made up his mind there was only one direction to go, and that was forward. He had a quiet confidence that was infectious, and I almost felt foolish and a little cowardly for asking now.

We made our way down the trail with me leading the way. I was glad that Willie had been this way once before. He had shown already that he had a sharp eye, and it could come in handy. Of course, it was dark now, and what light had been provided by the moon was now mostly lost to the thick canopy of trees overhead. I wasn't *too* worried about staying on the trail; there were only a few places where you could wander from it without knowing, and I had a pretty good idea of where those were even in the dark. We didn't talk much on the way out there. I guess we were both thinking about the same things. As many times as I had been in these woods, I don't think I had ever seen it so alive. During the daylight, I always had the sense that there were animals out there watching and hiding, but now it was *their* time to be up and around, and I found myself jumping at almost every sound.

"It ain't nothin'!" I told myself finally after having been spooked for the millionth time. Saying it outloud seemed to help me get a handle on my nerves and settle down.

"That's right," said Willie. "Just critters out there lookin' for something to eat. Right?"

"Expect you're right," I agreed. "Guess it's all right long as they ain't fixin' to eat us." I had never seen anything around here of that size, but that night everything seemed bigger and scarier than it really would have been in the light of day.

The trail seemed longer than usual, but I knew that was only because we were moving slower than we would have during the day. I had the lantern swinging from my hand by the handle, but I had not lit it yet. I wanted to save the oil for when we got closer, and after our eyes had adjusted to the darkness of the woods, the little bit of moonlight that did shine through the breaks in the leaves was enough for us to see well enough to stay out of any trouble we might run into. The night was cooling off from the heat of the day. It was still early enough in the summer that the evenings were pleasant and sometimes even cold, but this night there was a strong breeze blowing the leaves around and it felt good even though it was a little scary being out there. When we reached the part of the trail where it began to climb towards the top of the falls I came to a stop. There was another piece of a trail that led down towards the falls about halfway in between the upper and lower trails. Going up the trail would take us the long way around, but this was the one trail in these woods that I, and probably most anyone else, rarely ever used, so I was not very sure about it.

"Probably the closest way to go," I said after a moment of trying to decide. "But, I've only been on it a couple of times."

"If it's closest then we ought to have a look see," said Willie who seemed a lot more ready to jump into it than I did. "Maybe it's time to light up that lantern?" It seemed like a good idea to me. I took one of the matches from my pocket, struck it on the strike plate of the lantern and held it on the cloth wick until it lit. I blew out the match, dropped it onto the ground, and covered it with dirt with my shoe. I closed the glass pane of the lantern, and held it out in front of us. The light put an eerie shadow across the trees on either side of the trail, and we could now see how narrow the trail became after only a few feet. We moved even more slowly over the unfamiliar path. Not traveled as often as the others because it was in between the top and bottom of the falls, there was not much to see and no place to really go; the trail was more overgrown with shrubs and small seedling trees, which grabbed at our shoes as we walked. Five minutes down the trail, we stopped dead still at a rustling in the brush to the right, but it was only an opossum walking blindly into the lantern light before disappearing into the dense brush on the other side. The path wound around a small curve, and in the distance I could hear the sound of the falls crashing down. We rounded the end of the curve and came to a stop. There was something up ahead lying in the middle of the path, and I was pretty sure it wasn't a collection of brush or another animal. The lantern swung slowly from side to side in my hand, and the light played over the form in a way that seemed to make it move on the ground.

"Can you hold that thing still?" said Willie nervously. "Creepin' me out with that."

"Sorry," I said as I steadied the light with my other hand. "What do you 'spose it is?" From where we stood, it really could have been anything, but our imaginations were ready to invent any number of things. I know that mine sure was.

"Know what I *think* it is," said Willie. I did too, but I didn't want to say so as if saying it aloud would make it true. "Gonna have to get closer to find out." Willie started walking forward, so I took several steps as well. Five feet away there was no longer any doubt...even with only the feeble light of the lantern to testify.

"Reckon he's...dead?" Willie whispered with a mixture of fear and curiosity in his voice.

"Don't know. Wanna go over an' ask 'em?" I said. If the man wasn't dead, he'd picked an odd place to lie down and rest. "Ever seen a dead man before?"

"Saw my grandpa in his casket," said Willie. "Wasn't layin' out in the road or nothin' like this. Maybe we could poke 'em with a stick or somethin'."

"If you was dead, would you want somebody pokin' you with a stick?" I asked. I had poked at dead snakes and frogs to see if they would move, but there was no way I was touching this.

"Don't guess I'd care," Willie shrugged.

"I 'spose it was my idea to come out here," I said after a long minute. I took a few steps towards the form of the man lying with his body in the path and most of one leg in the brush. He was lying twisted with the lower body down and the top looking upward as if he had tried to get up, but his legs didn't want to. I could feel Willie coming closer, but he still hung back a little like I was sort of wishing I had. I leaned down and held the light forward a little more. I could see a lot of blood on the front of the man's shirt, with what looked like a small hole just below his ribs. I remembered the hunting trip that I had talked Claxton into taking me on. We had tracked a deer, and Claxton let me shoot it. I had seen dead deer before, and I'd even eaten the venison, but I had never seen one killed until then. My shot had been good, but not good enough. The deer had gone down and thrashed around on the ground. I had tried to give Claxton the gun back, but he told me that I had to finish it. That second shot was a lot harder to squeeze. I wondered if this man had been like the deer when he fell. I finally moved the lantern away from the bullet wound. Then I pulled it back suddenly and stood up. I'd seen a whole lot more than I'd wanted to.

"What'd you see?" Willie wanted to know.

"Reckon he's dead all right," I said sickly as I turned from the grisly sight. "Somethin's been gnawin' on his face. I think he would have somethin' to say 'bout that if'n he was able. Do you wanna see?"

"Was it as bad as you look right now?" Willie asked carefully. I nodded. I felt a little sick and knew that my face was probably as pale as Swiss cheese, but I was proud that I hadn't lost my dinner although my stomach was doing somersaults and there was still plenty of time for that.

"Do you know who it was?" Willie wondered.

"Couldn't tell," I shook my head. "Maybe if there was a little more face *left*..." My stomach lurched. I had to stop talking about it. I leaned over but that was all for the moment. While I was considering whether or not I was going to heave, I caught sight of a shiny glint in the dirt and knelt down with the lantern. There were some coins on the ground there in the light. There was a quarter, a few dimes, and something else there with them. I picked up the coins and handed them to Willie. The other thing turned out to be a coin also, but it wasn't silver. I stuck it in my pocket as I stood up. We had found a dead man, sixty-five cents, and an odd coin of some kind.

"I guess we know what that rifle shot was 'bout now," said Willie. "What do we do now?"

"Gotta tell Claxton," was the only thing I could think of to say. We couldn't very well keep this a secret, but I didn't want to say that we came out here to find this either. I took a step back up the trail and felt better already just being further away.

"What are you gonna tell him?" Willie said. "We're gonna be in trouble no matter what."

"I'll tell him," I said shaking my head. "I won't even say you were here. Just slip back in your window and don't say nothin' 'bout this."

"Don't seem right you takin' the blame when you wouldn't even a come out here if I didn't come along," said Willie. He had a strong sense of right and wrong about things, but this wasn't the time for it. He was new in town, and I didn't know how his folks would take it. Claxton wouldn't like it, but I knew we'd work it out.

"No sense in both of us bein' in trouble," I said with a thought on the talk Claxton and I were going to have. "Maybe you can come visit me while I'm doin' time in my own yard." It seemed like a crummy way to start the summer by being grounded for most of it, but it seemed to be a likely future prospect that couldn't be avoided. But, at least I *had* a future, bleak as it was, to look forward to. The dead man back behind us sure couldn't walk back into town on his own and report he'd been killed.

"Will you get a whupin'?" asked Willie as we now started to put distance between the dead man and us.

"Naw…" I began and then stopped. Claxton had only laid into me good one time with a strap, and it probably wasn't as hard as I remembered it, but as I thought about the schoolyard fight that had brought that on, it seemed like a minor offense by comparison to this. "I don't think so." I didn't sound any more convincing to myself than I did to Willie. We finally reached the place where the trail branched back into the main path back to town. We weren't jumping at every sound and movement anymore, and we didn't even see the man in baggy coveralls and a plaid shirt who stepped out into the trail right in front of us. I jumped back like I'd touched a hot skillet and Willie yelped like he'd run into the devil himself and been poked by his pitchfork.

"Whatchoo boys prowlin' round here so late fer?" the wild-eyed looking man demanded. I caught up to my wits a few seconds later and then grabbed onto Willie before he could run back the other way like a scared jackrabbit.

"'S okay, Willie," I managed to say after I caught my breath. "It's just Riley. He's all right. Just kinda spooked us, Riley. Didn't know anybody was out here." I was talking too fast, but I couldn't slow down. "What are you doing out here, Riley?"

"Asked you first," the old man grinned through a mostly toothless smile on his bearded face.

"Come out to get fishin' bait," I answered quickly with the first thing I could think of.

"Won't wash," the old man shook his head with a knowing smile. "Best bait's down t'other way. You know that. Been down there to show you myself. Now who's this 'un?" He stuck a thumb at Willie.

"This here's Willie," I said. "He's new in town. Just come here this week."

"Come up from Natchez," Riley smiled and nodded.

"How'd you know that?" Willie asked cautiously.

"Ole Riley *knows* things," the old man said with a nod and a point at his head with one crooked finger.

"So why are we out here then?" I challenged him. I figured I had him on that one.

"Come to see Dyle I reckon," the old man nodded. "Ain't that so?"

"Dyle?" I shook my head. "Dyle Courtland?" That was the only Dyle I had ever heard of.

"Yep," Riley nodded vigorously. "Couldn't miss 'em if you come from back there. Layin' deader'n a possum in the path an all. Don't spect you stepped over 'em…now did ya?"

"You *knew* he was there?" I said in surprise. Riley chuckled.

"*Course* I knowed that," he said with a roll of his eyes. "Ole Riley knows *everything* that happens in these here woods." He looked around. "Just me an' the trees…we *sees* everything…*hears* everything."

"Why didn't you…?" I began but he cut me off.

"But, I don't *tells* everything," he said with one bony finger across his lips. "Some folk say I'm p'culiar an all. Ain't so. Just not like other folks."

"Is he...touched?" Willie whispered cautiously. He looked like he was still ready to run.

"Touched by the Lord," said Riley earnestly. "Tole me one day to get up outa town, get away from folks, and live close to the land. Been doin' like He said ever since."

"So what you reckon we oughta do about Dyle?" I asked. "Don't seem right to just leave him out here." I was hoping that he might volunteer to go into town and say that he found him, but you had to be careful with how you talked to Riley because he could just as easily go off in another totally different direction.

"Wanna bury 'em?" Riley suggested with a shrug. "I could get a shovel. Grounds soft enough to do it."

"Might get in trouble with the law," I said with no thought in the world of going back there again much less to *bury* him. "Wouldn't want you to get in no trouble. I think it's illegal to bury somebody's been killed."

"That so?" said Riley as if he not heard about that before.

"Well, your daddy bein' a lawyer an all...I reckon you'd know 'bout such as that."

"I don't 'spose you might be of a mind to go see the sheriff and tell him where to find Dyle?" I suggested carefully.

"Don't seem like a right smart thing to do," said Riley. "Might want to lock me up for it."

"Aw, nobody'd think you done it," I said. "You ain't mean like some folks. You could just say you come across him while you was out froggin'...and maybe you could just forget you run into us tonight." I paused for a moment and stuck my hand in my pocket. My fingers found  the coin. I had really wanted to hold on to it, and figure out what it was, but I didn't have anything else to bargain with at the moment. I pulled it out. "Give you this if you'll do it."

Riley stuck out his hand and I dropped the coin in it. He held it up to the moonlight, and I was able to see it better than I had before.

"Where'd you get this, Nathan?" he asked as he flipped the coin over and looked at it with one squinting eye. He held it up to the red bandana around his neck and wiped it off and then looked it over again.

"Back down the trail," I said with a thumb over my shoulder.

"Twenty dollar gold piece…old 'un at that…1874," Riley said with interest. Then after a moment, "Got you a deal, Nathan. I'll tell Owen 'bout Dyle first thing in the mornin'. Don't 'spect he'll be totally et by the critters by then." I had to convince my stomach to be calm as I again saw the partially eaten face of Dyle Courtland in my mind. Now that I had a name to connect to a face, it seemed to make it worse.

"And you won't remember nothin' 'bout runnin' into us?" I reminded him.

"Yep…yep," said Riley tiredly. "Didn't see nobody. Not tonight, ner this afternoon when you *didn't* come by then, ner anybody else today." He winked at us, and I thought that maybe he really did know everything that happened in these woods. I breathed a sigh of relief. I stuck out my hand spit in it, and Riley did the same. Then we shook on it.

"Now you, Willie," I told him. Willie looked at me once and then shook as well.

"That makes it an oath," said Riley. "Ole Riley don't go back on his oath. T'wouldn't be right. Now you boys best get. I'll done forgot you was here by then." He held the coin back up in the moonlight, and we hurried on down the trail while he looked at his new treasure.

"I guess we dodged that one," I said. I was already missing the coin, but it seemed like a fair trade at the moment.

"Reckon," said Willie quietly, but he was thinking about something. "That old man all right in the head?"

"Wouldn't hurt nobody…if that's what you mean," I said. Willie nodded. I thought about it myself. Riley was odd by anybody's standards, but I just couldn't see him bringing harm

34

to anyone. He was a loner, but he was hard and fast on the Bible. Killing was against the Book except for food to put on your table, and I knew where he would stand on that. "Sure wouldn't shoot nobody."

We hurried up a bit, knowing this part of the trail pretty well, and made our way back to town. Things were still quiet there. I had no idea what time it was, but I knew it had to be late. We split up when we got to Willie's street, and I headed back to my house. I set the lantern back on the wooden table in the garage just about like I had found it. The oil was half used, and I wondered if Claxton would notice that. I checked the big glass bottle to see if there was any there that I could pour in, but it was just about empty. Well, I was boxed in there. Claxton would know that he was *just* about out of oil, but if the bottle were *empty* he'd wonder why. The only thing to do was to do nothing, so I left the lantern there, half full, and closed the door to the garage. Then I made my way to the big maple and climbed back up. As it turned out, I was able to balance well enough to walk out across the broad limb and jump the short step to the roof. There was a little more noise than I expected when I landed, so I hurried up the roof and back in the window. I jumped in the bed and covered myself up quickly. About ten seconds later, my door opened. I could feel Claxton's eyes on me, checking the room. I heard him walk silently across the floor and then saw him looking out the window. He glanced back at me, and I quickly closed my eyes before he could see me watching. A moment later he was gone. I think he stood at the door for just a second or two like he was giving me a chance to sit up there in the bed and tell him what he'd almost caught me doing. I think that I was about to do just that when the door clicked shut. I was a long time in getting to sleep even though it was just after three o'clock in the morning. I didn't know that I slept any the rest of that night, but I must have because I was sound asleep when Bertie opened the door at seven and told me to come on for breakfast. I got up and changed clothes and then went downstairs. Claxton was already dressed for church, drinking his coffee, and reading the Sunday paper. It occurred to me when I saw the paper that I could have very easily run in to the deliveryman when he dropped off the paper on the step. I couldn't have missed him by more than a few minutes.

"Thought you'd look fresh as a daisy this morning," said Claxton as I yawned and sat down. "Going to bed so early and all."

"Had me a busy day yesterday s'all," I said truthfully. "I expect I'll rest better tonight." Claxton nodded and went back to his paper. I started eating and wondering when things would start to happen today.

Chapter Four

Riley was sitting on the wooden bench outside of Sheriff Owen Mercer's Main Street jail when Mercer drove up in his car from church just after eleven am. I saw them walk inside as Claxton and I were just coming down the steps of the Baptist Church of God.

"Wonder what that's about?" said Claxton as he followed my not so innocent gaze down the street. "Reckon there must be a blue moon." I knew the answer, but the question wasn't really directed at me, so I said nothing. Minister Washburne's sermon had been about having patience, and then he went into a long talk about the importance of being truthful. I felt about as low as dirt when he finished up, and we walked out of there. If not telling the truth was even the smallest of sins, then I was sure enough going to hell for mine because I'd left out more truth in the last day than most people would ever know in a lifetime. Evan Washburne stood on the front steps that day like he did every Sunday, shaking the hand of everybody that came by, and taking the time to say something kind to even the least worthy of us there. I figured that had to be me today. He patted me on the head and said he hoped I had a good summer. I thanked him and walked on wishing that I felt better about things.

Claxton and I walked the short way home from church by cutting across the cemetery to the next street over, and I could smell dinner already cooking. Bertie attended the black church on the other end of town and always went to the early service, so she was almost done cooking dinner by the time we got home. It was fried chicken…one of my favorites. We had no more than sat down when there was a knock on the door. Bertie was up like a shot to get it before either of us could move.

"Sheriff Owen," I heard her say through the screen door. Her voice was full of worry because this was evidently not a social call, but she invited him inside just the same. "Come on in. We was just gett'n ready for dinner. Got plenty?"

"Sorry, Bertie," Owen Mercer was saying. "Appreciate it, but I can't stay. I need to see Claxton right quick." I heard them coming from the little foyer to the kitchen.

"Hate to interrupt your dinner, Claxton," Mercer began, "but we got some trouble. I need you to come and bring your bag." Except for the olive colored short sleeve shirt that said Josiah Falls Sheriff on the pocket, there was not much else to suggest he was the local law.

"What's the trouble, Owen?" Claxton said as he dropped his napkin on the table. He knew that Mercer wouldn't be here if it wasn't serious. Mercer looked at me and then at Bertie as if he wasn't sure he wanted to talk in front of us, but a moment later he started talking.

"Got a report of a body up in the woods," he said. "I'm headin' up that way. I'd appreciate it if you would hike up there with me and have a look." Claxton gave me a look.

"Praise, Lord," said Bertie. "Hope that ain't true."

"Me, too, Bertie," said Mercer. "But, I think it is."

"Give me a minute," Claxton said as he got up from the table. "I'll throw on something else and be right with you." He headed up the stairs quickly. Mercer paced around the front of the house until Claxton came back down the stairs. He was dressed in his old hiking jeans and boots and had his black medical bag with the US Army insignia on the side.

"Don't know when I'll be back," Claxton told me. "If you need me, I'll likely be back in town for a spell after we hike back down."

"Yes, sir," I said. I had a real good idea of what was going to happen. I heard the screen door slam shut a minute later and heard the sheriff's car start up and drive off.

"Reckon we might as well go on an' eat," said Bertie. "I'll put mister Claxton's meal up for later."

I began eating my dinner, but it was not with the same enthusiasm with which I had sat down. The sheriff had not mentioned anything about Willie or me, so I was safe in assuming that Riley had kept his word about not tattling on us, but it didn't make things any easier. I finished eating, went upstairs, and changed out of my Sunday 'go to meetin' clothes.

A few minutes later I was outside and headed back towards town. I knew I should probably be headed the opposite direction, but somehow I needed to know what was happening. I walked around town for a while looking into the shop windows. There was not much to do, and eventually I started walking towards the sheriff's office. As I passed by the church, I saw the cemetery caretaker, Carter Monroe closing up the supply shed and starting to walk back towards the church. He saw me and waved. I waved back. Carter was a hard man to miss. He was about as tall as Claxton, lean and strong looking. He was starting to go gray on top, but he still stood ramrod straight all time, and was usually the only black man around the Baptist Church. Carter kept to himself in town, but he would talk with you if it was just the two of you, and you said something first to get him started.

I reached the sheriff's office and sat down on the wooden bench outside. I tried to imagine what Sheriff Mercer and Claxton were doing right now. I was pretty sure that they were there by now. In fact, I knew that they had to have been there for quite a while now. I didn't know what you could *do* with a dead man for that long, but I figured Claxton would tell me if I asked. As I thought more about it, I wasn't all that sure I wanted to know. About twenty-five minutes later, I heard the car coming down the street and saw Owen Mercer's old Nash police car turn towards the curb. Claxton got out on the passenger side and pushed the door shut. I could see there was nothing in the back seat but a few small bags and one long thin one, and I was a little relieved at that. I had thought I might see Dyle sprawled out back there. I'd seen him up close once, and that had been plenty for me. I sure didn't want to see him after he spent the rest of the night in the woods as a cold snack for anything hungry that came along.

"Somethin' wrong?" I asked even though I knew well enough there was something very wrong.

"Somebody killed Dyle Courtland," Claxton said in his usual matter-of-fact voice with no more emotion than if he was reading the menu at the BBQ restaurant. Sheriff Mercer unlocked the office and we followed him inside. I sat down in one of the chairs by the wall as they set the bags on the desk and stood the long tall one up in the corner. Sheriff Mercer sat down behind his desk, and Claxton took the big padded chair right beside it.

"Well...here we go," said Claxton as he opened a filing cabinet behind the desk and pulled out some papers from one of the files. He slipped one of them onto a clipboard, took a fountain pen from the desk, and began to write.

"I think the 'cause of death' is simple enough," said Claxton. "A .22 caliber rifle shot in the guts from close up. No more than about eight or ten feet at most I'd say."

"I reckon," said Mercer. "Just about blew daylight clean through 'em. Suppose I ought to put it down as a homicide, Claxton?"

"Sure wasn't suicide," said Claxton as he continued writing. "Gun was way over in the brush. I think he was half dead when he hit the ground, so he sure didn't shoot himself and throw it there. It could have been an accident I suppose. Whoever it was...maybe got scared and ran afterwards." He was thoughtful a moment. "Might just hold off on that until all the photos and evidence are sorted through." I had known for most of my life that just about everyone around considered

Claxton the smartest man they knew, and I could see by his quick nod in agreement that Owen Mercer was one of them.

"I'll get Fletcher to get those developed right away. Probably find him out fishin' downstream," said Mercer. "Got some clear footprints at least. Place looked right busy." I hadn't thought about leaving footprints behind. I wondered if any of those prints looked like they belonged to a couple of ten year olds who were someplace they shouldn't have been.

"Can't figure how he got shot with his own gun," said Claxton as he finished the sheet he was writing on and took it from the clipboard. "Dyle was a lot of things, but he was no fool idiot." Mercer dumped the contents of a large yellow envelope out on the table. He picked up a spent shell casing with the end of a pen. I could see it was a .22 shell even from where I sat.

"If there's a print here, I'll bet its Dyle's," said Mercer. "I'll dust the gun. Maybe get lucky there. Do you think there was any sign of a struggle? Maybe a fight over the gun?" Claxton raised his head and shrugged and then went back to writing. I had no idea how anyone could have known that from what I had seen. Mercer picked up the phone on his desk and started dialing. "Put me through to Fayette. I need the homicide investigation unit. Yep…I know what day it is. I got a dead man here that don't know it's inconvenient to get himself shot on a Sunday." A few minutes later he had related the basic information over the phone. What they had was a man named Dyle Courtland, a local man his whole life, who was about twenty-six years old and who had been shot at close range with a .22 hunting rifle. Claxton estimated that he had been dead for no more than a day, but probably less. The weapon had been found near the scene along with one shell casing. The dead man had ten one dollar bills folded together in his front right jeans pocket and five more in his wallet with a restaurant dinner receipt folded up in between. The crime scene had a dozen or so footprints belonging to possibly as many as six to eight different people. A couple of men had been sent up to watch over the scene until the investigators could get there for a look. And that was it.

"I think that will work for now," said Claxton. "Might as well tell the next of kin. Let them know that you'll be holding the body for the investigation. Could be a while."

"Can't remember the last murder we had here," said Mercer with a shake of his head.

"I do," said Claxton as he set the clipboard back down on the desk. I thought there would be more, but that was all he said.

"Reckon you do at that," said Mercer. "Sorry I brought it up." Claxton shook himself out of his thoughts.

"Long time ago, Owen," he said with a smile. "Well, I guess I'll be on my way. Can't say I feel much like dinner now."

"I 'preciate you walkin' up there with me," said Mercer. "Didn't want the city boys jumpin' my butt for screwin' up the evidence." Claxton just nodded, stood, and clapped him on the shoulder in a way that seemed to always say that you'd gotten the job done. That kind of thing meant a lot coming from Claxton. I could see right away that it had that same effect on Owen Mercer.

"Come on, son," Claxton said with a sigh. "Let's go on home." Claxton picked up his bag from inside the door, and we headed back outside.

"Who got killed?" I asked after the door shut behind us.

"Dyle Courtland," said Claxton casually. "You heard that."

"No," I shook my head. "You said you remembered another killin' a long time ago." Claxton looked at me for a very long time and then started to walk down the sidewalk. I thought at first that he wasn't going to say anything. Then he started talking.

"It was 1932 when that...happened," Claxton said. He pointed across the way to a very tall maple. "Right over there by that tree...in fact, *on* that tree." He stared at the tree for a full minute, and I knew that he was seeing what had happened all those years ago just like I was seeing Dyle stretched out there on the trail with his insides running out. "There was a lynching right there. About fifteen or twenty men went into

41

the jail, opened up the cell, and took a man out of there and hanged him."

"Hanged him with no trial or nothin'?" I asked. I'd heard of lynchings, of course, but I never would have thought that something like that could have happened in little Josiah Falls. They happened other places, but not there.

"That's about the size of it," Claxton nodded.

"What'd he do?" I wondered. "Folks must have been plenty riled up to do something like that."

"Fact is, son," said Claxton with a pained expression on his face. "I don't think he did a thing. I guess I know he didn't."

"Killed him for nothin' at all?" I was amazed to hear that.

"He was just in the wrong place at the wrong time," Claxton explained. "He'd gone into the bank down the street to sell some land and had just walked out of the door onto the walk when a fella named Horace Greer stumbled right in front of him and went rolling out into the street. Well Horace got himself run over by a car that had come barreling down the way."

"Was he killed?" I asked. Getting run over couldn't be much good for you, and I wondered if there would have been a crunching of bones and stuff like that.

"Not right away," said Claxton. "Horace lived close to another two days, but he never woke up."

"So, how'd him fallin' out in the street get somebody hung?" I couldn't see how an accident could be blamed on somebody else just because he was standing there close by.

"See, when Horace went under those wheels," Claxton began, "there were a lot of people around close at the time, and one of them started pointing and yelling that the fella on the sidewalk had *pushed* him out there. Pretty soon a lot of folks who hadn't seen it happen were saying it, too. It sorta caught like wildfire."

"Who woulda said somethin' like that if it wasn't true?" I wondered. I knew people could get excited and do dumb things, but I would not have thought of anything like that.

"A man who, I guess, wanted to see that so bad that maybe he even convinced himself for a minute that he really had seen it," said Claxton.

"Then maybe he did see it," I said slowly. Just because one person says something and nobody else does doesn't make him wrong. Claxton had taught me that one although it had taken a few times for it to sink in.

"It didn't happen, Nathan," said Claxton with a slow shake of his head. "I was there on the same side of the street. There was five feet between them." He spread his arms wide apart for emphasis. "Horace just tripped on the curb, fell backwards, and got run over. I saw it as clear as I see you right now."

"But you saw. You told them, right?" I asked nodding my head, but I knew that something was horribly wrong.

"I told your granddaddy," said Claxton. "I told him just what I saw."

"So he told them," I nodded. But, something else must have happened because a man was hanged for it.

"No, son, he didn't," Claxton shook his head. "You see, he was the man who said he'd *seen* a fella named Carter Monroe…yes, the daddy of the Carter Monroe that you see in town sometimes, give Horace Greer a shove, and he told me that I didn't need to say anything else about it to anyone. He said that he'd handle it and sent me home. I did like I was told." Claxton had been walking slowly as we had been talking, but now he was barely moving. "They locked Carter Monroe up in the jail for two days. That second night, after Horace passed on that afternoon, that bunch I told you about had been drinkin' and talkin' big about what they ought to do. About eleven o'clock they came to the jail to do it. Some of them had guns with them, and they hollered into the sheriff that he could let them in or they would start shootin'. The sheriff just opened the door and let them in. They took that poor old man across the street, with him yellin' that he hadn't done a thing to anyone, and they strung him up right there in front of a hundred people who watched and didn't lift a finger to stop it."

"Why didn't your daddy stop it when it was goin' too far?" I asked sickly. "He could have just told them he was wrong. He'd made a mistake. Couldn't he?"

"He was leading them," said Claxton as he shook his head. "My daddy hated Carter Monroe. He hated that he was still gett'n by. It was the Depression on back then, when most folks were havin' trouble putting food on the table." Claxton was silent for a long while. I understood now why Claxton never talked about his father and why he had left home at fourteen and never came back until long after his father was dead.

"I'm sorry," was all I could say. I couldn't imagine how Claxton must have felt all these years living with that memory. "Did it ever come out? The truth 'bout it…I mean?"

"Like most things…it did," Claxton nodded slowly and painfully. "I spoke up, eventually. Turns out a few more people saw what happened, too. Some recollections got a little clearer, and a few consciences got a little heavier in the light of day after they'd had time to see what they'd let happen. But Carter Monroe was just as dead, and there was nothin' then that was going to change that. There was no trial and nobody ever went to jail. Things just went on."

"Wish I hadn't asked," I said after a moment. I'd never even met my granddaddy, but I felt bad about what he'd done. I wondered how Carter Monroe felt about waving to me. I'd probably talked with him fifty times over the years, and he never said a word about it. I wondered how I would have felt.

"You would have heard about it someday," Claxton forced a smile on his face. "Hard for people to forget something like that…even if they don't talk 'bout it much. Best that you heard it from me first." We walked home without saying much more that day. It's odd sometimes how you think you know someone, and then you find out that you really didn't know half of what you thought you did. I think that was the day that I first saw Claxton as something besides just my father. I could see him now as a boy, not much older than me, knowing something terrible and not being able to do anything about it. I thought in a way we shared that feeling, and I thought that if he could deal with that like a man, I could do the same.

Chapter Five

As the days wore on into June, the buzz about the killing of Dyle Courtland went from hot to cold. No less than five people were known to have threatened Dyle in the week before he was killed, and from everyone that knew him at all, that had been a fairly common thing for Dyle for the better part of his life. The crime lab in Jackson had not come up with much of anything. The only fingerprints that were identifiable had belonged to Dyle. The conclusion was that the killer had almost certainly worn gloves. Some of the footprints had belonged to Dyle and had matched his boot down to the missing part of one heel. The killer had worn anything from a size six shoe to a size fourteen boot, and there was no good way to tell how fresh any of those tracks were since there had not been any rain in at least a week and the weather had been brutally hot. Two weeks after the murder, no one had been charged or even arrested, and I heard Owen Mercer telling Claxton that he didn't think anyone ever would be. I must have thought a thousand times about telling Claxton the whole thing, but when it came right down to it, I really didn't have much to tell. Neither Willie nor myself had seen anyone, not even Dyle, until he was already dead. We had run into Riley, but not even the most suspicious person would have believed Riley would have done it. I wondered more than once if Riley might have seen something, maybe even who had been running behind us that day, but I was also sure that Sheriff Mercer would have asked him that. Then, of course, I had asked Riley not to mention anything about Willie and I being out there, and he hadn't, so there was no way to know what else Riley might not have mentioned.

Gradually, Dyle Courtland slipped onto the back pages of the paper. There was no mad dog killer on the loose as someone briefly speculated in the editorial column, and a week later Dyle was buried in the Baptist Church graveyard with only a few people on hand to see him off. Dyle had a little family left behind, but not many friends. Minister Washburne spoke over him at the graveside and somehow found a way to make Dyle sound almost as if he was a likeable man. Addie and Odessa were standing there behind him and even managed a tear or two for him. By the time the minister was done talking, we all felt a might sorry Dyle was gone now, but I knew in good time we'd all remember what a scoundrel he was. I stood there with Claxton a little ways off from everyone else. I wasn't sure why Claxton wanted to be there unless it was just because he felt connected to what had happened by writing up the death certificate. Mostly, Claxton seemed to be watching the people who showed up. I'm not sure what he was watching for, but he was studying on them close. Of course, not everyone there was touched by Minister Washburn's kind words, particularly those that had known Dyle best like several jealous husbands and the littered trail of women he had left behind. Most of Dyle's closest associations had been women, and none of them had parted with him in a friendly way, but three or four had come to see him put under ground. One of them laughed, and another dropped a gum wrapper into the grave as she walked by. I heard one of the town old-timers, Del Hardeway, ask if they had buried Dyle face down so he could see where he was going. Within a few days of the funeral, the talk about Dyle's murder was pretty much over. I saw Owen Mercer occasionally talking with people in town, and I wondered if he was still trying to follow up on anything. Whatever he found out must not have amounted to much because nothing ever came of it then.

I caught up with Willie over the next few weeks, and we played baseball several times, but neither one of us talked about what had happened, and neither of us mentioned much of anything about going back to the falls anytime soon. We had both had the lecture about staying clear of the woods after the shooting, and that was enough for me anyway. I would have only needed to get caught there once to lose the rest of my summer. We played three Saturday morning baseball games against the other team in town. We won twice and lost once. I couldn't figure out how we lost to a team after beating them handily two weeks in a row, but somehow we managed it just fine as they beat the dickens out of us twenty-four to two. I had to finish up the game as catcher when Buddy Lee was on his way to having a heat stroke, and Willie pitched the last two innings after Malicai Young said he thought his arm'd fall off if he threw one more pitch.

"Sometimes a game like that keeps you humble," Claxton said as we were walking back home.

"Don't do much for a fella's pride though," I answered.

"Losing is part of building character," Claxton went on. He was trying to put a good face on losing and that's always hard to do. It's even harder to do when you just did the losing.

"Reckon we got us a *big* dose a character today then," I shook my head. "Can't lose much more than that." Claxton laughed at that and rested his hand on my shoulder. It was just a baseball game, and I knew we would play again next week. By then, this game would be forgotten, and we would be walking home talking about that one.

"Seen anything of Riley lately?" Claxton asked after we had been quiet for a while. To tell the truth, I hadn't really thought much about Riley since I'd been out of the woods for so long.

"Can't say I have," I said after a moment. Riley didn't come into town very often. "Haven't been to the woods in quite a spell...case you forgot about that."

"And I'm glad to hear you finally listened to me on somethin'," Claxton said. "But...I expect there's probably no harm in you going out there again as long as you have somebody else along." I supposed that Claxton and most everyone else had figured that Dyle Courtland's murder had been personal. I smiled and nodded, glad that I was going to be able to go back out there again.

"Why'd you ask about Riley?" I asked him. "Somethin' wrong?"

"No..." Claxton began. "He just hasn't been seen around lately. I just thought I'd ask. I know you probably run into him out there from time to time." I nodded. There was no use trying to hide that. I had told Claxton about running into Riley quite a few times, and I always thought Claxton considered him harmless enough.

"At times I do. Maybe he's just stayin' up at his cabin," I suggested. "Could be the killin' made him think 'bout keepin' out of the woods some." I didn't really think Dyle's murder would have bothered Riley at all; it certainly hadn't the night we found Dyle's body on the trail. He slipped around like a ghost out there in the trees and hardly ever used the trails like everyone else.

"Maybe," Claxton nodded. That was all he said, but it did get me to thinking about Riley again. I knew that you could go for days, maybe even weeks, without running across his trail out there. And, if he didn't *want* you to find him, even Dan'l Boone and a bloodhound wouldn't have been able to track him down.

"'Spose I could take Willie up to the falls?" I asked even though I already had.

"Don't see why not," said Claxton. "Make sure it's all right by his folks first." I promised myself that I'd go by the rules this time, and I was glad to have permission to do what we already had done once.

"Thanks," I said as I was already planning ahead.

I went by Willie's house that afternoon and told his folks about the falls. They were a little slow about agreeing since it was so close to where there had been a shooting, but I convinced them that it was safe enough and that a lot of people had been going back out there in the last few weeks. I assured them that we wouldn't be going out on that part of the trail anyway. They gave in and said all right, and we didn't wait around for them to change their minds. By one-thirty, we were out at the falls. It had turned into the hottest day of the summer, and some of the other boys were already out there when we got there. We went over the falls until our feet got sore from hitting the water, so we finally just waded around in the stream up above the falls watching the fish dart in and out between our legs as we splashed our way along. I hadn't set out to look for Riley, but after a little ways up stream it occurred to me that we weren't all that far from his cabin, and it wouldn't hurt anything if we were to look him up.

"Wanna see Riley's cabin?" I asked Willie as we moved along.

"I don't know," Willie said slowly. "He's kinda…odd…dontcha think?"

"I 'spose," I said, "but he's harmless to folks…us anyways." We walked on along, and Willie didn't say anything about going back, so I took that to mean that he was fine with going on up there. We came around a small bend in the stream to a place where the trees started to close in again, and I pointed to a little log cabin just off to our right.

"Probably ought to get out of the water," I said as I began to walk up the gently rising bank. "Don't want to step on a hook. Riley's usually got a couple of fishin' lines out here." Willie followed me up the bank and we walked towards the cabin.

"Ain't got no bear traps 'round here does he?" Willie asked as he looked suspiciously around the ground.

"He ain't got no bear traps," I laughed. "Probably afraid he'd hide it too good and step in it himself. Besides, nobody's seen a bear out here in a long spell now."

We reached the cabin and looked around the outside. There were several different kinds of animal pelts hanging up on a line to dry. I recognized the fox and raccoon furs, but there were a couple I didn't. I knocked on the cabin door and waited, but there was no answer. We looked around. Except for the light breeze moving the leaves in the trees and the trickling of the stream, the day was quiet.

"Reckon he's out spookin' around," said Willie. "Musta found somebody else to scare fifty years outa."

"Aw, he ain't that bad," I said even though Riley had scared me plenty on a few occasions. "Maybe he's sick and can't get to the door." Usually there was a heavy padlock on the door if he wasn't around close by, but it was clearly not here now. I pushed on the latch and the door creaked open. I stuck my head inside. The cabin was pitch dark.

"Riley?" I called. "You in there?" I listened for any sound at all and heard nothing. My mind started immediately wondering if there was someone or something there in the darkness waiting. I pulled my head back out. "Think we oughta go inside?"

"I think we oughta get on outa here is what I think we should do," said Willie. It sounded like a good idea, but there were times when I just didn't catch on to common sense like I probably should have.

"Won't hurt to have a quick look," I said as I slowly pulled the door back a bit and had my head inside before he could argue against it. I opened the door all the way, and a little light made its way inside, but the two windows were closed up, and most of the cabin was still as dark as the inside of my pocket.

"Good enough for me," said Willie. "He ain't here. Now let's go." That sounded like an invitation to go on in to me, so I took a step inside the cabin and felt around on the little table to my right next to the lantern and finally found a match. The lantern was a lot like the one Claxton had, so I didn't have much trouble getting it lit. I shut the little glass door and turned up the wick about a half an inch. The lantern cast a flickering glow over the inside of the place. There was a bed to the left, fireplace to the right, and a table in the center of the single room. It didn't take much looking around to see that the place was a mess. Things were thrown just about everywhere. The mattress on the bed looked like it had been cut down the middle with a knife. I held the lantern out at arm's length so I could see the rest of the room and stepped carefully towards the table. There was something on it, but I couldn't make out what it was. When I got there and looked through the long shadow of the light, I saw that it was a long butcher knife stuck into the wooden board tabletop. It was coated in something dark on part of the blade and there was a spattering of it on the table. I couldn't be sure, but it looked like the same thing was on the mattress as well.

"Let's get on *out*," Willie whispered in a pleading voice. I thought it had the sound of wisdom this time. I set the lantern back onto the table and blew out the flame. We walked outside into the fresh air and light. It didn't look good in there, but it wasn't like we had found Riley dead like we had Dyle.

"Could have just been some critter he was skinnin'," I said after a moment. There were plenty of trapped pelts around, and I knew that he lived mostly off of trapping and fishing.

"Shoulda made sure that critter was done with that skin first," said Willie. "Looks like it put up a tussle for it before he got it...or maybe it got Riley's hide instead."

"It ain't right that the place ain't locked up," I said shaking my head, but I didn't know what to do.

"Maybe whoever killed Dyle come lookin' for Riley," said Willie. I considered that for a moment. Anyone who knew the woods very well would probably know about Riley. Maybe Willie was right. Maybe they got to thinkin' about what Riley might have seen or heard and came lookin' for him. Then again, maybe Riley was just fine and had taken off for a while. He did that sometimes.

"Let's head on back," I said after one last look around. Willie nodded. He was ready. I wondered if I would ever talk him into coming back out here again, but I figured that once the goose stepped off his grave, he'd be game enough.

"Which way you figure on going back?" Willie asked as we started back along the stream. We had left our shoes back up above the falls to let them dry out until we got back, and we had to get them first.

"Thought we might take the high trail back," I said after a few steps. We were already hot again after being back in the sun for just a few minutes, and we stepped back into the water.

"If you figure on the high trail...guess we oughta take the low trail then," Willie grinned. I laughed at that one, but all the way home I never quite stopped thinking about Riley's cabin up there by the falls and just what might have gone on inside there.

We passed back through town still drying out in the hot summer air. Anyone with a fan in the window was finding a reason to stand in front of it, and I saw through the window that the grocer had decided that this was a good day to stock the frozen foods. As we walked past the Baptist church we both attended I got the usual flutter in my stomach that I'd felt since the Sunday after we'd found Dyle. For whatever reason, I felt like God was watching me closer around the church than anyplace else and that if I were to get struck by lighting this would be the place. Minister Washburne and Addie were out front tending the flowers along the walk to the front doors.

"Kinda hot dontcha think?" I said to Minister Washburne. He looked up from his knees.

"Flowers have to be tended even when we'd rather be doing something else," said Minister Washburn. He was sweating heavily.

"Reckon that could be just about anything right now," I said.

"Don't answer that, Evan," said Addie without looking up. "I know just what you're thinkin'." She brushed her forehead with the back of her gardening glove. "These flowers were planted by the wife of Minister Redding more than twenty years ago. Won't be said we let them wilt an' die just 'cause we was a little shy o' the heat."

"No, mustn't be said," said Washburne with a shake of his head. I looked at the flowers. To me they looked a lot like weeds I'd seen in the woods, but I figured that was something I ought to keep to myself. I took a step to my right and created a bit of shade over the minister.

"Bless you child," said Washburne as he was allowed at least a moment's relief from the afternoon's blistering sun. "Moses was sent out into the desert...and survived. It must have been much as this I think."

"Now Evan," said Addie with a warning tone. "We coulda been workin' at a cooler time o' the day if your hours at the church wasn't runnin' so late." I had never thought about a minister having work besides the hour and a half we saw him at church every Sunday, so I was surprised to hear that.

"Quite true, Addie," said Washburne with a nod as he returned to his work of pulling out the weeds and grass. I could hear in his voice that he had lost this argument, and I didn't reckon that he won very many with Addie Washburne.

"Reckon we ought to be on our way," I said.

"I was goin' to say a prayer for our baseball team," said Willie, "but I reckon you could use it more'n us." Washburne looked up and smiled but said nothing. Thinking back, I think that was probably the wisest thing he could have said. We had started to leave when I noticed an even larger shadow spread out over the ground. I looked up and saw the scowling face of Garson Ashe. I tried to recollect if I had ever seen the man smile and came up empty.

"Nice day to you, Garson," said Washburne as he looked up again from his work.

"Hot as blazes if'n you ask me," said Ashe. "See she's got ya' doin' woman's work again." He shook his head in disgust.

"Must be my English blood," said Washburne with a strained smile. "The British were always very fond of gardening."

"Limies," Ashe scoffed. "Got no use for them either."

"Tell me, Garson," said Washburne as he seemed to be losing his temper, "just what have you a *use* for? I've not seen you wearing out a pew in church on Sunday."

"Come on out to the river an' preach, parson," said Garson with a laugh. "That's where you'll find me come a Sunday morning."

"Perhaps I will one Sunday," said Washburne thoughtfully. "John the Baptist had no more than the Jordan River for his church, and Christ preached to the faithful on the mount."

"You've got one for every one I give you," said Garson with a sneer.

"Evan…don't pay him no mind," said Addie as she moved protectively closer to her husband. I saw the fear in her face. I kind of thought Minister Washburne would hold his own if it came to fists, but I could see right off that she didn't.

"I think I have *two* for every one you give me," said Washburne. I knew then that between the heat, the weeding, and Garson that this was starting to look ugly, but I figured if the minister just kept on with his gardening, Ashe would get bored and leave. Still, I wasn't counting on that. I nudged Willie in the ribs with my elbow and we ran across the street and down to Claxton's office. I pushed in through the door and went straight to Claxton's examination room. I opened the door without a second's thought about who might be in there.

"Nathan," said Claxton as he looked up. "You know to knock first...could have had a lady in here."

"Sorry, sir," I said a little winded. I saw now that he did have a patient, Gerald Williamson, sitting on the table. "I think there's 'bout to be trouble. Garson Ashe is havin' words with Minister Washburne out front of the church. I think they're 'bout to fight!"

"Must be the heat messin' with people's brains," Claxton sighed. "Let me see what this is 'bout Gerald. I'll be back in a minute." Claxton took off his white examination coat and dropped it into his chair and then was promptly out the door and on the street taking long strides to the church.

"This a private gettogether, or can anyone join in?" asked Claxton as he walked up on them. Washburne was on his feet now and his gloves were lying on the walkway like he had tossed them down.

"Just chewin' the fat with the parson," said Ashe. "Havin' us a difference of opinion on some things."

"On just about all things I'd say," said Washburne angrily.

"Kinda hot to be stirrin' up the blood an' all," said Claxton with a peacemaking smile. "Garson...you still boatin' up on the river these days?"

"Whenever I can," said Garson. "Bass are 'bout jumpin' in the boat 'bout now."

"Well, 'spose you might send a few o' them rascal's my way?" asked Claxton with   another of his amiable smiles. "Give you three a piece for 'em."

"Reckon I could fix you up with a couple," said Garson. "Soon as the parson an' me finish up…" Garson took a step in Washburne's direction. Claxton put a hand on his shoulder. It looked like it was just a friendly pat, but I saw that it was more than that. There was strength in that hand that stopped Ashe cold in his tracks. I saw Ashe check the hand on his shoulder and then look straight at Claxton. I could tell that he was surprised by how easily Claxton had stopped him in midstep.

"I've got a powerful taste for those bass," said Claxton. "Sure would like to fry 'em up for supper tonight." I thought Ashe tried to push past him, but if he did it didn't work, as he didn't budge Claxton an inch. Claxton only smiled. Ashe licked his lips. Any fight he'd been spoilin' for a few minutes before was now gone. He might have wanted a go at Minister Washburne, but I could tell right off he wasn't feelin' up to takin' on Claxton today.

"Reckon I'll see to those fish," said Ashe as he eased back a half-step. "All right if I drop them by the house 'bout four?"

"It'd be right neighborly of you," said Claxton. Ashe gave him a nod and stepped back another step.

"Washburne maybe we'll run into each other again sometime. Ma'am," said Ashe. He turned and began walking quickly down the sidewalk.

"Garson's a troubled man," said Claxton with a shake of his head as he watched him leave. "I'd be careful talkin' with him, Evan."

"He has a way of getting under my skin," said Washburne. "For the life of me, I can't recall offending the man, but everytime we meet, it gets worse. I know I should turn the other cheek, but mostly I just want to punch him."

"Garson has a problem with God…not you Evan," said Claxton. "He can't take God to task, so you're just here in person for him to take it out on."

"I think sometimes he sees this collar and forgets I'm a man," said Washburne. He was still a little angry, and that surprised me, too. I'd never seen him that way before, but listening now, it seems that he and Garson might have a running feud.

"You've got nothing to prove," said Claxton with a smile. "Takes a bigger man to not fight. Garson's not worth it." Washburne shot a look at Addie. Claxton saw it. "Nothing to prove there either," he added just above a whisper.

"If Garson has a problem with God, perhaps that is something I *could* help him with," said Washburne. He was calming down now. "It is my job to help those who've lost their way."

"I'm not sure he would let you," said Claxton. "But, if anyone needs the help, it's him."

"What is the nature of his…issue…with God?" asked Washburne.

"Blames God for his problems, Evan," said Claxton. "Parents died in the flood of '24, two brothers killed in France, wife left him. Probably just scratchin' the top of the list."

"I hadn't known all that," said Washburne. "I must keep that in mind when we meet next."

"I'd tread light on those things," said Claxton. Well, I got a patient to see. Hope you get out of the sun before you're my next one." Claxton looked at Addie. "Even the county lets the prisoners drink on work details, ma'am. Probably best if you didn't spend much more time out here either." Claxton was probably the only person in town that could have said that and gotten away with it. He turned and was on his way back to his office before she could say something that she might regret.

"Glad you boys stopped by to say hello," said Washburne. I thought what he really meant was to say 'thanks for getting Claxton in between them', but that was fine.

"Yes, you boys ought to come by and get some cookies," said Addie. "I've got fresh bakin' most ever Wednesday and Saturday."

"Yes, ma'am," I said. "Reckon Willie an' I could keep any from goin' to waste." We said our good-byes and were on our way.

"That fella' Ashe...was he born in a bad mood?" asked Willie as we went down the street.

"Maybe," I said. "Don't rightly recall the last time he ever said howdy an' meant it. Wouldn't pay him no mind."

"Thought he was aimin' to have him a fight," said Willie. "Never knowed anybody wantin' to fight with a *minister* an' all. Seemed to go right out of him when Claxton showed up."

"Yep," I said. "Sure did." As much as I could recall, I couldn't remember Claxton having a great appetite for bass, but that night we had two fifteen pounders, and I guessed them to be the pick of that day's catch.

Chapter Six

As it turned out the heat kept on like it had with no breaks, and most days were clear and cloudless, so Willie and I went back up into the woods just about every day for the next week to enjoy the cool cover from the canopy of the trees. We never did run across Riley, but we never went back to his cabin either, so there wasn't a lot of chance of it happening. I was hoping that Riley had just decided to make himself scarce and that somebody hadn't helped him along in that direction. He was wily as an old fox, but I also recalled that he had a number of fox pelts hanging on his cabin wall, and they had probably been pretty wily, too, and yet he had their skins. Claxton was fond of saying that there was always somebody out there in the world that was little bigger, a little stronger, a step quicker, and a hair smarter, and if you lived long enough you'd run into him. When you did, you had better have an ace up your sleeve because that would be the time to play it. I hoped Riley had that ace up his sleeve, but I really hoped that he hadn't needed one. I had thought about telling Claxton what I had seen up there at the cabin, but I knew deep down that no one...not even Claxton...was going to spend their time looking for a crazy old man, so I kept it to myself and hoped for the best.

Josiah Falls

If Dyle's murder and Riley's untimely disappearance had been the only things that had happened that summer, most folks would have probably forgotten about the summer of 1950 by the time the next one rolled around, but any possibility of that happening soon changed right after the night of July Fourth.

Josiah Falls was usually a quiet place, but on the Fourth each year, it was as loud as Times Square on New Year's Day. There were fireworks of all kinds; firecrackers, roman candles, bottle rockets, whistlin' chasers for the kids while the adults loaded up the big sky rockets and put on a show. There were charcoal grills going up and down Main Street on both sides with people grabbin' a hot dog off one and BBQ ribs off another. There was also plenty of beer and liquor, but Claxton reminded me that those were off limits for at least another year or two. I didn't put up much of an argument on that. I had already tried a beer and some rum a year before when Ranson Hayes and I got into his daddy's liquor cabinet and helped ourselves. We got pretty sick, and since I could still remember yaking up everything but my shoes into the kitchen sink, I really didn't have a taste for it now.

I walked around with Willie most of the time. The Fourth was one of those few times when the whole town, black and white, got together and had a good time. I saw Carter Monroe about half way down the block. He had a big open grill cut from a metal barrel stood up on a heavy steel frame. The smoke was pouring out the top and he was flipping ribs, chicken, and steak on it in between throwing the cooked ones onto plates. I sneaked into line between two elderly black men, and stuck my plate out.

"You passin' for colored these days?" Carter winked at me when he saw me there.

"If'n it'll get me a piece of chicken I am," I smiled back.

"I'll keep it under m' hat," Carter said without the slightest smile to anyone. He forked up a sizeable piece of chicken breast and dropped it on my plate. I winked back and moved on down the way.

The night wore on and finally the firecrackers and rockets began to die down. I saw most everybody in town there at one time or another. Even Minister Washburne was there. He was wearing his little white collar, but he had gotten rid of the black coat he always wore after a couple of bouts with Stu Armondson's twelve-alarm chili. His wife, Addie, was there with him. She was dressed up like she was going to a wedding puttin' on airs and such, and I couldn't believe that she was wearing a fancy dress and gloves in this heat. I shook my head at that. I was hot wearing nothing but a T-shirt and shorts. Figured if I lived to be a hundred I wouldn't figure out girls. Before long Addie Washburne got sick from the heat or something she ate and left for home a few hours into the night, but she insisted on her husband staying on without her. I saw him looking after her as she went, but he did like she asked and stayed there.

Claxton finally found me again about eleven o'clock. I could tell he was ready to leave, but he seemed to be hanging back like he was expecting something to happen. He hung around close by when Garson Ashe surprised a lot of folks and showed up in town. Usually he stayed away from church, town meetings, and other get togethers of the kind. It didn't seem to take long before he found Minister Washburne. Like Claxton, I was kind of curious to see if there might be more fireworks there than in the sky. I saw Claxton take a few steps closer, but not so close that he was in the way. I knew what he was doin'. He wanted to be nearby in case the talk became more than that. I didn't think he could hear what was being said, but if the voices got hot he'd know it.

"Are you familiar with the book of Job?" asked Washburne tentatively.

"My mother was a church goin' woman," Ashe grunted. "I recollect some of it. Was 'bout that fella that had durn near everything an' lost it 'cause God an' the devil was bettin' on him. That the one?"

"Yes," said Washburne. "Job was put through many trials by the devil who was trying to break his faith in God."

"An' God just set back up on high an' let his best man get skint by the devil," Ashe snorted. "Ain't that a fine howdy do in the mornin' for a fella that was God fearin' all his durned life. Fella tryin' to do what was right an' gett'n dirt kicked in his face for doin' it. Yeah…reckon I know *all* 'bout that one."

"When I first read Job," said Washburne. "I was very angry. I was angry that God would do that."

"Well, then we're o' the same mind on it then," said Ashe with a nod. "Kinda surprised me on that, parson."

"It took me a long time to understand that it was not just a test of *Job's* faith that was on trial," said Washburne. "It was also a proof to the devil of *God's* faith in Job."

"God's faith?" said Ashe scratchin' the back of his head. "Ain't never thought 'bout it like that. Figured God always *knew* what was to come…steered things the way He pleased an' damn what the rest of us wants."

"He knows," said Washburne, "but it's up to us to *choose* and steer. You see, Garson, you may have lost your faith in God, but he never lost his faith in *you*."

"Oh, now parson," Ashe shook his head. "I been gone from the light a powerful long time. I done a heap o' things I ain't proud of. likely I'll do a heap more."

"God always forgives," said Washburne simply. "The only thing left is for *you* to forgive. The light never left you. It's just behind a cloud waiting for you."

"Reckon you done give me a heap to think on," said Ashe. "Sure would like to talk it out…private like."

"Doors of the church are open to all," said Washburne. "Let me know sometime when you want to talk. Any time." They went on for a while, and I was right surprised to hear Garson Ashe talkin' like a man that wasn't spoilin' for a fight, but he was just as apt to change his mind anytime. After a bit, I saw Claxton movin' on down the way. The serious look was gone off his face, and that told me that he wasn't lookin' for anything to happen right then.

As it turned out he was right about *something* happening, and so was I; it just wasn't between Garson Ashe and Evan Washburne. As the partying died down, some of the drinking turned serious. It wasn't long after that before the talk started to get loud. The subject of the church burnings had surfaced again, and someone was wondering very loudly if maybe that had led to the untimely demise of one Dyle Courtland.

"And maybe you made good on layin' ole Dyle out," said a very intoxicated Dwight Bishop. "Last I seen him...Dyle shore was laid out for good."

"I ain't laid a finger on Dyle," said Carter Monroe. "You done had you too much, mister Dwight, sir." I could hear something smoldering in his voice, but he wasn't drunk and it was clear he didn't want trouble. He went back to getting his grill ready to move, willing to let the talk stop right there. But Bishop wasn't ready to let go.

"Everybody knows that ole Dyle was handy with a match...liked to watch things burn...and wasn't exactly partial to colored folks." Bishop went on. If it was clear to me what he was implying, I'm sure it was clear to everyone else. "Would'a took a strong man ta' take his gun from 'em and blow a hole in 'em."

"Jes what you trying to say?" said Carter Monroe. He stopped working on his cleaning, and I could see his fists clenching and unclenching.

"You got clogged ears, Monroe?" said Bishop. He pointed a wavering finger in the general vicinity of Main Street. "Everybody heard you talkin' 'bout what oughta be done. Well sure looks like you gone and *done* it all right." He took a step in the direction of Carter. I felt my blood run a little cold. I didn't think Carter Monroe was going to back down or run even if he didn't want trouble.

"You're makin' a damn fool of yourself, Dwight," said Claxton as he walked part way out in the street, took Bishop by the shoulder and pulled him back towards the sidewalk. Bishop tried to pull away, but I was close enough to see that Claxton was bearing down on him with a very strong grip even though to everyone else it probably looked like he was just gently guiding him along. I had seen how easily he had convinced Garson Ashe that one more step might be his last. Dwight Bishop was not nearly the size of Ashe. Claxton forced a smile on his face. "Let's not have any trouble tonight, Dwight."

"Good thing you stopped me, I'd a given him…" Bishop began as he wobbled unsteadily on his feet.

"Carter's as strong as a country mule," said Claxton cut him off quietly. "He'd a broke you in half an' used the pieces for kindling." Bishop turned and stared at Claxton with a bit of comprehension starting to seep inside his foggy brain.

"You know…you're right 'bout that," said Bishop drunkenly, but not too drunk to take that fact in. "Now who are you?" Claxton pulled Bishop's glasses from his pocket and put them on his nose. "Claxton, I didn't even know you were here. Good party this year…ya think?" I watched Claxton walk Dwight Bishop down the walk; Bishop seemed to have forgotten what was going on entirely. Carter Monroe watched them go, and he hadn't forgotten. I could see his jaw still working away the anger, as he went back to getting his grill packed up. I hung around for a few more minutes to wait for Claxton to get back. Dwight Bishop only lived two minutes away. I figured Claxton would see him to his house to make sure he got off the street and nothing else flared up. Carter Monroe picked up the end of his rolling grill and started pushing it back down Main Street where he had parked his truck.

"Tell your daddy, I'm much obliged," said Carter with a nod as he walked past. I nodded in return.

"I will," I said. I only knew that there could have been trouble, but I didn't really understand what Carter meant. He would have handled Dwight Bishop for certain, drunk or not.

"I'm glad Claxton was here," I heard Minister Washburne saying over my shoulder. "That could have gotten ugly…and we've had way too much of that lately." I was wonderin' if he was thinkin' about his own run-ins with Garson Ashe.

"I reckon it could have," I said. "But…you don't reckon Carter woulda hurt 'em do you?"

"Not meaning too. But, every man has a breaking point, Nathan," Washburne said seriously. "It's not good to see when it happens. I might ask Carter to take some time away from the church and let things cool off a bit..." I looked at him, but I knew right then that he had been thinking out loud and not really talking to me.

"Evan?" said a voice from behind him. It was Odessa, Addie's friend that she was almost never seen without. "Could we talk for a bit? I could use some more advice, if that's okay."

"I suppose we can talk," said Washburne. "Is it something private?" She only smiled and nodded. "Well, go on to the church, and I'll be along shortly. I guess I know what it is." She nodded again. I turned at that moment and saw Claxton waving at me.

"I gotta go," I said. I ran over to Claxton and we started walking right away.

It was two fifteen that morning when we awoke to the town fire alarm. I sat up in bed, still half asleep, and looked around. There was an orange glow outside my window. Less than a minute later, Claxton, tossed open my door, and I was just then beginning to realize what the sound was.

"Nathan!" he called to me. "Grab some clothes...find my bag downstairs. I'm heading to that fire." He was stepping into his pants there in the doorway. I jumped up out of the bed to find the clothes I had just taken off a few hours before.

"What's burnin'?" I asked. "Reckon the fireworks done lit somethin'?"

"Don't know yet," said Claxton. "But it must be big. Comin' from downtown. Bring the bag and find me...hope we don't need it."

"Yes, sir," I called back but he was already gone from the door. I could hear him on the stairs. He stomped on his boots on the wood floor and was out the screen door. I was probably only two minutes behind him and running fast.

"Where you goin' child?" called Bertie pulling on her housecoat.

"Claxton told me to get his bag and come on," I said. "That's what I aim to do." I tied my shoes and burst past her down the stairs.

63

"You stay clear o' that fire!" she called after me.

"Yes'm, Bertie!" I yelled back. Then I was out the door and running with Claxton's heavy bag. Once outside, I could smell the burning, and the orange glow covered the skyline. A lot of people were walking and looking, but only a few were going that way. It seemed like most everyone was in a daze. I ran past them, turned onto Main and saw that the fire was coming from the Baptist Church. There were several men already there. Three of them were attaching a big fire hose to the yellow hydrant out front and Claxton was working the huge wrench on top. I saw the hose on the ground slowly come to life as it filled up with water, and five men grabbed hold of it and started trying to spray down the church. Owen Mercer was up on the front of the hose wearing only his shorts and an undershirt.

"Put it on the door!" Mercer was yelling at the men with him. It took some doing, but they managed to guide the powerful stream down to the front doors. I could see the heat and the steam coming from them, and once it cleared, I could see that the outside of the church was not really burning. The roof was completely lit up, but rest of the flames seemed to be coming from inside. It then occurred to me that the doors were heavy oak and the church itself was mostly brick on the first level, and brick and wood on the second.

"Owen!" I heard Claxton yelling over the blaze and everyone else. I looked and saw Owen Mercer running for the front doors of the church with the hose arcing a line of water in over him. There were burning timbers falling down around the place when he got there. He tore off his undershirt and grabbed for the handles, but I could see that they were not opening and were probably red hot by the way he flinched back. He took a step back and threw himself shoulder first at the middle of the doors. Owen Mercer was a strong man, short but stocky and wide across the shoulders, but those doors were four-inch thick oak and didn't budge much at all. He took several steps away from the doors all the way back to the edge of the brick steps, and I thought he had caught a sudden attack of good sense. Then he did what might be the bravest thing I ever saw a man do. He ran full force into the middle of those doors with everything he had. There was a thump that some people later said was heard a block a way. The doors buckled in as the old creaky hinges started to give. He grabbed at his right shoulder once, then gathered himself and hit the doors once more, and they gave. There was a blast of heat and flame from the mouth of the broken doors, and probably only the left-hand door flying back out and completely off its hinges kept him from taking the incinerating heat head on. Mercer and the door went flying off to the side of the entrance while all the fire of hell seemed to come from within. After a full minute of keeping the water on it, the fire pulled back from where it had fed on the fresh air, and Claxton went running up the steps with Norm Abernathy and began dragging Owen Mercer back down the steps away from the inferno.

"What the blazes were you tryin' to do up there?" Claxton was yelling at Mercer over the roar of the fire and the commotion around it. They were back behind the hose now, and Claxton was looking at Owen Mercer's shoulder.

"Heard somebody was in there!" Mercer yelled back.

"At two in the mornin'?" said Claxton shaking his head.

They went on fighting the blaze as best they could for the next hour, but mostly they were fighting to keep it from spreading by then. Luckily, it was a calm night, and there was only a little damage to the next-door bakery. The fire went on through the morning and finally burned itself out just after eight am. When it was done, there was nothing left above the first level except for a few columns of bricks here and there, and the insides were entirely gutted. Owen Mercer had a broken collar bone, cuts and bruises, and looked like he had fallen asleep on the beach for about a week, but other than that he was going to be fine. It wasn't until late the next evening that we found out that he was the lucky one. He had been on the outside.

Chapter Seven

What Owen Mercer had heard was true. Two bodies were found in the church. They had been burned beyond recognition and it was some days before the state forensics lab was able to identify them positively, but everyone in Josiah Falls knew who they were since that first morning. Only two people had not eventually shown up at the church, Evan Washburne and Odessa Hendricks, and most everyone figured that was pretty good evidence that they'd been there all along. I told Claxton what I had heard the night before about the two of them planning to meet at the church. I don't know if it really solved the mystery, but it certainly helped confirm the answer, and I felt a little less guilty about some other things. There were, however, a few left over questions. First, the two of them were locked inside. Claxton asked around about that and found that it was not uncommon for Evan Washburne to be at the church late at night, and that he typically would lock up after hours. The problem, though, was that he didn't have the key on him when his body was found and neither did Odessa. Those keys did not turn up in the debris of the church either. The second mystery was how the fire started, but it did not remain a mystery very long. Fire investigators from Jackson only needed a short time to determine that the fire had been set deliberately. They saw the signs of it everywhere. This was a case of arson, and whoever set the fire had taken some time to do it because the place went up almost at once. It didn't take long for people to begin looking for a connection between this church fire and those that had claimed the two other churches several weeks earlier.

There was a lot of angry talk around town over the next several days, and just about everyone had a theory about who had done it. I think about the only person that wasn't accused at least once might have been Dyle Courtland, but somebody did suggest they check the graveyard just to make sure he was still there as it was the first time that Dyle had been shot at and stayed dead. After that, the talk started to shift towards Owen Mercer. Nobody could deny that Owen was a good man at heart, and he certainly had more backbone than most; his busting in the church doors was proof of that, but folks were not real happy with the lack of progress he had been making on what was now three murders all in just a few weeks time. Some wondered if maybe they needed to bring in some help from outside, and a few wondered loud enough to be heard if maybe Owen just wasn't the right man for the job. After all, it wasn't like he was neck deep in a metropolitan crimewave and such that he couldn't throw himself on the task full time. In a small town, talk like that circulates quickly, and it came back around to Owen in due time; he took it just about the way Claxton figured he would. He got out of bed, busted shoulder and all, and went back to work, making a point of talking to just about every living soul in town and even close by. Inside of three days, he filled up a notebook with more than two hundred people who had good reason to want to kill Dyle. A few even owned up to having *tried*, and he found a sizeable number of men who had been at least somewhat romantically involved with the late Odessa Hendricks. None of them seemed to harbor a grudge bad enough to want to roast her alive like a Christmas goose, but there was the odd loose end or two she had left behind while she husband hunted through the biggest share of Josiah Falls' eligible young men. The only one that nobody seemed to have a problem with was Evan Washburne. Except for some run-ins with Garson Ashe, everyone that had had occasion to cross his path liked him, and there weren't too many dry eyes mourning his passing. In fact, the only person I'd ever heard have words with him had been Garson Ashe, but if Garson had killed everyone he'd had words with, there wouldn't have been anyone left in town. And besides, the last time they had talked, it had been almost friendly from what bit I heard. There was one other small fact that came back from the state lab. It seems that Odessa Hendricks had been with child. It hadn't been long enough for her to show, and no one in town mentioned knowing. Even Claxton had not known about it, and evidently she had not told anyone. I only knew because I had heard Claxton and Owen Mercer mention it, and they had decided that it wasn't anybody's business, so it didn't go any further than that.

Eventually, Odessa Hendricks and Evan Washburne were laid to rest in the cemetery beside the church, but it was not until the crime scene tape around the Baptist Church of God came down, and the last of the cleanup got started. I think the whole town turned out to see Minister Washburne sent off. The Haywood brothers, who sang in the church choir at the black Baptist church that got burned down on Emerson Avenue on the far end of town, came out to the cemetery and sang 'Amazing Grace' over him. I was pretty sure that just 'bout everyone in town had come up with one reason or another to have been walkin' by Emerson Avenue early on Sunday morning just to give them a listen, but I do believe it was the prettiest singin' I'd ever heard. Harlan Clary, who had been one of the church elder deacons and was probably most responsible for bringin' Evan Washburne to Josiah Falls, read over him at the graveside. By the end of the day you couldn't see the grave for all the flowers coverin' it. Strangest thing though was that early the next mornin' there was a brand new headstone ready carved and stood up in place. It was a fine stone with Evan Washburne's name and the day he died on it, but nobody ever owned up to havin' the work done. I know that Claxton asked around tryin' to find out, but all he found out was that Harshburgher's, who made just about all the tombstones in town, didn't make it. After that he kinda let it rest, but I know he was still puzzlin' over it.

It was decided that the bottom foundation and walls were good enough to be saved, but there was nothing left on the inside except for the church books and some cash donations that had been left inside a big fireproof box. Since it was technically evidence, Owen Mercer took the box to his office for safe keeping until the church leaders could decide where they were going to move for a while.

I don't think anybody really expected Owen Mercer to get to the bottom of anything much except maybe his next beer, but everyone was surprised when they heard that something important had been turned up, and that he was going before Judge Harlan Clary to get an arrest warrant. It was a little late for a warrant, however, as he already had a man with him that he wanted to charge. Claxton had gotten a call from Judge Clary to come down to the courthouse for what he called 'an impromptu hearing', and I went along with about half the town to see what was going to happen. By the time we got there, the courthouse was just about filled up. I squeezed onto a piece of the bench on the end of the front row while Claxton went up front to see what the judge wanted with him.

"Got your message to come down, Harlan," said Claxton as he walked up to the judge who had yet to take his seat up behind his high desk.

"Claxton," said Clary as he signed a paper and handed it to the bailiff. "I'd like you to sit in on this…maybe lend a hand to Junior." He motioned to the table out front of the desk where Junior Preston sat with a notebook, three-dozen pencils, and a legal book ten inches thick.

"I haven't practiced criminal law in a long time, Harlan," Claxton said with a glance at Junior.

"Junior's been before me three times since he come home from law school," said Clary. "I expect you know a little more than he does right now. As an officer of the court, I'd be obliged if you'd keep him out of trouble during this hearing. I don't want any claims of incompetence coming back later on."

"All right," said Claxton with a sigh. "I'll act as co-counsel. You can put my name down if you think it helps."

"It'll carry more weight than a public defender practicing law for the fourth time," said Clary. The judge turned around and walked up behind the desk while Claxton walked over to the table, shook the hand of Junior Preston and took what looked like the weight of the whole world off of his scrawny shoulders when he sat down. I could see him leaning close to Junior and saying something, and it looked like Junior was trying to fill him in on what was going on. About that time, Owen Mercer walked into the courtroom with Carter Monroe beside him. I was a little surprised to see Carter, but like everyone else I expected that he had come on in to talk about something he knew. The real surprise came when he took a seat over beside Junior at the defendant's table.

"All rise and…" began Woodrow Silas the burly bailiff in his court uniform. Nobody past the first row could have heard him over the noise.

"Everybody hush up!" Woodrow bellowed in his deep baritone voice that rang out over the courtroom like a foghorn on the Mississippi. The place didn't go silent all at once, but it got a lot quieter. "That's better! Now all rise and knock it off!" That put an end to it. Most of the people there were already standing anyway, but they did finally shut up and listen. "Honorable Judge Harlan Clary presiding. This hearing is now in session."

"Thank you, Woodrow," said Clary as he pulled out his chair and sat down. He looked around at his packed courtroom. This was probably the first time most of them had been here. "Y'all can sit down now, but keep it quiet. I like to hear myself think now and then." People began sitting down then. "Now…just so's y'all know…this is a *hearing*. It ain't no trial. We're here to talk about some things and see if we can get 'em straight." He waited a minute for all that to sink in.

"All right," Clary said. "Owen…you go on have your say." Owen Mercer, still a bright orange from the fire, walked out in front of the table on the left. He was carrying a small clear bag in his left hand. His right arm was still in a sling.

"Well…Harlan…your Honor…sir," Owen Mercer began.

"Just pick one," said Clary. "I'll answer to it." Mercer nodded.

"Well, I went by the church this mornin' to see if Carter had the key to the box with all the church papers and such in it."

"I know the one," said Clary with a nod. "Go on…"

"…well, I run into Carter back by the old tool shed. He was just openin' up to do some trimmin' work," said Mercer. "So I walked inside and asked if he had the key."

"Did he have it?" asked Clary.

"He did," Mercer nodded. "Had it on his ring of church keys 'long with the rest. We were about to walk back out when I saw another set of keys there on the shelf right inside the door. Looked just like Carter's...'cept for one thing..." He walked up to the judge's desk, reached up and set the bag in front of him. Clary lifted the bag and looked at it closely.

"Seems there's a little wooden ID with the initial's 'E.W.' on it," said Clary. "Is that the difference you mean?"

"That's it your honor," said Mercer. "I asked Carter where it came from. He said he didn't know how they got there, but that they were sure enough Minister Evan Washburne's."

"That right, Carter?" asked Clary. "You need to see these up close?"

"Done seen 'em up close," said Carter as he stood up. "Those is mister, Evan's keys, sir. I seen 'em a bunch of times. Couldn't be no other like 'em. Got five keys. One's a key to the front door, one's to the little side door, that small one...well we don't rightly know what that one's to. One's the shed key, and that last one's the key to the records box." He took out a set of keys from his pocket and held them up. "'Cept for his 'nitials, these here is just like them."

"And this set...here in my hand...was locked up in the shed?" asked Clary.

"Yes, sir, your honor," said Carter. "They was settin' there just like mister Owen said, sir."

"Does anybody else have a key or any of these keys?" asked Clary.

"Might have been one of the deacons, sir," said Carter slowly, "...but don't recall when that was. Must be near ten years since they been seen."

"Do you know which deacon?" asked Clary.

"Was Riley as I recall," said Carter, "...afore he got a notion to go live up in them woods yonder." Clary smiled and almost laughed.

"Done forgot Riley was deacon for a spell," said Clary. There was a murmur in the crowd of people. "Simmer down now," Clary raised his hand, and everyone started to quiet again.

"Well, judge, it kinda raises a question now don't it?" said Mercer. "The keys to the church was right there in the shed. The shed's been locked up tight since the fire, and the church was locked up when it burnt...and there ain't but one other key that opens that shed door."

"Those keys with you all the time?" asked Clary. "Ever outa your sight? Evev so much as an hour?"

"No, sir," Carter shook his head. "They's with me lessen I'm washin' up. I never knows when I might needs 'em when I'm in town." Clary nodded.

"Anything else, Owen?" asked Clary. I could see that he was all serious now and a lot of things were going on his head. Claxton was leaning across to Junior saying something.

"There's one more thing," said Owen. "When I was in the shed, I smelled gasoline real strong. There was a big ole five gallon jug, empty 'cept for a drop or two, settin' under the shelf with the keys. The top was just settin' on it. I think it's the same oil 'n gas mixture the lab boys turned up in the fire."

"What's that fuel for Carter?" asked Clary.

"Your honor," said Junior Preston standing up quickly. Everyone could see that he was plenty nervous. "I think my client might not should answer any more questions under the Fifth Amendment"

"Don't see why I cain't answer the judge," said Carter as he stood back up.

"Junior's thinkin' that you might say somethin' that might cause you trouble later on," said Clary. "Just doin' like he's 'sposed to do. Junior, this here is still a hearing. Nobody's been charged with any crime yet, but Carter...do you want to have a word or two with Junior before you say anything else?"

"Cain't see how I needs to," said Carter. "Ain't done nothing wrong. We uses that gasoline to run that big ole gen'rator out back when the power goes out."

"You put something in that gasoline?" asked Clary.

"Yes, sir," said Carter. "Puts a bit o' cylinder oil in it...just like it says on the printin' on the plate." He sat back down.

"Carter..." Judge Clary began. He looked around the courtroom for a minute as if he had to say something that he didn't want to say. "I'm goin' to have to have you go with Owen over to the jail. Afraid there's goin' to have to be some charges."

"Charges...for what?" asked Carter. "I ain't done nothin'!"

"We got a shed locked up with *your* keys. The only other keys to the church were locked up inside, and the gasoline used to burn it down was in there too," said Clary. "Folks around here know you were riled up about those other church burnin's."

"Riled is one thing...killin' is another," said Carter shaking his head.

"I don't like this myself, Carter," said Judge Clary, "but I don't have no choice. I'm postin' a charge of arson in the burnin' down of the church."

"Judge," said Owen, "You addin' murder on that too?" Clary shook his head.

"Goin' to call in a prosecutor," said Clary. "Let him look the case over first. Then he can decide if he wants to do that."

"Your honor," said Junior, "I'd like to request a bail hearing." Clary looked at him as if he would like to slap him upside the head.

"You would?" said Clary. "All right. Bail is set at...five hundred thousand dollars."

"Your honor!" said Junior. He was standing up an' all excited now. "The United States Constitution forbids unreasonable bail."

"Please define *unreasonable*, counselor," said Clary sternly. "I am vaguely acquainted with that document you're talkin' 'bout, son, and it does allow for some…latitude in making such decisions." There was a low snicker in the courtroom by some, but for most they were shocked by what they were hearing. Junior was about to say something else, but Claxton grabbed him by the forearm and stopped him.

"Your honor," said Claxton standing for the first time. The courtroom quieted immediately. "May counsel approach the bench?"

"I'd be obliged if you would, Claxton," said Clary. He motioned for Owen to come up as well. "Concerns you, too, Carter. Come on up here and listen. Claxton stood and walked up in front of the bench and the rest joined him.

"I'm guessin' that you're settin' bail so high so that it *can't* be met?" said Claxton with a tilt of his head at Carter.

"I am," said Clary with a nod to him. "I think Carter's a whole lot safer over there in that cell with Owen than out walkin' round town right now." Claxton nodded.

"Don't know that no jail cell can protect a man," said Carter. I think everyone knew what that meant.

"Ain't openin' that door to nobody," said Owen. "Judge, I want you to appoint me a couple of deputies." Clary nodded in agreement.

"Who you want, Owen?" asked Clary. "Name 'em."

"I'd like Ted Fiedler. He was with the police force in Fayette 'afore he retired here…he don't scare none," said Owen. "…an' Gerald Edmundson."

"Reckon they'll do," said Clary. "It's so ordered, and they are appointed. You swear them in proper like…issue guns as you see fit. They don't want to serve, you send them to me, and I'll persuade them otherwise."

"But, Judge, sir," said Carter, "I ain't done *nothin'*. You think I could do somethin' like that?"

"Nobody here wants this, Carter, but it don't matter what I think," said Clary. "The state has a case here. They got opportunity. they've got evidence, and they've got motive. Now you gonna have your say in this, but hear me real good now. You need to get you a top o' the line trial lawyer." He looked at Junior Preston. "No offense, Junior, but you ain't ready for this yet." Carter seemed stunned by what he was hearing.

"Carter…you takin' all this in?" asked Clary.

"I hears you, judge," said Carter almost in a daze. "What happens now?"

"We…all of us," Clary started and then stopped. He looked up. "Let's go on and do this right. Ted…Gerald…y'all come on down here." I saw the two of them stand up and walk down towards the group around the judge's desk.

"Ted, Gerald…y'all are now acting deputies, and the first thing to do is to get Carter over to the jail," said Owen. "I'll swear you in when we get there." A moment later the whole group was on the way out of the courtroom while everyone sat or stood and watched in amazement. Judge Clary stopped just before he reached the door and turned to the people in the room.

"Hearin's adjourned," he said. "Now y'all get on home." With that they were on their way…but not necessarily home. I hurried to get moving before everyone caught on that everything was really over, and I managed to catch up with Claxton about halfway down the steps of the courthouse. Inside of a minute, we were across the street and at the jail. Owen Mercer unlocked the place, let everyone in, and then locked it up from the inside. He went over to the front window and looked outside.

"Looks like they're thinkin' 'bout whether to leave or wait 'till everyone comes back out," he said. He walked over to the desk drawer and came up with two pin-on badges. "Gerald, Ted…raise your right hands." He waited for them to raise them. "You solemnly swear to uphold the laws of the state of Mississippi and of these here United States and act as official deputies of Josiah Falls?"

""'Gainst my better senses," said Gerald Edmundson. He was about sixty and ran the outdoors and sporting goods shop that specialized in hunting and fishing equipment. He was well respected in town and generally had no patience with nonsense.

"That mean 'I do'?" asked Owen.

"Reckon it does," said Gerald with a sigh.

"I'm in," said Ted Fiedler. Fiedler was seventy-eight but still looked like the tough cop he had been on the streets of Fayette. He had shot it out in 1926 with bank robbers and had sent four of them to the graveyard. I figured that Owen Mercer had picked a couple of men that not many folks would want to cross if there was trouble, and by the looks on the faces around the room, I could see that nobody was really sure what to expect. Owen unlocked a cabinet on the wall and took out a pair of handguns in holsters and handed them to Ted and Gerald. He then pulled out a shotgun and a couple of boxes of cartridges.

"Won't need but one," said Ted with a smile. "You fire a round over their heads and they'll scatter."

"Hope we don't need even one," said Owen. "I'd like you and Gerald to have a seat outside and just keep an eye on the street. Let everyone see you. Let 'em know."

"All right," said Ted as he checked the gun and holstered it. It looked right at home on his hip. He and Gerald walked out of the office, and Owen locked up behind them.

"Well," said Judge Clary. "I'll send for the prosecutor right away. Carter, you take a bit and think 'bout what you want to do for a lawyer."

"Done thought about it," said Carter. "Reckon I could talk to Claxton…private like?"

"Claxton?" asked Clary. Claxton nodded that it was all right with him. Owen handed Claxton the key, and Claxton locked the door after they went outside. Nobody asked me to leave, so I sat quietly over by the sheriff's desk.

"All right, Carter," said Claxton. "What's on your mind?"

"Reckon I'm gonna need me a lawyer," said Carter.

"I think so," said Claxton. "I can recommend some very good ones that I know. Be glad to make some calls if you like."

"I 'preciate that, mister Claxton, sir," said Carter, "but I already knows who I want."

"Well, just tell me and I'll get in touch," said Claxton.

"I wants you to talk for me, mister Claxton, sir," said Carter.

"Me?" said Claxton. "I haven't practiced in years. You need the best there is right now. Now, Merlin Applewhite over in Jackson is probably the best trial lawyer in the state."

"Think the best trial lawyer be standin' right here in this room," said Carter. "Think it's 'portant that a man know the men sittin' in the jury. Ought to know the little things 'bout this place."

"There's more to it than that," said Claxton. "There's some history involved here that could prejudice the jury against you just 'cause I'm your lawyer. They might think that's why I'm takin' the case."

"I knows maybe you be worried 'bout what folks might say if'n you take on a colored man," said Carter deliberately. "You right to think it. Folks real quick gonna think I done this here thing. Judge Harlan be right 'bout that."

"I'm not worried 'bout what people might say or think about me," said Claxton with a shake of his head. I could tell that he was serious. "Never worried 'bout that before...won't start now. I could live with that."

"Then what got you worried?" asked Carter. Claxton was thinking but he didn't say anything. "I ain't never thought no less o' you. Never put no blame. You ain't got to account for what your daddy did." Carter looked at me. "Nathan, you know what we's talkin' 'bout, boy?"

"I think so," I said. "You're talkin' 'bout what happened to your daddy. Claxton told me 'bout it."

"Same for you," said Carter. "You ain't never got to have no shame. Was none o' your doin' any more than your daddy's. Don't never hang your head 'bout it or let nobody make you." Carter smiled at me. "Probably more words than I said since I knowed you."

"Reckon it might be," I said. "Claxton, what do you aim to do?"

"I don't know, son," Claxton shook his head slowly. "I just don't know. It's a powerful thing to have a man put his life in your hands. It's nothing to take lightly." He looked back at Carter. "My family's got your blood on their hands already. I don't want to have any more of it."

"Well, mister, Claxton, sir," said Carter, "some folks say I'm stubborn as a mule. They'd be wrong. You'd talk the mule out of it…but not me. You done stuck with me."

"You're sure about this?" said Claxton very slowly. Carter nodded. "I'm not sure it's for the best. First thing any lawyer ought to do is consider what's best for the man he's standin' up for. Sometimes the best thing he can do is walk away and let somebody else do the job."

"Never more sure of nothin'," Carter said, "…but I tell you what…I'd be obliged mightily if you would ride out to my place and tell my family what's goin' on here. You think 'bout this away from here, an' when you come back this'a way you make up your mind. I'll lives with what you say then."

"All right then," said Claxton with a nod of his head. "I'll ride out there and tell your family…and I'll think on it"

"Cain't ask for no more," said Carter as he sat down on the bunk in the open cell. "Reckon I best be get'n used to this. 'Spect I'll be here awhile." He looked back at Claxton. "Tell my family that they ought not worry, an' don't come 'round here directly. Don't want them runnin' into no trouble."

"I'll tell them that you'll be all right here," said Claxton as he started towards the door.

"Ain't worried none," said Carter. Claxton tried to smile, but somehow it just didn't work, and I could see that he was thinking of another time. He turned and opened the door. Owen Mercer was right there when it opened.

"I'm goin' out to Carter's place and let the family know not to worry," said Claxton.

78

Josiah Falls

"I 'preciate that, Claxton," said Owen Mercer as he scratched his head. "I was puzzlin' over who to send out there." I followed Claxton out the door. It was locked and bolted before our shadows were off of it. I looked around the street. There were still quite a lot of people standing around talking, but it didn't look like a mob ready to drag a man out of the jail. I saw Ted Fiedler and Gerald Edmundson walking around and talking to people.

"Probably lettin' 'em know that nothin's goin' to happen," said Claxton as we walked down the sidewalk. "Want to ride out there with me?"

"Sure," I said. I'd never been out to the Monroe place except to pass by it now and then. It looked big from the road. "Used to be a plantation didn't it?" I thought I recalled something about that.

"Yep," said Claxton. "Right up 'till the war ended in 1865." We walked quickly on to the house and told Bertie where we were going. She had a lot of questions, but Claxton put her off saying he'd tell her everything when we got back to town.

"Want me to wait dinner on y'all?" Bertie asked. "Goin' on three o'clock now..."

"Don't imagine we'll be back to the house 'till after six," said Claxton. It wasn't a long drive, so I figured Claxton thought that we might be there a spell. Claxton picked up the keys to the Studebaker Champion and we went to the garage. Claxton pulled back the heavy cover over the car and dropped it on the back table. It was quite a car, and I was already looking forward to the day I might drive it. Claxton had bought it brand new in 1946 after he'd come home from the service. He seemed to like it, but he didn't drive it much unless he was going too far to walk. Even though it hadn't been out of the garage in almost a month, the engine turned over on the first try, and we were on our way down the road. Most folks would say that if you blinked you'd miss Josiah Falls when you drove through it. I think it's a *might* bigger than that, but a really long yawn could be enough.

Josiah Falls

Claxton turned the convertible out onto the long dirt and gravel road that was marked as county road 3140. About every other year, the county would come out and drop some more gravel on it, but within a month, the gravel would tend to mound up in the middle and on the sides. There was room for two cars to pass just as long as they got over to the edges, but usually there was not any traffic, so the best place to drive was on the two middle dirt ruts that straddled the middle of the road. Usually Claxton would talk about the things and places we were passing, but he was quiet, and I could tell that he was thinking, so I let him be and just watched the fields and old falling down barns pass by. About ten minutes later, we turned off of 3140 onto a road that didn't really have a name. It was narrower than the county road and was only hard-packed dirt. Two cars couldn't pass on this road unless one of them got part way into the field of soybeans growing on either side. This was the road that led to the old plantation. About a mile and a half later, I could see the big white house standing back off to the left facing the road. Claxton turned down the dirt drive leading up to the house. Before we reached the house, Claxton turned into a little stand of trees to the right of the drive and stopped. He got out of the car, and I followed him through the trees to a little wooden rail fence with a small latched gate on it. When we got closer, I saw that it was a small graveyard. Claxton opened the gate and we went inside. Once inside, I saw that it was really pretty big.

"Lot o' folks buried here," I said as we started to walk along the first row. Most of the graves had at least some kind of marker, mostly small rough-cut stones, but there were others that had nothing at all.

"Monroe Plantation was here a long time," said Claxton. "These here graves up front…some go back close to one hundred thirty years maybe." He walked on towards the back, and I saw that the markers here all had names and dates on them. He finally stopped at a large white marble stone.

"Isaac Monroe…" Claxton read. "Born 1800 and died 1882. his wife is there beside. And there on that side…" he pointed to the right, "…is Carter Monroe the first…born in

1845 and died in 1925." I looked the stone over. It was the same marble as Isaac Monroe's. Claxton took a step further down. I saw that after Carter's grandmother was Carter's father. All I needed to see was the year 1932 on it. I knew the rest. Claxton stopped right there for a while as I walked down and looked at some more. I saw where three girls all died as children in 1918, and there appeared to be more groups of families that had been buried together a long time before that. I walked on back around past the very old unmarked graves and headed back to the car. Claxton met me there a few minutes later. We got back in and drove up to the house. Claxton pulled the car up on the side, and we walked around the front on a stone paved walkway to the front doors. There were ten steps going up to four tall pillars that held up the roof over the big front porch. Claxton gave a loud knock on one of the tall wooden doors. We waited for a few minutes and finally heard someone moving inside. The door on the right opened slightly and an elderly, slightly bent black woman craned her head outside.

"Yes?" she said with a slightly confused look. She pushed her glasses back up onto her nose with a crooked looking finger. "Can I helps you?"

"Luwuana, my name's Claxton Delaney," said Claxton. "It's been some years."

"I remembers you," the fragile looking elderly lady nodded with a smile as she leaned heavily on a cane. "It *has* been some years. I got the rheumatis' real bad an' don't get 'round so good no more. Cain't hardly ride in the truck. How's you doin' Claxton?"

"I'm tolerable," said Claxton. "This is my son, Nathan."

"Ma'am," I said.

"You nearly growed as tall as me," she said with a smile. "Course…I be get'n shorter near 'bout every year now." She opened the door. "What brings y'all out this way. Ain't trouble is it?"

"I'm afraid it is," said Claxton as we walked inside. "Carter's in jail down in Josiah Falls."

"What that fool old man done?" she asked as she walked slowly to the sitting room off the side of the entryway. "Gots to sit down. Cain't stand up no more'n a few minutes." She sat down into a small high-backed padded chair.

"Carter's been accused of burnin' down the Baptist church in town and of killin' the minister and Odessa Hendricks," said Claxton. "He wanted me to come out and tell you not to worry 'bout him. He's all right."

"Burnin' down the church you say?" she said. "They done give him a trial and such?"

"No," said Claxton with a shake of his head. "There won't be a trial…not for a while anyway. Right now he's just locked up."

"My daughter-in-law's gone off to Natchez for the day with the children," she said. "Goin' be back tomorrow. Reckon we might come see him then?"

"I think it'd be all right," said Claxton.

"Can't figure he'd be burnin' down the church," she shook her head slowly. "Done been workin' there since the war. Always say'n what a good fella that mister Evan be."

"Do you remember the night of the Fourth?" asked Claxton.

"Took me some pills and gone to sleep early," she said. "Didn't wake up 'til next mornin'. Was already light outside. Don't recall the time."

"Did anyone see Carter when he came in?" asked Claxton. "Maybe know what time he got back here?"

"I reckon he didn't come to bed 'till late," she said. "Would have gone out to tend the stock when he come in. I'd have'ta ask the family, but I wouldn't reckon they'd be up."

"Well, if you think of anything about that night, let me know," said Claxton. "Could be real important. We'll be goin' now. Let you get your rest."

"Reckon I'll need it if'n I be goin' to town tomorrow," she said. "I thanks y'all for comin' out here. Carter goin' be needin' some help. He be a proud man, but he's a good man. Couldn't be that he done what they said." Claxton just nodded.

82

"We'll see our way out," he said as we turned to leave. I could see that the old lady was worn out just from doing what little she had.

"How old you reckon she is, Claxton?" I wondered.

"'Bout ten years older than me I 'spose," Claxton answered. I was surprised at that. "Bad health can age a body real quick."

We drove back to town in silence, just about the way we had come. I had a lot of questions for Claxton, but I thought they could wait until night and he'd had a chance to work things through in his mind. Claxton didn't stop at the house, drove on into town, and parked right outside the jail.

"It's Claxton. Open up, Owen," said Claxton as he gave a sharp rap on the door. The door opened a moment later, and Owen Mercer let us inside. He locked it right back after a quick look outside, and then walked back to his desk where Carter was sitting to the side. They had been playing cards while we were gone.

"Didn't seem to make no sense," said Owen as if he somehow had to defend himself. "Him being locked up in there doin' nothing, and me bein' locked up over here doin' nothin'. Thought we could get together and do nothin'." Claxton just smiled. "Want me to give you some time again? Thought I might check up on my new deputies anyway."

"That'd be fine, Owen," said Claxton. Owen Mercer stood up and went to the door. "Just open up when you want me back in. I won't be far." He disappeared out the door, and Claxton locked up behind him.

"Reckon you been out there," said Carter. "Seen my wife?"

"I did," said Claxton. "Didn't know she was get'n on so poorly. Used to be one to work from can to can't."

"Started get'n real bad last year," Carter said. "Rankles her that she cain't get out and tend things." He was thoughtful a moment. "Did you look in on my daddy when you was there?"

"How did you know?" asked Claxton quietly.

"Seen you out there now and again…payin' your respects when you passed by." Carter nodded.

"You never said anything," said Claxton. "I didn't want to intrude."

"You's always welcome," said Carter. "Never wanted to keep you from vistin' daddy. He knowed you from when you was a boy. 'Spect he'd be glad to hear from you now." I had never known that Claxton stopped there sometimes, but he had known just where he was going. "Mister Claxton, sir, I was born on that there piece a land, and I aims to die there. My daddy was born there, and now he's restin' there. So's his daddy." He paused for a long minute. "You know the story 'bout that plantation?"

"A little," said Claxton. "I know the plantation dates back a long time. Isaac Monroe owned it at one time."

"Yep. And, my granddaddy was born a slave on that land and was a growed man when the War Between the States was over. Now, when the fightin' was done most of the field hands run off, but my granddaddy had him a wife and some young'uns and didn't have no place particular to go, so ole mister Isaac comes to him and says, 'Let's you an me farm this place together. If'n we can make a go of it, I'll pay you wages out of what we make.' Well, they done just that. Had them a couple o' lean years, but by 1880 they was makin' good money out of it and buyin' up more land. Had them a bunch o' hands workin' it, too. But ole mister Isaac was get'n on and startin' to be sickly. He and the wife didn't have no children. The two twin boys was killed up there at Shiloh and the youngest was killed up at Gettysburgh, so he decides to make the farm into a company and they be equal partners. Well, the papers was drawn up right an proper, and when mister Isaac passed a couple years later, my granddaddy took on the whole thing and seen after mister Isaac's wife 'til she passed 'bout a dozen years later. That land passed to my daddy when my granddaddy passed. Come to almost two thousand acres, but along come the Depression, and my daddy had to sell off just 'bout all of it. Hung on to the homeplace and 'bout a hundred acres with the graveyard. Now it belongs

84

to me, and I been buyin' back that land. Only 'bout four hundred acres left to get. That's why I works me a couple jobs. I'm set on leavin' it to my grandson, Carter."

"I didn't know all that," said Claxton. "What happened to your son…Carter the fourth?"

"Got hisself killed over in Germany in 1945," said Carter with a sad shake of his head. Claxton nodded. "All my young'uns is gone now. Lost my three little girls to 'fluenza while I was off to France in the first war and was over in Germany in the second war…seen where my boy's buried." It seemed like a lot of bad luck for one man to have in just one lifetime, and I didn't understand how he seemed to take it in stride.

"The Lord's ways is mysterious to us," Carter said after a moment as if he knew what I was thinking. "But we cain't question what He do."

"I've been thinking a lot about what you're asking me to do," said Claxton. "I still think you could do better for a lawyer, but I'll take it on if that's what you want."

"Don't think I could do no better," said Carter. "You be a fair man. I'll let it set with you."

"All right. From right now, I'm your lawyer," said Claxton. "First thing I think we need to do is file with the judge for a change of venue."

"What do that be…a venue?" said Carter.

"Means we ask the judge to move your trial someplace else," said Claxton. "Maybe Fayette, Natchez, or maybe Vicksburg or Jackson."

"Don't reckon I want to do that," said Carter with a shake of his head. "I lives right here, sir. I wants folks to know I didn't do nothin'. If it comes from a bunch o' men they don't know…just won't set right with them."

"Good chance we might lose if we fight it out right here," said Claxton. "Local juries are hard. Evan Washburne was a well-liked man. His widow will be sittin' there in the courtroom, dressed in black and wipin' her eyes, and you're a…"

"And I's a colored man that speaks his mind more'n he ought. I knows that," said Carter. "I wants my trial right *here*. Want to walk the streets with my head up so's folks know that there was justice done.'

"All right," said Claxton. "We can appeal. There might be grounds for it if the jury could be proven partial to the case." Claxton looked at me for a moment. He didn't look convinced that fightin' it out in Josiah Falls was the smart thing to do, but we could both tell that Carter was set on it.

"I'm going to need some things," he said finally. "I'll be back in an hour or so. I'll have a lot of questions when I get back, and I need you to be absolutely honest about everything. I'm your lawyer, so you can tell me anything at all. Anything you say is confidential… don't worry 'bout hurtin' anybody's feelin's."

"Won't be no problem talkin' honest," said Carter.

"That's good," said Claxton. "Now, Owen Mercer or anyone else asks you anything about the case, you just tell them your lawyer doesn't want you to talk about anything unless he's here. You go on and talk about the weather, dinner, or anything else you want."

"I hears you," said Carter.

"I'll call Owen back on in here and be back in a bit," said Claxton. I'd only seen Claxton in the court one time, and that was in a boundary dispute between two property lines. I felt like I was seeing something change in him right there in front of me. Claxton went to the door, unlocked it and called for Owen to come in. I followed him outside and down the walk as we heard the door lock up tight behind us.

Chapter Eight

Claxton and I were at the house just long enough to eat a little something of the meal Birtie was keeping warm for us, pick up some pencils and notebooks and the rest of the meal that Bertie had packed up for us, and head back to town.

Carter and Owen finished off the pork chops, potatoes, cornbread, and apple cobbler before Claxton sent Owen home to get a shower and a few hours sleep. Gerald Edmundson was going to stay on outside, or until we left, and Ted Fiedler was going to spell him about four am. Ted said that he was always up by then anyway.

Claxton asked Carter a lot of questions and looked like he was taking down just about every word he said along with making his own notes. I learned a whole lot about Carter Monroe that night, and I think Claxton did to. Carter didn't much understand why Claxton wanted to know so much about things that didn't quite figure into a church being burned down, but he answered everything that he could. It was probably almost midnight before Claxton got around to asking about the night of the Fourth.

"So, what time did you leave town that night?" Claxton asked.

"Took me a bit. I dumped the ash from the grill," Carter began, "…seen my watch 'bout then and it was near on twelve thirty. I let the heat die off some and then loaded it up in the truck. 'Spect I drove off 'bout one o'clock."

"Did anybody see you leave?" Claxton said as he scribbled some notes. "And did you see anyone then?"

"Cain't be certain," Carter said scratching his head. "Streets was about empty by then…don't reckon I took notice of anybody. Most everybody that was left gone and took off 'bout then. Seen Garson Ashe talkin' with the minister 'bout midnight out front of the church. Seen Grady after that, but he don't see no more'n a foot in front of him, so I don't reckon he coulda seen me."

"Was Garson giving Evan a hard time?" asked Claxton.

"Wasn't close enough to tell what they was talkin' 'bout," said Carter. "Coulda been. They was pointin' a lot." Claxton only nodded, but I could see that he was filing that away for later.

"Anyone see you when you got home?" Claxton continued.

"I unloaded the grill from the truck and went directly to see after the stock…make sure they was bedded down," Carter answered. "Went out on the back road by the old Pritchart farm and fixed me a piece of fence. I got me a cow kept trying to get through it. Everybody was done asleep when I got back to the place. Luwuana ain't been restin' well. She been takin' some pills to let her sleep some. I 'bout certain she didn't wake up."

"Did you happen to see either Odessa or Evan Washburne that night?" asked Claxton.

"I seen mister Evan off an on," Carter recalled. "Last time was 'bout midnight with Garson Ashe like I said. Looked like he was on his way to the church. Don't recollect seein' Odessa for a spell there. I figured she done went off with Addie when she took sick. Thought I saw them both leavin'. Then I seen her back real late talkin' with mister Evan." Claxton wrote for a little while after that.

"Did you happen to hear anything that was said?" asked Claxton.

"No," said Carter, "they was a ways off from me. But that Odessa always kinda troubled me…"

"How's that?" Claxton wondered as he picked up his pencil from the page and looked up.

"Took to comin' by the church…often like…to see mister Evan," said Carter. "Was usually after she got off her job at the hair fixin' place when it closed up about seven o'clock."

"How often was she comin' by?" asked Claxton.

""Bout three, maybe four times a week," Carter answered. "Didn't seem…proper…Addie bein' home sick an all most of the time. I knows they's like sisters."

"Addie wasn't there when Odessa was talkin' with Evan?" Claxton said as he wrote some more. "Did you ever see or hear anything that seemed improper?"

"Cain't say I did," said Carter. "They was in his office most the time when I was there. Wasn't none of my business…course, but did seem like she was needin' a whole lot o' spiritual comfortin'." Claxton turned to a fresh page in his notebook, and was quiet for a moment while he thought.

"Well, I reckon a lot of folks would have a tough time provin' where there were that night," said Claxton. "But, Carter, we've got to think about the evidence. We need to figure out how Evan Washburne's keys got locked up in that shed. With just one other key to the shed…that is a piece of evidence that's not just circumstantial."

"I been studying on that a lot," Carter nodded and shook his head. "Cain't figure how that could be."

"Would the church have been locked up on the Fourth?" Claxton said as he added some notes.

"'Bout certain it was open all night," said Carter. I seen him come out a few times bringin' some tables and chairs outside. Never saw him usin' a key."

"All right," Claxton nodded, "Evan's in and out of the church all night. Maybe a few other times, too. Could be he doesn't even have his keys. We know they're goin' to turn up in the shed, so let's say he *doesn't* have them. So who does?" He wrote some more. "Now somebody comes along after he and Odessa are in the church. The fire investigator said the fire could have been burnin' for a while before anyone knew about it. Could have been set as early as one thirty. First anyone heard was when some of the roof came down around two. Somebody had to lock the doors, lock the keys up in the shed with the gas can…and leave without being seen." Claxton set down his notebook and pencil, got up and walked around the small office.

"Could anyone else have a key to that shed…for any reason?" said Claxton after a trip around the jail.

"Ain't been a third key for long's I can remember," said Carter. "Got to go back to before the war." Claxton nodded.

"Could Evan have made a spare?" Claxton wondered more to himself than to Carter. "I'll check on that." He went back to the notebook and made some notes on another sheet. "Did you ever loan out your keys to anyone?"

"'Bout never out of my pocket," Carter shook his head. Claxton took out his pocket watch. It was almost one o'clock in the morning.

"I'll be most of the day tomorrow," Claxton said as he wrote, "taking depositions from folks in town. Don't worry if you don't see me. If you need me for anything, or you remember something important tell Owen to have somebody fetch me, and I'll come on directly."

"What gonna happen next?" asked Carter anxiously.

"Judge Clary will probably have the prosecutor in town in a few days…could be a week, but probably not that long," said Claxton. "Harlan will give him some time to get his feet on the ground, figure out the case, and such…then he'll come out with charges against you. The charges are going to be arson and two counts of murder in the first degree, and he's likely going to ask for the death penalty. Best if we just go on and plan that way."

"Figured that," said Carter, but I still thought that hearing it out loud hit him like a hard punch in the stomach.

"Then, there'll be an arraignment in the courthouse where they'll read the charges to make it official," said Claxton. "The judge will ask for a plea of guilty or not guilty. I'll tell him that you plead not guilty of all charges. Like as not the judge will go on and set a trial date…unless there are motions to delay it."

"You 'spect there to be any?" Carter wanted to know.

"I think the prosecutor will want to get on to the trial," said Claxton. "Probably think those keys are all the evidence he needs to convict. I'll file a motion if I need more time for anything. We'll let him be in a hurry. We got all the time in the world, so no need to rush in unless we're ready. It's possible, but not likely, that the prosecutor might offer a plea bargain."

"What that be?" asked Carter. I was curious myself.

"Sometimes," Claxton began, "the prosecutor isn't *sure* he can get a conviction, so he might offer a lesser charge for a guilty plea…that way he doesn't have to try the case, and the state still gets a conviction."

"Reckon he'll do that?" asked Carter slowly.

"No," Claxton answered quickly with a shake of his head. "But, would you take it if he did? Might keep you off death row."

"You knows me better than that," Carter smiled and shook his head. "Ain't gonna admit to somethin' I ain't done. Might as well be dead as be alive an' my name dead."

"It ain't right. I know it," said Claxton, "but sometimes a man just doesn't have a choice. A lot of innocent men have done a little time to keep from doin' a lot of time, and some would do life just to keep living it."

"Well, my mind's made up on that," said Carter.

"I figured that," Claxton smiled. "Just doin' my job and tellin' you everything you need to know."

"Sounds to me like you slippin' back into that lawyer hat now don't it?" said Carter with a smile.

"Suppose I have at that," said Claxton. "Well, now you go on and get some sleep. You'll have company here all night, and Owen will be back in the morning. He'll have meals comin' in regular by tomorrow, but I reckon Bertie will be sendin' some things your way too." Claxton closed up his notebooks, but I could see that he was thinking about what he would be doing the next day. I was dog tired when we walked out of there, but Claxton looked like he was ready to wake up the town and get started. I sure was glad that he didn't. I needed some sleep.

Chapter Nine

Claxton was up early the next day making his rounds in town. I tagged along with him as he walked up to the cemetery beside the burned out church. He didn't say what he was lookin' 'round for as he walked almost all the way up to Norm Abernathy's house and turned back to look at the back of the church.

"Whatcha checkin', Claxton," I asked when he never said anything.

"Just figurin'," said Claxton as he walked across Abernathy's yard from one side to the other. Claxton looked over at the house, saw Norm at the window, and waved to him. Norm gave a little wave back and then disappeared from the window. I thought maybe he might come out to talk, but when he didn't I supposed he knew what Claxton was up to and probably everyone else in town did, too. A minute later, Claxton walked over to the old tool shed. It was old but still solid. The lock was made into the door, so there was no padlock. Claxton gave the locked door a tug, but it didn't move an inch.

"You findin' what you was lookin' for out here, Claxton?" I asked.

"I don't rightly know, Nathan," said Claxton. He looked back over at the church like he was tryin' to remember what it had looked like before it burned. I looked, too. The brick was still standin' there like it had been, but the wood was all gone. There was still the bottom piece of the minister's upstairs window, but not much else on this side of the church. We walked across the graveyard, out the little wrought iron gate, and back onto the sidewalk.

"Well, reckon I'll get on with my depositions," said Claxton. He planned on trying to talk to everyone he could and figured it would take him about three or four days at least, so I didn't figure to see him much for a spell.

"I'm goin' to Willie's house I reckon," I said. Claxton nodded and we split up. Willie and I got together at his house and went into town, but we stopped at the jail to drop off some of Bertie's cooking.

"Claxton ain't here, Nathan," said Owen as he cracked open the door.

"I know. He's down yonder talkin' with mister Bishop," I said. I had seen them as we walked past. "We just come to bring y'all some of Bertie's fried chicken and a couple pieces of cake." I handed him the big shopping bag.

"Tell Bertie thanks," said Owen.

"Thanks, Nathan," Carter called from inside.

"Hey, Carter," I called back. I turned to Owen Mercer. "Reckon you could lock me up when you get Carter on out of here? I could sit in there for some cake brought to me regular." Owen just laughed.

"Y'all boys stay out of trouble," he said as he closed back up. I told him we'd try, but I also knew that trouble had been finding us regular like without us looking for it that summer. We left there and went down to the Outdoors Place. Gerald Edmundson was sitting inside looking like he was only half awake.

"Need anything done today, Mr. Edmundson?" I asked as we walked inside.

"Reckon I might," said Edmundson. "Got some freight in back that needs to be unboxed and put out on the shelves. Don't much feel up to it myself right now."

"We'll get on it," I said as I walked with Willie to the back. We went through the double swinging doors into the stockroom and found a stack of about fifty boxes waiting there. It was a mix of things from hunting equipment to tents, and it took us most of the morning to take care of it. When we had finished breaking down the cardboard boxes in the back, we went back up front.

"'Preciate it boys," said Edmundson. He hit a big key on the cash register and took out two quarters and gave us each one.

"Thanks," I said with a big smile. "I expect we'll see about spendin' this quick as we can."

"Just stay out of trouble," he said with a wave.

"Reckon we'll try," I called back as we left.

"You get in trouble a lot 'round here?" asked Willie as the door shut behind us and we were back on the street.

"Didn't think so 'till now," I said. "Was a spell there, though, that I was in trouble 'bout as regular as the sun comin' up, but Claxton done put me on the straight an narrow." Willie looked at me with a sly smile, and I had to laugh. "…well mostly anyhow." I added. Sneaking out to the falls, running around at night, and finding dead bodies could be seen by some folks as getting in trouble, but I hadn't really gotten in trouble since nobody knew about it. Nobody except Riley of course. That got me to thinking about Riley again.

"Reckon Riley's come back from wherever he lit out to?" I said as much to Willie as myself. Willie shook his head.

"I dunno," he said. He looked out towards the woods in the distance, and I thought I knew what he was thinking. "Don't 'spose we'll find out either." I nodded. We were just about of one mind on that. It was about that time that I saw Claxton coming out from the little downtown bank with a couple of notebooks under one arm. I remembered that I was supposed to ask him something for Bertie, so I nudged Willie in the ribs and started that way. We hurried down the walk, crossed the street, and ran to catch up to him.

"Claxton!" I called when we got closer. He turned part way and saw us.

"Kind of hot to be runnin' 'round," he said.

"Bertie wanted me to ask you if you was goin' to be by the house for supper or if you was goin' to be takin' it down at the jail." I asked.

"I 'spect I'll be by the house," Claxton said. "Let Bertie know when you get out that way."

"I will," I said. About that time Bubba Drury, the town barber, was coming down the walk.

"Mornin' Bubba," said Claxton as he got near.

"Ain't true is it?" asked Bubba without so much as a 'hello'.

"What's that Bubba?" asked Claxton although he seemed to already suspect what was on Bubba's mind that morning.

"You lawyerin' for Carter Monroe," he said with a frown. "Was told, but I flat didn't believe it."

"It's true," said Claxton with a nod. "He asked...and I accepted." I knew that it hadn't been as easy as all that, but that was Claxton's way; when he promised something it was done.

"Claxton, it's clear as day that he done it," said Bubba. "Blind man could see it in the dark! How can you stand up for him?"

"Man's entitled to a lawyer and a fair trial," said Claxton with a serious look on his face even though he held onto his smile. "It's what this country is all about, Bubba."

"But he's guilty as sin, and we both know it," said Bubba angrily. "I thought you was Evan's friend. How can you defend his killer?"

"I'm still Evan's friend," said Claxton. The smile was gone from his face though. "Evan would want justice to be done. If you knew him at all you'd know that. He wouldn't want an innocent man convicted."

"Innocent! Come on, Claxton. Justice'll be done when he rides the lightin'," said Bubba hotly.

"This was still America when I woke up this mornin'," said Claxton. He was still talking calmly, but I could hear something in his voice now. "Man's innocent 'til a jury says he's not."

"Don't reckon that'll take long to decide," said Bubba. He stepped around Claxton and said something real low that I couldn't hear, but I saw from Claxton's clenched fist that he had heard just fine.

"I'm gonna forget you said that, Bubba," said Claxton without turning around. His voice was calm but dead serious now.

"Why don't you do somethin' 'bout it instead," said Bubba with a big grin on his face.

"Bubba, I've got twenty years on you, but don't let this gray on top fool you. Wouldn't look good for a young man like you if I was to lay you out on this sidewalk," said Claxton.

"I'd kill you first," said Bubba with a snarl, but I noticed that he took a step back. I think anyone with sense who'd seen Claxton in a T-shirt would have done that too. Claxton was probably the slowest man to anger that I ever saw, but you sure enough didn't want him to take that anger out on you if you were fool enough to let it out of the box.

"Is that so?" said Claxton evenly. He took a step towards him. "I'm right here, Bubba." Bubba took a couple of steps further back as he realized that he might have asked for more than he wanted.

"I got no time for you," he said shaking his head. "Got business to tend to." Bubba Drury turned on his heel and left down the sidewalk a whole lot faster than he'd come along.

"What's he so mad 'bout?" asked Willie as he watched Bubba disappearing in the direction of his Main Street barbershop.

"Just upset 'bout the minister I 'spect," said Claxton. "You boys might see more o' that. I've been runnin' into it all mornin'. Don't pay it no mind. Bubba will get over it…in time. So will everybody else." I wasn't so sure about that, and

I'm not sure Claxton believed it either, but I didn't say anything.

"How's the depo...sition...in' goin'," I asked trying to change the subject. I was still trying to get a hold on that word even though I'd heard it often enough lately.

"'Bout like I thought," said Claxton. "Most folks don't know much 'bout anything, and those that do got different stories. Sure wish..." He stopped right there.

"Wish what, Claxton?" I asked when he didn't go on.

"I was just thinking about that lost set of keys," said Claxton. "I talked to Harvey Walker this morning first thing. I showed him the keys to the church and the shed, and he said he'd never copied any of them. Said he didn't even have a blank for the lock on the shed. Said he'd have to special order it. The shed lock is real old, older than the church even."

"What do you reckon happened to those keys?" I asked. I recalled from the hearing that they had mentioned Riley once having them when he was a deacon of the church.

"Probably long gone," Claxton said. "Sure would like to run across Riley an' ask him though." Willie and I looked at each other, and I knew right away that was a mistake. Claxton had a knack for reading peoples faces. Sometimes I wondered if he could read their minds, too. I figured if he was reading mine, I was in a real pickle.

"All right, boys," Claxton sighed. "Reckon you've got somethin' on your minds. Best come on out with it."

"Don't reckon it's nothin'," I said after a long minute of thinking. "Me and Willie was up at the falls a time back and walked up to Riley's cabin. He wasn't there, but it sure looked like somebody'd been in there. It was tore up like somebody went and robbed it."

"Why didn't you say something about it?" asked Claxton.

"It's just *Riley*. Folks don't pay him no mind unless they want to make fun of him or mess with his traps and stuff," I shrugged. "Didn't think nobody'd care 'bout what goes on up there."

"Any other time, I 'spect you'd be right," Claxton sighed. "You boys feel like hikin' on up there with me and show me what you found? Maybe he'll even be there."

"Riley's kind of skittish 'round folks anymore, 'cept maybe Willie 'n me," I said. "Kinda thought he might a just picked up and run off." I looked at Willie. "Reckon we can go on up there." Willie shrugged.

I knew this was serious when Claxton didn't bother to go by the house and get his hiking clothes and boots. He just rolled up his sleeves and started walking. We followed the high trail up above the falls and found our way to the stream. Claxton asked some questions about Riley, and we answered as much as we knew...except for one incident, of course. It took us about forty minutes to reach the cabin. Claxton stopped and checked the bass and trout lines. There were some fish on the lines, and even I knew that there were more fish than there ought to be. Willie and I turned loose the live ones before we walked up to the cabin.

"Looks 'bout the same," I said as we got close. The furs were still hanging on a line on the side of the cabin, and were now fully dried after several days of hanging in the sun. Claxton pushed open the unlocked door, picked up a heavy bucket from just outside and set it inside to block the door open. He then found the same lantern I'd found and used before, lit it with a match from his matchbook, and then went to open the window blinds. Claxton set the lantern down in the middle of the table. The big butcher knife was still stuck in the table where it had been before. I couldn't tell that anything had been touched.

"Is this how you found it?" Claxton asked as he inspected the place, carefully looking around.

"Far as I remember," I said after a long look of my own.

"Me, too," said Willie.

"Sure looks like somebody was lookin' real hard for something," said Claxton. "Any idea if Riley had anything...anything somebody'd want bad enough to do this?"

"Furs and fish are still here," I said. "Usually a lot more furs hangin' up though." I thought about that now. I had been here before when there were sometimes a few hundred of them. There were probably no more than a dozen this time, and those had looked fresh then. I knew that he traded the furs and sometimes some fresh fish, but I didn't know more than that. Claxton was careful not to move anything, but he combed over the little cabin about as thorough as the person who had been there before. He didn't come up with any money, so it was possible that the place had been ransacked for cash.

"What do you reckon happened with that knife?" I asked Claxton. He looked it over again.

"I'd wager that's blood on the handle and on the blade," he said after a moment's look. "There's some drips on the table and on the floor...and over there on the mattress. Somebody got cut for sure."

"Don't think it might be from some critter he was cuttin' up?" Willie asked.

"I don't reckon he'd be cuttin' up a critter on his dinin' table," said Claxton. "'Spose he'd do that out back."

"Cut enough to be dead?" I wondered.

"I wouldn't think so," said Claxton. "A body's got a sight more blood than what's here. Whoever was cut up left here breathin'. Now, he could have stopped it up here and bled the rest of it out someplace else." That seemed to give him an idea, and I thought maybe he wished that he hadn't said it out loud. Claxton walked outside and looked around. "I want you boys to stay put right here. I want to have a look around outside."

"Yes, sir," I said as he walked out behind the cabin. I knew that he was going to look and see if there was any sign of Riley, and he was leaving us here just in case he found something we didn't want to see up close. We went over to the stream and waded around in the cool water while we waited. Claxton was gone for the best part of an hour. I wasn't worried about him getting lost out there since he probably knew these woods better than I did, but I did start thinking that whoever had gotten Dyle and maybe gotten Riley might also be looking to get one more. Of course Claxton was about the size of Dyle and Riley put together, and I had seen Bubba Drury, a strong man himself, decide that Claxton was a might bigger bite than he wanted to try to chew all at once. I was worried for nothing. A few minutes later, Claxton came back from behind the cabin brushing himself off after hiking through the thick brush and trees.

"See anything?" I asked as he came past the cabin towards us.

"Found a couple of traps full," said Claxton with a shake of his head.

"Nothin'…buried…or ought to be," I started.

"No, nothing like that out there," Claxton smiled. "Well, I'm not sure what all this means, but we didn't find any keys, and we didn't find Riley." We hiked back down the trail. I kept an eye on the woods just in case Riley was out there somewhere watching us go by, but if he was there, he wasn't coming out to talk.

Chapter Ten

When we got back to town, Claxton was headed back to the jail. Willie and I went along with him with the thought that it was still early enough in the day that we might scare up some work and make enough for a soda.

"Think you boys could find Junior Preston and send him over to the jail?" Claxton asked as we reached the first sidewalk after crossing over the baseball field.

"Reckon he's at his office?" I asked.

"That," Claxton considered, "…or maybe the courthouse."

"We'll fetch him," I said. I nudged Willie. "Come on." We started running down the sidewalk and then crossed over to the other side and kept going. When we reached the middle of town, Willie ran off towards the small one room office of the public defender while I jogged up the steps of the courthouse and went inside.

"You seen Junior 'round here lately?" I asked when I saw Woodrow Silas coming out of the courtroom.

"Was here this morning," said Silas with a point back at the courtroom with one big thumb. He opened up a folder that was under his arm. "Don't see no more cases this afternoon."

"Thanks," I said and headed back outside. I went down the steps two at a time and hit the sidewalk running. I saw Willie coming away from the small office down the way.

"Find 'em?" I called down to him.

"Naw," said Willie when he got closer. "Locked up tight." I thought for a moment where else he might be. It didn't take a lot of thought, and I wondered why I hadn't thought of it first. "Bet he's down at the five 'n dime makin' time with Gertrude." We crossed the street and went down a few blocks. I peeked in the window, and sure enough Gertrude was behind the counter at the cash register and Junior was leaning on the counter talking to her.

"Hey, Junior," I said as we walked inside the glass door. A little bell rang over our heads as we came through.

"Hey yourself, Nathan," said Junior Preston. He had one of those big law books opened up on the counter, and I knew that he was probably boring Gertrude to death with stuff he was finding in something that big that didn't have pictures.

"Claxton had us come ask if you could come by the jail and see 'em for a spell," I said.

"That so?" said Junior with a puzzled look on his face. "Well, Gertrude, I hate to just run off."

"You go right on," she said with a smile that might have been partly relief. "Might be somethin' important."

"I'll catch up to you later," Junior said as he closed up the book entitled *Cases of the Supreme Court* and something else below it. I supposed it was interesting as could be to a lawyer, but I didn't think I'd care to spend the day listening to it any more than Gertrude did. We led the way back outside with Junior right behind us.

"Claxton say what he wanted me about?" asked Junior.

"Just said to fetch you if we could," I said. "I 'spect it's some lawyer stuff."

"Probably," Junior smiled. We hurried along as fast as Junior could walk. I thought he was a little excited but was trying not to show it. A few minutes later, we reached the jail. I pounded on the door twice with my fist.

"Still keepin' locked up?" Junior said with a frown.

"Night 'n day," I nodded. "It's Nathan, Willie, an' Junior." The door opened and Claxton let us inside.

"Claxton, you sent for me?" asked Junior as he came inside and set the big law book down on Owen's desk.

"Yes, I did, Junior," said Claxton. "I was wonderin' if maybe you had some time to help me out on this case."

"I suppose I do," said Junior with a surprised look on his face. "You really want me to help?"

"I do," said Claxton. "You've been doin' a fine job 'round here since you came home from school. Might be good for you to do some work on a tough criminal case."

"Well," said Junior slowly. "Can't say I've done a real bang-up job. My only steady client was Dyle Courtland. He'd get paid on Friday, drunk on Saturday, jailed on Sunday, bailed on Monday, fined on Tuesday, and let out on Wednesday on time served."

"Good thing Dyle only got paid once a month," said Claxton. "Still, I could use your help."

"What would you need me to do?" asked Junior.

"Well, to start, I want you to act as co-counsel," said Claxton. "I'll arrange it with Harlan to list you as co-counsel on the case. First thing I want you to do is go over my notes. I've got about four-dozen interviews and sworn depositions. I'd like you to see if you can come up with any questions I might have missed. I've also got another forty or so that need to be done." Junior picked up the thick folder and opened it. There was a long list of names in four columns on the inside left cover. He read through part of the first deposition quickly.

"It looks pretty thorough. Is there a *particular* question that you might already be thinking about?" asked Junior after a moment.

"In fact," said Claxton with a smile, "there are a *couple* of things." There was something in that smile that told me that maybe Junior was a little sharper than anyone thought. He had already put together what I had been thinking about. Sometimes there are reasons for doing things...inside of those reasons. Claxton's mind worked like that. He wanted Junior to help with some of the legwork, but he also wanted to put a fresh face in front of some people...one that they just might let down their guard for.

"I'd like you to ask about Dyle Courtland," said Claxton. "I'd like to know more about his habits, anybody he was around much over the last few weeks he was alive. Anything he might have talked about with them."

"You think Dyle's murder might be important to this case?" asked Junior.

"I don't know," said Claxton with a shake of his head. "Right now, I'd say probably not, but you might come across something else that is. Sometimes it's just a matter of gett'n folks to start talkin'. Dyle was one of those fellas that you either liked or you didn't, but nobody sat on the fence about him."

"Anything else?" asked Junior as he pulled out a pencil, turned to a fresh page at the back and began writing.

"Yes," said Claxton slowly. "I'd also like you to find out anything you can about Riley Shimmerhorn."

"Riley?" said Junior in surprise, but he nodded and scribbled some more. "All right, I'll get started right away."

"Say, Junior," said Carter from the open cell where he was sitting. "Whatcha read'n in that big ole book there? Must be a heap o' law in there."

"I'm reading about a Supreme Court case from 1825," said Junior. "It's a very interesting case involving interstate commerce laws between two states."

"Reckon they done decided that one by now," said Carter. "Justice be slow sometimes, but that be *real* slow."

"Yes, they did," Junior smiled. "I'll let you know how it turned out when I get finished." He picked up the law book and closed up the folder. "Claxton, I appreciate you doing this for me."

"Nonsense," Claxton smiled, "you're helpin' me out. I'll do the appreciatin'." Junior laughed at that.

"All right, we'll *say* I'm helping you out," said Junior. "Any advice on doing this?"

"Yep," said Claxton with a serious nod. "Most important thing you will ever learn as a lawyer. Be yourself all the time. Folks will see through a phony in a New York second. Do that one thing, and the rest will come. I think you'll find that folks around here will like the Junior that became a lawyer a sight more than they might like the lawyer that *used* to be Junior." I could see that Junior was thinking about what he had just heard. Maybe I imagined seeing it, or maybe I really did. I don't really know, but it seemed like something changed in Junior right then and there. I wasn't sure what it was, but I thought it was good.

"Maybe I'll just leave this here," said Junior as he put the book back on the desk. "I'll see how many I can get through today and stop back by with an update later."

"I'll be here 'til six at least," said Claxton. "I'm gonna start goin' over questioning with Carter. The prosecutor will likely be along soon, so we need to get started with that."

"Do you know who'll be trying the case?" asked Junior.

"Not yet," Claxton shook his head. "Marty Slaton's a possibility, but it could be George McCluskey."

"I'd rather draw Slaton I think," said Junior thoughtfully.

"Me as well," said Claxton. "But that's up to the judge and their schedules. Can't worry 'bout who they send. Burnin' daylight."

"I'm on my way, Claxton," Junior grinned. I think that was the first time I had seen him look relaxed since he had come back from law school. He turned and went to the door. I let him out. Owen Mercer came back inside and bolted it back.

"You done a good thing there," said Carter as he stood up, stretched, and walked out of the cell.

"Junior's gonna make a fine man," said Claxton. "Just helpin' him along a bit. Be a good lawyer one of these days, too. You'll see."

"Reckon so," said Carter. He looked around. "Sure wish there was somethin' I could do. Man gets used to workin', it's hard to just sit 'bout."

"Wish I could take you on home with *me*," said Owen from behind his desk. "Got me some roofin' work to do. Could do with a good roofin' man."

"Don't 'spect Judge Harlan be able to let me do that," Carter laughed. "Folks might not look on it right." I knew that was right. I'd heard some ugly talk around town from some.

"Well," said Owen, "it was just *wishin'*. Cell ain't big enough for both of us. Reckon it's time for me to make the rounds and let you talk."

"Hate to chase you off all the time, Owen," said Claxton, "but you might be called as a witness in the trial. It could put you in a bad spot if you had to answer somethin' that maybe you ought not to have known 'bout."

"Sure don't want that," said Owen with a smile. "Like I said, the cell ain't big enough for both of us." He picked up his hat and left. I started to bolt the door back.

"Why don't you boys go on and have some fun," Claxton suggested. "Not gonna be much fun around here." He glanced over at Carter. "I'm gonna be playin' the prosecutor for a bit, and I don't think Carter's gonna like me much 'til I get done." I didn't know exactly what he meant, but I figured it meant that they were going to talk about some things that he didn't want anybody else to hear about.

"We were gonna pick up some work anyway…maybe enough for a coke or somethin'," I said as I opened the door. Willie followed me out into the bright sun, and Claxton closed up behind us.

We walked down the sidewalk and stopped at a few shops. Gerald Edmundson was full asleep when we went in this time. He complained for a minute about how he was hoping the trial would come on because he was just about dead for sleep and didn't have anyone to watch the place part of the day. He hadn't had anything come in that day, so he didn't have any work for us. I told him that I wished I could help out. He just nodded and seemed to doze back off. After a few more stops, it didn't seem like we were in time today to find anything. It was past middle of the day, and most everybody did the hard work early to beat the heat, so I thought maybe we would do better tomorrow. I looked down the street. There were a couple of places that I had never tried before. One of them was the jewelry shop. It wasn't the kind of place that attracted ten year-old boys, but I thought it was worth a try. Every place needs sweeping and fixing up. We went inside Bardwell's Jewelry and walked past the glass counters of rings and watches. I looked across to the other side and saw that there were some other things there also.

"Hey," said Willie as he got there first, "they've got stamps, coins, cars...baseball cards..." I glanced inside the case. I wasn't much of a collector although I did have a small collection of baseball cards.

"I didn't know they had this stuff," I said with a glance down the counter. Old Simon Bardwell slowly made his way down the backside of the counter.

"Don't reckon you boys come to buy an engagement ring today did you?" asked the elderly man with bifocal glasses and a blue bowtie.

"That'd be for a girl wouldn't it," I said with a shake of my head. "I ain't gone foolish in the head just yet." Bardwell laughed at that.

"You got plenty of time for that," he said with a nod. "Maybe you'd be interested in some cards 'till then?"

"Maybe," I said. "Willie, you got a coin collection."

"And some stamps, too," said Willie. I hadn't known about the stamps, but he had mentioned the penny coin collection before, and I had briefly seen it when I was at his house once. I could see the way his eyes lit up, that collecting was really a hobby for him. He had a birthday coming up at the end of the month, so I filed that away to think about when I got him a present.

"You boys go on and have a look," said Bardwell. "If you see something you like, let me know." I looked at few of the stamps and coins. I noticed right away that the prices got steeper as you moved closer to the back of the building, so I stopped right there.

"Mr. Bardwell," I said. "Do you ever need any work done 'round here?"

"You mean stock, cleaning, and such?" he asked. He shook his head. "I don't have much of that, but I might *could* use some young eyes for sortin' coins and stamps. Got to look close to judge quality, and my eyes are not as sharp anymore. Come by on Wednesday mornings when I open up at eight. I've got a man from Fayette that comes by once a week with stock to look at."

"All right," I said with a smile. "We'll see you again on Wednesday." I looked at Willie who was still looking through the glass at the coins and stamps. "You might see *him* before then." Bardwell smiled.

"I can spot a collector a mile away," he said. "My eyes work good going that direction."

Chapter Eleven

Willie and I spent part of the morning the next day helping Gerald Edmundson out at his store. Willie even watched the cash register for about an hour while Gerald got a few minutes of sleep in the back room on top of the desk where he handled his paper work. He gave us a dollar each that day, and said it was worth it just to close his eyes a few minutes. We left there and went out into the woods for a while just to be out of the heat in town. On our way out, we saw Junior going door to door on the next street over. Claxton hadn't mentioned the night before whether Junior had actually come up with anything he could use, but I was kind of hoping that he would. Claxton had been up late working on the case, and he didn't seem too happy with where it was headed. I was only ten, but even I could see that it was going to be real hard for Claxton to find a way to put Carter's keys in somebody else's hand.

And that was exactly what he was going to have to do if he was going to come out on top.

Late that afternoon, we came out from the woods filled up on wild mulberries and our lips and fingers stained purple. Back in town I saw Junior heading towards the jail, so I thought we might drop by for a few minutes to see what he might have to say. Claxton had already told us that he didn't mind us hanging around just so long as we didn't talk with anyone about anything that was said. That was fine with us since we didn't really follow everything they were talking about anyway. We managed to catch up with Junior and slide in with him when the door opened. The office was a little full, so we took the two chairs just inside the door to the left under the barred window that stayed closed up with heavy wooden shutters these days.

"Had to break up some drinkin' that was gett'n out of control over at Elias's place," said Ted Fiedler. He had only needed about five seconds to slip comfortably back into the routine of patrolling a town.

"Were they talkin' 'bout the case?" asked Claxton.

"Yep," Fiedler nodded. "Some folks just get plain mean when they get liquored up. Mostly just wonderin' when the trial's comin'."

"Won't be long," said Claxton. "Harlan gave me the word today that George McCluskey will be in town tomorrow to start in on the case. I'll probably spend some time with him first thing to discuss any discovery and evidence. Then he'll line up some witnesses to interview. I'd 'spect him to need about a day. Come Friday, Harlan will likely have the arraignment. Jury call will go out right away. Harlan's already got two dozen on the list, and Monday we might be startin' the trial."

"I didn't think it would move this fast," said Junior. "I've got ten more people to interview, and I was thinking about these." He showed Claxton a few more names he had written down. Claxton nodded thoughtfully.

"Might be worth the time," he said after a moment. "Go on and squeeze 'em in if you can."

"I started this one," said Junior as he underlined a name on his list. "But I wasn't getting anything much, so I was thinking that you might want to handle that one yourself."

"Reckon I know the one," said Claxton. "Probably need to do that one personally. I'll look over your notes." It took me a minute to realize that Junior and Claxton were having a private conversation in a room full of people without really saying anything anyone else would understand. I was a little more impressed by Junior every day now. He seemed to be catching on really quick now, and I think he was actually giving Claxton some help. Claxton took out his pocket watch.

"It's almost four," he said as if he was thinking about twenty different things at one time. "I'll go on ahead and take care of this interview. Junior, I want you to work with Carter. Get a good background, character, references, anything you can. Then start looking at putting together a witness list and the order you'd call them in. Character witnesses first. Then move on to anyone who might testify to any evidence." Claxton pulled out some papers from the stack. "Have a look at this one, again. Tell me if you thought there was somethin' held back."

"Got it," said Junior as he made a few notes. Claxton gathered up one small notebook and left. We followed along behind. I had thought Willie and I would go to my house for a while and maybe check on an apple pie that Bertie had been working on that morning that might be in need of our attention. I wasn't sure if I had room for much on top of the mulberries, but I was willing to try if he was.

"You boys got a few minutes?" Claxton asked as we passed the burned out church.

"Need us to do somethin'?" I asked. I sort of hoped he did as it might give us a few minutes to work off the mulberries.

"Just wonderin' if you might come on with me while I stop in and talk with Addie for a spell," he said.

"Reckon we can," I said. I looked at Willie and he only shrugged that it was okay by him. "What you need us to do there?"

"Just be there," Claxton answered. I didn't have any idea how that could help, but it was fine with me, and like always I knew that Claxton had his reasons; he had reasons for everything he did even if nobody else ever knew them.

"Don't 'spose we can mess that up," said Willie with a grin. We followed Claxton to the corner past the church and then down the street that offered a view of the graveyard through the old black wrought iron fence that marked the front and one side. It only took a few minutes to reach the minister's house. It was an old house that had been lived in by just about all the town ministers that had been there before, but it was in good repair. Evan Washburne had been a tireless worker when it came to saving souls, and he had just about been as tireless in fixing up the old place after quite a few years of neglect. We followed Claxton up the three steps to the wooden floored porch in front of the door. He rang the bell and waited. There was a swish of the window curtains that told us someone was checking to see who was there, and then a few moments later the front door opened.

"Was wonderin' if you was going to stop by, Claxton," said Addie through the screen door. "Talked with Junior for a bit, and he said you might."

"Sorry I haven't been by before now," said Claxton as she opened the screen door. She was dressed in mourning, wearing a black dress with small black gloves, and looked like she hadn't seen the sun in weeks as she squinted out at us.

"Don't be," she said. "I've had too many people as it is. Come on in. You, too, boys. I've got some cookies in a jar on the table. Go on an' help yourselves."

"Thanks," I said as we walked on past to the kitchen. It turned out that there was oatmeal and peanut butter cookies in the jar. They weren't fresh baked, but a quick sampling told us that they were still pretty good. It wasn't pie, but cookies were good in a pinch. We sat down at the table to make sure we didn't drop crumbs anywhere. From where I sat, I mostly just listened and looked at the pictures on the walls. They were mostly pictures of people I didn't know, but there was one that was kind of different. It was a picture of some playin' cards with something else in it, but it was across the room, and I couldn't see it any better than that.

"Done told Junior 'bout everythin' I know," Addie said as she sat down in the front living room in a rocker and Claxton took a seat on the sofa.

"Well," Claxton smiled, "I mostly just wanted to check on you and see if you were holdin' up okay. Thought you might come by and see me at the office."

"I had me a spell of the heat that night…" she said but trailed off. "Been tolerable since, though."

"You eatin' like you should an' gett'n your rest like I said?" Claxton went on.

"Yes, sir, mister Claxton," she said with a weak smile. "I know I got to do right by this child. It's just hard right now."

"I know," said Claxton. "If you need anything at all, just let me know." He said nothing for almost a full minute.

"Reckon this ain't just a social call is it?" she said finally. "Heard you was doin' the lawerin' for Carter."

"Hope you don't take it bad that I am," said Claxton. "Some folks didn't take very kindly to it."

"I ain't like other folks," Addie shook her head. "You just doin' what you think is right. You was a good friend to Evan. Nothin' gonna change that."

"I'm glad to hear that," said Claxton, and I thought I could hear a little relief in his voice over that. "I was kind of thinkin' that I'd run into Evan while he was passin' out cigars, but the couple times I ran into him he didn't let on he knew."

"Never got a chance to tell him," Addie sighed. "Was plannin' on makin' it an anniversary surprise. Woulda been five years this July thirtieth. Claxton nodded.

"Did you get a chance to see him again that last night?" Claxton asked. I noticed that he had not opened his notebook or even taken a pencil out of his shirt pocket, and it occurred to me that maybe he wasn't as interested in what she said as much as how she said it.

"I went on home and directly to bed," she shook her head. "Next thing I heard was all the commotion goin' on at the church."

"So he didn't stop by the house that night at all?" Claxton continued.

"Didn't see him if he did," said Addie. "But, Evan wouldn't have woke me if he had. He was consid'rate that way when I was feelin' poorly."

"He was a good man," said Claxton softly. "I miss him…miss him a lot."

"I know you do, Claxton," she said. "You a lot like him, you know, in a lot of ways. Probably why you two got on so well together."

"I 'preciate that," said Claxton, and then after a moment, "'Spose I ought to get on with the business part, so you can get supper and get to bed."

"Tell you what I can," she said, "but it probably ain't much."

"All right," he said, "do you recall ever seein' anyone with another key to the church or even another key to the graveyard shed?"

"Oh, Evan would sometimes loan the key to somebody while he wasn't there I reckon," she said, "but I don't remember there bein' another key 'cept Carter's since I was a little girl. Used to belong to the deacons so's they could get into the church when the minister was gone." Claxton nodded. "Somewhere I reckon one of 'em must of lost 'em or maybe died and they got packed up. I don't rightly know."

"Seems to be what a lot of people recall," said Claxton.

"Any idea why Carter'd do somethin' like this?" Addie said. "He got on so good with Evan."

"He says he didn't," said Claxton.

"You believe 'em?" she asked quietly.

"I'm his lawyer," Claxton answered without really answering.

"Now you're even talkin' like one," she shook her head. "Reckon you cain't answer on that. Probably don't make no difference no how. Got to do what you got to do whether he's guilty or not. Anything else you want to ask 'bout?"

"Well, I was wonderin' 'bout Odessa," said Claxton. "This thing kinda caught you both ways I reckon. How you doin' there?'

"It's a hard thing, Claxton," she said, "ending a friendship you've had a lifetime. Cain't even put that kind of thing into words."

"Were you two still as close as ever these last few years?" asked Claxton. "Sometimes when a friend gets married, it's like they moved away."

"Was nothin' like that with us," she said. "Odessa was over here a lot. Sometimes the three of us would go drive over and see the picture show. And, then this summer…something I thought was never gonna happen…she found God…or maybe He found her."

"Was there anything special goin' on in her life?" asked Claxton. He didn't seem surprised. "Was she seein' anyone?"

"Think she was husband huntin' 'bout the time we turned three," Addie laughed. "Was somebody *special* just 'bout every other day seems. But no, I don't think there was nothin' new with her…same old Odessa."

"All right," said Claxton as he stood up. I figured that meant we were about to leave, so Willie and I grabbed a few cookies to take along. "I think that 'bout covers the official part of the visit. Now as your doctor, I want you to keep on with your vitamins, and make sure you're gett'n plenty of calcium. Keep eatin' regular, and get your rest." When I got into the front room from the kitchen, I walked over to the picture on the wall, but when I got there I saw it wasn't a picture like the rest. It was four old playin' cards behind glass in a frame. There was a pair of black eights and a pair of black aces. It seemed like an odd thing to have on the wall of a house.

"I promise mister Claxton," she smiled as she stood up from the rocker.

"Missus Washburne," I said, "what's these here cards all 'bout?" Claxton gave them a glance. I thought he was goin' to say somethin', but he didn't.

"Jes somethin' that been in the family a long spell, I reckon," said Addie Washburne. "Don't reckon I know much 'bout it. All the rest of them pictures is relatives of mine an' Evan's."

"Yes ma'am," I said. Claxton gave her a pat on the arm as he walked by, and we joined him on the way out. I heard the front door close quietly behind us as we walked down the steps, and then I caught just a glimpse of the window curtains rustling as we turned in front of the house. Norm Abernathy was rakin' some cut grass in his yard, so Claxton headed over there to say hello.

"See you got that blade sharpened up," said Claxton as he walked up to him and nodded at the old rotary push mower.

"Yep," said Norm. "Had to. Yard was growin' up."

"Mine, too," said Claxton. "You got a few minutes? I been takin' depositions of the witnesses 'round here. Thought I might see if you got anything to add."

"Done talked to Junior," said Norm. "'Cept for the fire, don't know that I could tell him much."

"Guess, I forgot he had you on his list," said Claxton. "You know, I was out this way the other day lookin' the place over."

"Right," said Norm. "Believe I saw you. What was you lookin' for…if it ain't somethin' secret?"

"Nothin' secret," said Claxton. "Just tryin' to see if I could see what you saw that night from your house. I reckon only you and Evan's house even got a view of the church with it settin' back off the road. Lucky you heard somethin'. Could have lost half a Main Street."

"Wish I'd a seen it when it started," said Norm.

"You see anything else when you came outside…or before?" asked Claxton.

"Like what, Claxton?" asked Norm.

"Somebody walkin' 'round… maybe by the tool shed or the church door?" asked Claxton.

"'Spose I could see the *back* of the shed, but I didn't see nobody by the church door when I looked out the back," said

Norm. "Didn't see nobody anywhere. Place was all lit up. Don't think I coulda missed anybody runnin' 'round."

"All right," said Claxton. "Just thought I'd ask. Probably goin' to be called to testify 'bout the fire, so you might want to get that suit pressed."

"Sure, Claxton," said Norm. "Anything else?"

"See you in court, I reckon," said Claxton. We walked with Claxton down the next block and onto the house where we smelled Bertie's meatloaf simmering in the pan fifty feet from the front door.

"Claxton," I said. "What was you 'bout to say 'bout them cards back there at Missus Washburne's house?"

"I was goin' to say that somebody had put together a Dead Man's Hand," said Claxton. "Then I thought it might not be good to say with Minister Washburne bein' dead an' all."

"What's that?" I asked. "A dead man's hand?"

"Aces and eights...a poker hand that Wild Bill Hickock was holdin' when he got shot an' killed playin' poker," said Claxton. "Now, that smells awful good in there. You boys go wash up and see if she needs any help settin' the table." We ran inside and up the stairs. When we got back down, we found that she did need plates and silver put out. Claxton joined us a few minutes later, and we all started eating.

"Don't know where you boys be puttin' it," said Bertie with a shake of her head. "You still stained from eatin' them mulberries."

"And they had cookies," Claxton added.

"It's meatloaf," I said as if that explained everything.

"Reckon it's the fresh air and runnin' 'round," said Bertie. "You boys eat up, but save you a space for some pie. I done fixed it special for you since you was havin' Willie over tonight."

"Don't figure on missin' on pie," I said with a shake of my head.

"Sure is good," said Willie as he was nearly finished with his slice of meatloaf.

"Got plenty," said Bertie. "Go on an get you another.' Willie did, and even I was surprised that he could eat another.

The pie after dinner was maybe some of the best I'd ever had. Bertie said she had gotten the apples fresh yesterday off the tree at the orchard.

"Now I gonna 'spect you boys to roll out for breakfast at first light," said Bertie. "Don't want no hibernatin' on all you done et today."

"We'll be up," I promised. "We've got business in town first thing. Got some work with old man Bardwell inspectin' stuff for 'em."

We listened to a few radio shows that night. My favorite was a mystery show where the detective put together all the clues and solved the crime right there at the end. I was just about sure that the old man gardener had stabbed his boss in the back with the shears, but it turned out it was the next door neighbor getting back at him for stealing some of his prize roses and beating him at a show with them. The detective went through how he'd gotten at the answer, and I had to admit that all the clues were there. I just hadn't found them out. Willie was way off track. He guessed that it was the milkman, but already knew that he couldn't have done it because he had been out sick that day and no milk was delivered. Claxton was barely following along as he was going over things in his notebook, and Bertie only stayed for half the show before she went off to bed. I'm not sure if Claxton really knew we went upstairs to bed or not, but he did say goodnight.

"Wish I was detective Brent Hardcastle," I told Willie after we got to my room and got into bed. "Might be able to help Claxton out a little on this."

"Reckon he could use him a detective all right," said Willie. "But, it's not like the show. There ain't all the clues layin' out there to be found."

"But I'll bet they're there *somewhere*," I said. "You know how sometimes you don't see somethin', and then one day you look at it from another way, and you see it was there all the time?"

"Yeah," said Willie. "I lost a stamp once and couldn't find it anywhere. After a week, I figured it was just gone. Then I picked up a letter, and that stamp was sittin' right on top of the real stamp. I'd probably looked at that letter 'bout everyday, I just wasn't *seein'* it like you said."

"I think that's what's happenin' here," I said. "Just don't know that stamp's sittin' there."

"Well, maybe Claxton will come on it," said Willie.

"Maybe," I said. I thought about it a lot while we talked that night and finally got off near sleep. I started wondering if maybe Claxton was just too close to see all the clues, and that if he took a big step back from the picture he'd see stuff he'd missed. Then I started to wonder what might happen if there just *wasn't* any clue to be found. It wouldn't matter how much you looked or where you stood to look at it if it just wasn't there.

Chapter Twelve

"I'm goin' to stop by the office for a bit this morning an' see a few patients I've been puttin' off a few days," said Claxton as Willie and I came down the stairs. It had taken three tries, but Bertie had finally chased us up out of bed. We sat down at the table to two plates of hotcakes and bacon while Claxton was finishing his morning coffee and reading something in the paper.

"We're goin' to Bardwell's," I yawned. "It really six-thirty?"

"Yep," said Bertie as she set down two glasses of orange juice. "Took me forty minutes to get these here young'uns out o' the bed. Sleepin' the day away." She ruffled my hair with her hand as she walked past on her way back to the kitchen.

"I had 'bout forgot," Claxton dropped his paper down and looked over it. "He's a good ole fella, mister Bardwell." He folded up the paper and dropped it onto the small stand beside the wall. "I'll likely be over at the courthouse later to meet with George McCluskey. Could be the rest of the day."

"All right," I said as I started in on the hotcakes. Claxton got up from the table and picked up his notebooks. Then he was on his way. Willie and I finished eating and took our plates to the kitchen. I thought we ought to get back on Bertie's good side, so I rinsed off the plates and the cups before standing them up in the drainer.

We got to Bardwell's Jewelry store about ten minutes before eight just in time to see him opening up and letting in a very tall, thin man wearing a brown jacket with elbow patches. We came inside and mister Bardwell introduced us to Bernie Chesterfield of Fayette. I think he was probably the tallest man I'd ever seen outside the circus. He must have been a whole head and shoulders taller than Claxton but only about half as wide.

"Howdy boys," said Bernie Chesterfield with a big smile on his face. "Simon's telling me that you boys are gonna do some of his coin and stamp gradin'."

"That's right," I said.

"Having good eyes is just part of it," Chesterfield said as he craned his head and neck down just a bit. "Real trick is in knowin' what to look for." He handed each of us a silver dollar. "Tell me what you see there." We each looked at the coin we had.

"Year says it's 1886," I said. "Got the Statue of Liberty's head on the front and a big ole eagle on the back."

"Mine's the same," said Willie.

"You sure 'bout that?" he asked. "What else you see there?" I looked closer.

"Got a little letter on it...a 'D'," I said.

"Mine has an 'S' on it," said Willie. "And it looks like a little piece of the 'L' in Liberty is broke off. Guess that makes it worth less."

"Makes it worth *more*," said Chesterfield. "There was a mistake on the die and about two hundred of those got made by accident before they saw it and fixed it. That other one was made after they fixed it. Probably millions of those. Rarity, even if it looks bad, can make a coin more valuable."

"What else do you look for?" I asked as I looked at the coin even closer. I took Willie's coin and held them up together. "I can see the feathers on this here eagle of his, but mine's just about rubbed clean off. Same with the Liberty's face."

"That's it," Chesterfield nodded. "You done answered your own question, son. Usually a coin's value is tied up in how much wear's on it and sometimes how old it is. That coin over there don't go nowhere but my pocket, and I don't keep nothin' in that pocket with it to rub on it." I handed him back the coins. We followed him over to the counter where he spilled out about two hundred coins onto the glass. There was an assortment of pennies, nickels, dimes, quarters, half dollars, silver dollars, and a few I didn't even recognize.

"How 'bout you boys look through these and put them into five groups," Chesterfield said. "Best ones go on the left, and worn out ones go on the right." We went to work on the coins while Chesterfield and mister Bardwell started talking about some old stamps he had come across.

At first it seemed like an easy job. The really good coins were pretty easy to sort, and so were the worn out ones, but putting the other coins into three groups in between got tricky. I'd find a coin that I thought was pretty good, but it'd have something wrong in one spot. Then I'd find another that was good there but messed up somewhere else. I moved coins in and out of groups, and finally gave up and let Willie try his eye on them. Eventually we had the coins sorted, but I thought only fifteen were really good and about forty-two were really bad. The other hundred or so were in between, and I think we could have put them in any of the three groups or maybe just made one.

"You boys 'bout got it?" Chesterfield asked as he mister Bardwell finished talking about the stamps.

"Not sure 'xactly what we got," I said scratching my head, "but they're sorted some." Chesterfield looked through the good ones and bad ones and nodded. Then he started looking through the rest. He picked up one from the good pile second from the left and the not so good pile second from the right.

"Have a look at these here," he said. They were both Lincoln pennies from 1909. "These are first year pennies. Now this one here looks a little worn on the face, but the wheat ear on the back is not too bad. That one is worn a might on both sides, but I'll tell ya' it's worth more. See them initials on the bottom? 'VDB'? That's the initials of the engraver that done this picture of Lincoln. Makes that coin a sight more rare than the other that was minted later that year. Now if you boys run across one of them with an 'S' mint mark on it, you look me up cause they're ain't but ten of them ever made and we might just do some business." I was a little amazed by everything there was to know about this job, but it was like a lot of things that look like nothing on the outside until you look closely at the inside.

"I've got a book for you boys to study," said mister Bardwell. He handed us a coin book. "This book will tell you what to look for on just about any coin minted in the last two hundred years, will tell you how rare, and other things 'bout it. Use it to look at those coins for me. You boys go on an get on it, while we settle up."

Bardwell and Chesterfield walked off to the other side of the counters to figure out the cost of the coins we were looking at as well as the stamps we'd not yet seen. I opened up the book to the Lincoln penny and started reading off some of the things to look for while Willie started checking one. Willie knew some of the things already from his own collection, but there was just about always something about a coin that we hadn't known until we looked it up in the book.

It wasn't long before we were using one of mister Bardwell's big magnifying glasses that had a bright light clipped to the handle. We compared each coin against a picture of it in the book to figure out what kind of condition it was in, and then we looked up the value of the coin by its condition. Then, we wrote down what we'd found on a little tag and stuck it to the little plastic sleeve that we put the coin into. We finished up with about half of them by lunch, and I could see that we were going to fill out the afternoon getting the rest done. That was just about what happened. Willie dropped the last coin into place at five o'clock.

"You boys done a fine, fine job," said Bardwell as he sifted through the little packs and checked the writing on the back. "Couldn't have done better myself." He motioned towards the counter. "You can go on pick out anything in the place up to a dollar each, so if you got some empty spots in your collection, you can start fillin' 'em up."

"Thanks, Mister Bardwell," said Willie with a broad smile. "Sort of had my eye on a couple already."

"Thought you might," said Bardwell. He started picking up the little packs of coins and putting them into place under the glass.

"Don't reckon I've decided on anythin' today," I said to Mister Bardwell as Willie went over to look right away. "'Spose I could save it up for a spell? Maybe get somethin' worth more than a dollar?" I did actually have a coin in mind. It was an old penny that I knew Willie didn't have because he'd mentioned it when were looking through the book, but he got un-excited about it in a big hurry when he saw that it was three dollars and a half. I'm not the quickest one with figuring numbers, but I figured I could save that much by Willie's birthday and buy it for him.

"All the same to me," said Bardwell. He picked up a little ledger book from the shelf behind him and wrote quickly across the top. "All right. I got Willie down as havin' worked and been paid, and I got you down for a dollar on account. Cash that in whenever you want."

"Thanks, Mister Bardwell," I said. I hung around while Willie found the 1881-penny he was looking for. Mister Bardwell said that he'd expect us the same time next week, and that he was expecting some baseball cards with the coins next time.

When I got home, it was almost time for supper. I asked Bertie if Claxton had been home yet, and she said that she hadn't seen him yet. When he finally did get home, it was almost seven o'clock, and Bertie finished cooking his dinner that she had started hours before. I sat at the table while he was eating and told him what Willie and I had been doing all day.

"Sounds like you sure kept busy enough," said Claxton. "Learn a little, too?"

"Man name of Vincent D. Brenner was the one that done the engravin' for Abraham Lincoln on the penny," I said a little proudly that I had recalled that fact. "They done it in 1909 'cause it was a hundred years since he was born."

"I reckon you did learn a few things," said Claxton with a whistle of admiration. "Don't hold that against Mister Bardwell now."

"Aw, I ain't 'gainst learnin' stuff," I laughed. "Just don't come as natural as playin' ball." I leaned on the table on one elbow. "Claxton, how'd your day go down at that courthouse with Mister McCluskey?"

"I don't rightly know just yet," Claxton shook his head. "We didn't spend a lot of time on much but the evidence, and then he was off early in the afternoon to talk to folks that he might be callin' to testify. I reckon he thinks this one is goin' to be mighty quick to try."

"What you thinkin' 'bout it, Claxton?" I wondered. "Think it'll be quick like that?"

"I think he'll throw the state's case out there right quick," said Claxton. "He'll be more interested in what the defense might be up to." He paused for a minute. "Come to think 'bout it, I'll be mighty interested to see what the defense comes up with myself." I laughed at that. I knew Claxton probably already had his case all planned out because that's just the way he did things. But, I also thought that he was plenty worried about what might be up ahead. He had mentioned more than once that you never quite knew what a jury might do no matter how you thought it was going to turn out. There was a knock on the screen door.

"Claxton?" a voice called from out front.

"Come on in, Junior," Claxton called back as he stood and started picking up his plate. I heard the screen door shut, and a minute later Junior came walking into the kitchen.

"Go ahead and start layin' things out," said Claxton with a motion of his hand at the table. "Be right with you."

"Looks like you been doin' a heap o' work there, Junior," I said as I gazed at the stacks of handwritten pages he was putting on the table.

"It is that," said Junior. "A heap...that is. I just hope there's a *case* in it somewhere."

"So...do...I," said Claxton as he came back in from the kitchen. "So do I." He pulled up his chair and sat down in front of the spread out work. "All right, what am I lookin' at here?"

"I've got Carter's stuff right there," said Junior as he pointed to the first stack of papers. "Witnesses there that might help us, and witnesses there that wouldn't spit on us to put us out if we were runnin' down the street on fire." Claxton nodded and began reading over them.

"This is good here on Carter...real good," he said after a moment. He tapped another paper. "Yes, that's what I want to see. Get down what they say, and give me what you *think* right there with it over on the side. If you think they're addin' in or leavin' out, go on an make the note." He read through some more, nodding occasionally. When he finally finished with the last stack, he set it down.

"There's good work in here, Junior," Claxton said. His eyes trailed to the stack of witnesses on the right. "And you're right 'bout these here witnesses. They could be trouble for us if George puts them up there to talk."

"It's mostly hearsay," said Junior. "When I pinned them down, they didn't really know anything for sure, but they don't like Carter very much and don't mind sayin' why."

"And I want you ready to jump in there if they start talkin' that way," said Claxton. "You and I know it's hearsay. George and Harlan know it, too, but the jury's goin' to *hear* it. Now Harlan can tell 'em to forget all 'bout it. He can say that 'till the cows come home, but he can't take it out of their heads once it gets in there. I've seen innocent men gone to jail on it before." Claxton tapped the table with his fingers. "Trouble is...if we jump up and object to everything, the jury starts wonderin' what *we're* hidin' from them. That can start to work against you, so we have to pick and choose the time."

"Sounds tricky," said Junior. "I've been kind of wonderin' though about our case."

"Oh...me, too," said Claxton with a smile. "The prosecution is really only goin' to do one thing...and that is show that the only way those keys could have got into that shed was if Carter put them there. And if he put them there, then he had to be the one that locked up the church with Evan Washburne and Odessa Hendricks inside, and if he did that he's the one that used the gasoline from the shed to burn the place down. Now that's murder in the first degree...thought out and done. George will put some of those folks in that stack up there on the stand, but nothin' they say will matter much."

"So what does that leave us with?" Junior asked.

"We've got to plant the seed of reasonable doubt in the mind of the jury," said Claxton slowly. "We've got to water that seed and make it grow. We have to *prove* that it's possible there could be another key out there."

"Kind of hard to do when you don't have it in your hand to show the jury," said Junior.

"It would help if we did have it," said Claxton, "but we can make that key just as *real* as if it was there, and the prosecution can't prove it *don't* exist...any more than we can prove it was used, but *that* right there is reasonable doubt, and if we win that fight, then the jury has to look at the man at that table and ask themselves if they really think he could do somethin' like that. Could he really have soaked the place in gasoline, locked the place up knowin' there was two people in there, and then lit it up before calmly goin' back to the shed and lockin' up for the night."

"You still lookin' at an arraignment on Friday?" Junior wondered.

"I am," said Claxton. "We'll pick the jury that afternoon most likely, and go to trial on Monday."

"You worried 'bout the jury?" asked Junior.

"Always," said Claxton. "Just takes one juror with an axe to grind, an' he'll grind it on everybody in that jury room when they go to deliberate. We'll try to excuse anybody that really has it in for Carter, but I might as well tell you, there'll be a couple that have done made up their minds before they sit down."

"Are you putting Carter on the stand?" Junior asked after that soaked in.

"Got to," said Claxton. "He's the only one that can really speak to the jury. If he didn't testify in a case like this…well, we might as well just drive him up to the state pen at Jackson ourselves." Junior nodded in agreement.

"I guess we need to go over all this and talk it out," said Junior as he started with the stack of witnesses on the right. Claxton nodded and they started in on it. It was late that night when I heard the screen door shut, but I was half asleep when Claxton looked in on me on his way to bed.

I was pretty sound asleep when I heard a commotion outside and then the sound of someone walking and then running. I sat up in bed. There was a sharp crack followed right away by the sound of shattering glass. Then there was another almost just like it. I got out of bed and started toward the door, but when I reached for the handle, the door opened and Claxton was there. He grabbed me by the arm and took me over behind the dresser.

"Stay right here," Claxton told me as he started back to the door. It was then that I saw he had his old service revolver in his hand.

"What's happenin'?" I asked. I hadn't been worried until I saw the gun.

"Just stay put," he said and then he was gone. I heard him going quickly down the stairs and heard the front screen door open. Then there was another crack, and I knew that was a rifle shot. The next four shots were different. They were quick and steady, and I heard more glass breaking and a truck engine suddenly fire up. If there was anything else, it was lost in the scream of tires burning up on the pavement. There was a chorus of whoops and shouts as the truck sped away from the house. I waited where I'd been told and was just starting to figure out that someone had been shooting at our house. Maybe shooting at Claxton, and him maybe shooting back at them.

"Claxton?" I called out. Everything had happened so fast. Now that it sounded like it was over I was finally scared. There was no sound from downstairs, and I started wondering if maybe he'd been shot out there. My mind started seeing a lot of things. I wondered if he'd look like Dyle, his insides running out of him and all. "Bertie!"

"Stay where you is child!" Bertie called back somehow managing to yell and whisper at the same time. "Claxton be back directly." I stayed where I was, but I wasn't so sure about him coming back. I'd already seen him killed in the wide-awake nightmare I was having. I was just about set on going down there, when I heard someone on the stairs. Then I crouched down even lower into the little space behind the dresser wondering if someone was coming upstairs to do some more shooting.

"It's all right," I heard Claxton say from somewhere on the stairs. I felt a wave of relief spilling out of me about then, and I went running out from behind the dresser.

"What was all that shootin' 'bout?" I asked as I saw him coming in the room.

"Seems there was some fellas payin' us a call after a long night of drinkin'," said Claxton.

"Was they shootin' at you, Claxton?" I asked. It was just then that I noticed that I was shaking. I saw Bertie in the doorway behind him.

"You ain't been shot or nothin' has you?" asked Bertie as she clutched her housecoat up tight around her.

"Not even close," Claxton shook his head. "Don't even think they knew I was there. They were just shootin' at the windows 'til I put a few rounds into the truck out there on the street. They kinda lost interest in bein' 'round here then."

"Did you see who they was?" asked Bertie. She looked like she was about as scared as I was. Only Claxton seemed all right.

"It'd be hard not to know that old '31 Model-A made into a truck," said Claxton. "Don't reckon they'll be back. Probably halfway to Natchez by now."

"Them Gaston boys," Bertie fumed as she shook her head. "They ain't never been nothin' but trouble." She glanced over her shoulder down the stairs. "Now what? What do that be…" She walked away from the door. "Now that just ain't right! They done burnt up a cross in the yard!"

"Who do they think they is? The Klan or somethin'?" said Bertie angrily as she came back up the stairs. I'd heard a few times that the Gaston's did have some Klan ties, but this was the first time that I knew of that it had shown out.

"Just drunk I imagine," said Claxton.

"Is it still burnin' out there?" I asked.

"I put it out with the hose," Claxton shook his head. "It'll keep 'til mornin'. Just stay out of the front room. We'll need to sweep out the glass."

"Reckon I'll start in on it," said Bertie. "Don't 'spect I'll be doin' no more sleepin' *this* night. Done scare't me out o' ten years o' breathin'." She was still mumbling as she headed down the stairs to get her broom. "Just no account white trash is what they is!" She hollered back up from downstairs.

"What do you aim to do, Claxton?" I wondered.

"'Spose I'll catch up with Owen in the mornin' and swear out a complaint," said Claxton. "He can pick 'em up when they show up in town again."

"I reckon they done this 'cause you're Carter's lawyer," I said after a moment. I'd heard of things like this happening other places, but I never thought it could really happen here. Just one more thing I'd been proven wrong about.

"I reckon so, Nathan," he nodded. "We'll talk more 'bout it in the mornin'. Right now, you need to get back to bed."

"'Spect I'm 'bout as sleepy as Bertie 'bout now," I said, but I did as he said and crawled back into bed. There was the sound of people outside.

"Probably the neighbors," said Claxton. "Reckon I ought to tell 'em it ain't the Russians shootin' at us." He patted me on the head and left to go outside. I pulled the covers up to my chin and tried to shut my eyes, but they wouldn't close for the longest time. I don't remember going to sleep that night, but somewhere along there I did. The next morning the broken glass had all been swept up off the living room floor, and the burned cross was gone from the front lawn. Claxton was already dressed and drinking his coffee when I got downstairs, and I could tell that neither he nor Bertie had slept a wink.

"Reckon I'll have me a nap," said Bertie, "…now that the sun be up. Y'all take you a key when you go out, an' don't be surprised if the doors be locked up tight when you come back." She yawned and then started on her way upstairs.

"I'd like you to stay in town today," said Claxton. "Keep 'round folks you know well. Might even think 'bout spendin' a night or two over with Willie." I nodded. I'd spent four or five nights over there this summer, and he'd stayed with us that many or more.

"All right," I said. "Don't mind doin' that. Just don't like you bein' here alone…just you and Bertie."

"I 'spect Owen will put a deputy over here for a spell," Claxton said.

"How 'bout Mr. Edmundson?" I suggested. "I reckon he'd like to sleep on the couch."

"Could be," said Claxton with a laugh. Gerald Edmundson's long days of double duty were starting to become legendary around town by now, and a few folks who'd woken him up at the store had started calling him Rip instead.

"You gonna have to carry your gun with you now?" I asked as Claxton began gathering up his things.

"Don't reckon I'll need it," said Claxton with a shake of his head. "Try to get last night out of your head. Ain't nothin' worse than lookin' over your shoulder for somebody that ain't comin'."

"All right. I'll try anyhow," I promised, but I didn't really think I'd be forgetting about this anytime soon. And I thought that maybe I ought to be looking over my shoulder now and then. Dyle, the minister, Odessa, and maybe even Riley might be around right now if they'd had just a glance or two in the rear view mirror now and again. I knew from cold hard fact, that sometimes there *was* somebody coming for you, and sometimes they *do* catch you.

Chapter Thirteen

I started spending the nights with Willie starting that first night after the Gaston's came calling. Willie's father was all right with me being there for a while, but I did notice that he locked up the doors at night, and the next day he was cleaning his shotgun. He said it was just due for cleaning, but I wondered if he might be thinking he'd need it.

The arraignment came on Friday just like Claxton said it would, and I was sitting in the courtroom with just about everybody that could squeeze in that little place that ordinarily seemed pretty big. The folks that had been there for the hearing caught on quick to what they needed to do and they hushed up mighty fast when Woodrow Silas stuck one big hand up in the air. The rest was a bit slower on the uptake and didn't close their mouths until Woodrow said he'd boot them out in the street with his size sixteen shoes. When the courtroom settled down, Judge Clary walked in and came up to his desk. Woodrow had everyone up on their feet and said just about every word he'd said the first time. We all sat down when he said to be seated.

"Got a nice turn out today, Woodrow," said Harlan Clary as he settled into his chair. "Didn't know there was such an interest in law an' order 'round here." Silas nodded and smiled.

"Now, just so y'all know it," Clary began, "there ain't but a couple lawyers, one bailiff, an one judge here today, so don't nobody out there get to thinkin' that you're one or the other." There was a low rumble of laughter. "All right. What we are doin' is having an arraignment today. For those who don't know him, or done forgot from when he was here before a few times, the prosecutor for the state is Mister George McCluskey." He pointed to the man in the dark blue suit at the table next to Claxton's. McCluskey turned and gave a little bow to the audience. "And over here is Mister Claxton Delaney and Mister Junior Preston for the defense. George, you go on and get things started."

"Thank you, your honor," said George McCluskey in a remarkably smooth voice that seemed to carry throughout the room. "The state is entering a charge of two counts of murder in the first degree and one count of aggravated arson in the commission of a capital crime against Mister Carter Monroe the third of Josiah Falls, Mississippi. He is being charged in the deaths of Minister Evan Washburne and Miss Odessa Hendricks…both of Josiah Falls…and with the burning down of the Baptist Church of God of Josiah Falls. The state will waive the request for an arrest warrant as the defendant is already present and detained without bond being met."

"Thank you, George," said Clary. "The charges are so noted and so entered. Claxton? Are you ready to answer the charges today with a plea of guilty or not guilty?"

"Yes, your honor," said Claxton as he stood up from the table with both Junior and Carter beside him. "The defendant in this case, Carter Monroe the third, answers with a plea of not guilty on all charges." There was a bit of talk throughout the room after that, but Woodrow Silas ended that with only a single step towards the gallery of people.

"A not guilty plea has been so noted and so entered," said Judge Clary. "Thank you, Claxton, Junior." He looked around the courtroom. "Thank you all for coming out today. I reckon there's no secret that Carter Monroe will be stayin' on as a guest of Owen Mercer 'cross the street. I don't want nobody botherin' anyone over there 'less'n you got one big life'n death crisis. I'd be obliged if nobody'd have one of those." There were a few laughs at that. "Now y'all go on back home or to work 'cept for some of y'all that have already been told to stick 'round for a bit." Judge Clary banged his hammer on the desk. "Arraignment is adjourned." He stood up and walked out of the courtroom through the back door.

Everyone else stood up and started milling around and talking. I couldn't exactly figure out why. It wasn't like anything surprising had just happened, but I guess that's the nature of folks. I saw Claxton talking with Owen Mercer and Ted Fiedler. They were getting ready to walk Carter back over across the street when the crowd thinned out. There were a few dozen men that were evidently not leaving, and I saw that Claxton was also right about that. The jury was probably going to be picked in just a little while. It took Woodrow Silas the better part of fifteen minutes to clear the courtroom, and after everyone was gone except for the men that might be on the jury, they were just about ready to get going.

"Sorry 'bout it, Nathan," said Woodrow. "Got to ask you to head on out." I looked over at Claxton, but he just nodded.

"Reckon I'll find something to do," I said as I got on my feet and started out of the courtroom. The door closed behind me, and I heard the bolt being thrown making it pretty clear that nobody was going to interrupt them. I checked around for Willie outside, but he must have already gone on home.

With nothing much to do, and nobody to not do it with, I just started walking down through town to see what I might find to do. I eventually ended up at Bardwell's Jewelry and stepped inside to have a closer look at some of the coins while I was there. I'd never had much of an interest in them before, but after spending a whole day learning about them, I thought I was developing just a bit of an itch to collect them.

"Just goin' to look 'round some," I said to Simon Bardwell as I came inside. He was back behind the counter in the left corner reading a book and gave me a wave with one hand before he went back to his reading.

I looked through some of the less expensive coins for a while before I began to work my way into the higher priced ones. I'd not really taken any time to look at them before because I knew I'd never be able to buy one, but I had the time today, and I had become a little curious about what they might be. The first expensive coin I saw was a shiny silver dollar that was listed for fifteen dollars. I walked down the line taking them all in. The further I walked the higher the price got. About two steps from the end of the coins, the price went over one hundred dollars. I picked up the coin book from the counter and looked a few of them up and saw how few of them had been made. Then I saw a price on one for three hundred dollars. I looked at the gold coin to see what it was, and I felt my skin turn cold and tingly. Behind the glass was a dead ringer for the coin that I'd found in the dirt and later given to Riley.

"How long you had that coin?" I asked without taking my eyes off of it.

"Which one is that?" he said as he looked up from his reading.

"This here three hundred dollar coin," I said slowly.

"Oh that one," he smiled. "Got it last week from Bernie."

"He say how he come 'cross it?" I asked. I tried to take my eyes off of it, but they were stuck.

"It's right rare," Bardwell said, "but he said he got an anonymous phone call from somebody looking to sell it."

"What's 'nonymous?" I asked scratching my head. "Never heard o' that kind a phone call before."

"Just means whoever it was didn't give a name," Bardwell smiled. "Some folks just want to keep stuff private like I reckon."

"Well, how'd they sell it then?" I wondered.

"I think he said that they dickered a bit on the phone but agreed on a price, and it came special delivery the next day. Bernie gave the deliveryman the cash in an envelope just like it was talked about and then got on the phone to sell it to me. Next day, he was here in town, and I looked it over and bought it."

"You might be stuck with it a spell," I said. "Cain't believe many folks 'round here got that kind o' money to spend on a coin." I also couldn't believe that I'd held this coin worth more money than I'd ever seen outside of a cash drawer, and had given it to Riley. But, I couldn't figure how it had gotten here. Riley didn't have a phone, and I didn't think he would have sold that coin anyway. It sort of began to settle into my mind that maybe somebody else had come across Riley's coin. Maybe while they were tearing his cabin apart. Then I started to wonder if maybe somebody had been up there looking for that coin 'cause they lost it out there where Dyle was killed. Everybody knew that Riley had come in to town and told Owen Mercer about Dyle. My mind was racing like a car downhill without brakes.

"You're probably right on that, Nathan," said Bardwell, but I only partly heard him. "I'm goin' down to New Orleans in about a month. Gonna set up a booth at a flea market. Figured I'd take it along. Ought to be able to sell it there."

"Reckon I'll be on my way, Mister Bardwell," I said after a last look at the coin. He waved at me as I was leaving. I stepped outside into the sunlight and tried to think about what that coin being in there really meant. It didn't sound like whoever sold the coin to Bernie Chesterfield wanted him to know who they were. But it also came to me that whoever sold that coin must have been from around Josiah Falls. That same person must have gone up to Riley's cabin and stolen it...or maybe took it from off of him. I tried not to think about that. I walked back down the sidewalk trying to think it all out, but it didn't make a lot of sense. Nobody knew about the coin except three of us...four if I counted Dyle maybe, but he sure didn't tell anyone about it. I didn't tell and Willie didn't tell, so that left Riley, and Riley didn't tell anybody much of anything. That only left whoever took it from Riley. Since the coin never turned up when they picked up Dyle, that *somebody* must have figured Riley had it. If that was right, then whoever killed Dyle must have paid Riley a call, too. While I was walking, I decided that I needed to find Willie and tell him about it. Maybe he would have an idea I hadn't thought of. I wasn't sure of anything, but what I was thinking wasn't making me feel too good.

Chapter Fourteen

I didn't see Willie that day or that night because he had gone with his family down to Natchez for a few days to visit some family that still lived down that way. Claxton came in about four-thirty with Junior Preston and Ted Fiedler. Owen had sent Ted along to start keeping an eye on the house until the trial was over. He  figured that no one would try anything with Ted sitting out there on the front porch smoking his Lucky Strikes all night, and I pretty much agreed with that. I also figured that we'd sleep better knowing he was out there.

It didn't take long for the trial papers to take over the kitchen table. I'd never thought anything could take up so much paper, and I was beginning to think that I had it downright *easy* just going to school. Claxton and Junior spent most of the next three hours just reading. I spent most of that time sitting in the front living room looking out the windows thinking about a certain 1874 double eagle gold piece. The coin book backed up what Simon Bardwell had said about it being a rare coin. The Carson City mintmark meant that only a little more than a hundred thousand had been made. The only thing that hurt the value was how much wear it had on it. Still, a coin that rare had to have a history behind it and maybe a story to tell. Mostly, I was interested in what kind of story it might be able to tell about where it had been this summer. But, that was going to be hard to find out about. Someone had gone to some trouble to keep their name away from Bernie Chesterfield, and it seemed like they had done it. It didn't take me but half an hour to figure out that Nathan Delaney wasn't going to come up with a name, but I started to wonder what Brent Hardcastle might come up with.

I thought on that for some time. On the radio shows, he usually solved the crime or the mystery by either starting at the beginning and working his way to the end, or by starting at the end and working his way to the beginning. I scratched my head at this mystery. I knew the beginning already…at least the one that counted. The gold piece started up by the falls not but a few feet from where Dyle Courtland took his last breath on this earth. There were three possibilities as I saw it. The coin could have been his and fell out of his pocket after a scuffle with whoever killed him. It was close enough that it could have spilled out of his pockets when he fell. It also could have been dropped up there by somebody just walking through, and ole Dyle just happened to get himself killed right about on top of it. Or, that gold coin just might have been dropped by whoever blasted some afternoon sunshine through Dyle's inards. Could be that same somebody was the one running down that trail right behind us. I stopped right there. It didn't really matter who the coin belonged to, I heard Detective Hardcastle whispering in my ear. The only thing that mattered about the coin is that it tied whoever was in the woods to Dyle and probably at Riley's cabin to Riley. I listened for a while, but Detective Hardcastle didn't have any more hints for me.

Back in the kitchen, I could hear Claxton going over some of the things that they were going to hear in the courtroom, and he wanted Junior to be clear on what they were going to object to and what they would let go. They also started going over who they thought might have an axe to grind on Carter Monroe. They talked about a lot of folks. The night wore on, and I finally went to bed. Junior spent the night on the living room sofa, and I got the idea the next morning when I got up and left the house on my way to see Willie that I might as well get used to seeing him there for a while.

"What do you reckon I saw at Bardwell's yesterday?" I asked Willie as we walked along to the ball field. I already knew Claxton wasn't going to be there for this game, and I figured there would be some others missing as well.

"I dunno," said Willie as he flipped a ball in the air and caught it as we walked. "Figure we'll have enough fellas to play today?"

"Saw me a 1874 double eagle twenty dollar gold piece," I answered.

"Gold piece? Same as what you found up by the falls?" asked Willie. He stopped and looked at me.

"Yep," I said. "I'd say it was the same one." I went on and told him what Simon Bardwell had told me.

"Sounds like a right odd thing to do," said Willie.

"Unless somebody had good reason for not wantin' anybody to know they ever had, an' I 'spect they did if'n they killed Dyle," I said. Willie nodded.

"So how you figure on findin' out who it was?" Willie asked.

"Sort of hopin' you might know," I said as we started to walk on.

"Cain't say I do," Willie smiled. "Who do you figure toted that coin all the way out to Fayette?"

"Don't rightly know," I shook my head, but Willie had just given me something new to think about. Maybe I didn't know who had the coin, but *somebody* knew because somebody drove it out there and came back with the money. "You might be on somethin' there, Willie."

We got to the baseball field and found that there was only enough for us to have a practice game. Most everyone was getting their chores and work done over the weekend so they could be at the trial on Monday. We went ahead and played by sharing a couple of players back and forth. It wasn't as much fun as a real game, but it was something to do, and it was good practice anyway. After the game, Willie and I headed downtown to talk about the coin some more and to see if we could think about who might have carted it out to Fayette. I knew just about every business in town, but I sure enough couldn't come up with any place that specialized in fetchin' coins back and forth.

I passed the afternoon Sunday listening in on Claxton and Junior making their final run through the trial. They finally took a rest from it long enough to eat some dinner. I was just biting into a buttered roll when I thought maybe I ought to just ask.

"Claxton," I began, "if you was to want to send something 'spensive like someplace to sell it and have somebody tote the money back to you, how would you go 'bout that?"

"You thinkin' 'bout sellin' somethin'?" Claxton asked as he sliced into a piece of chicken with his knife.

"Ain't got nothin' like that to sell," I said with a shake of my head, "just wonderin' how a body'd go 'bout it."

"Well," said Claxton as he thought about it a moment. "Reckon I'd look for somebody'd that be insured…maybe bonded by a company'd that guarantee your property if it was to get lost or somethin'."

"Anybody do that kinda work 'round Josiah Falls?" I asked.

"You'd need a good car if you're thinkin' 'bout it," Claxton said. I shook my head.

"Naw," I said. "Don't reckon I am."

"Cliff Masters," said Junior as he took a bite of chicken.

"Thought he just run the wrecker service," I said. I'd seen Cliff Masters drive by a number of times with somebody's car hangin' on the hook behind his truck. Usually he didn't take them far, but sometimes they had to go to Fayette or Jackson for engine work.

"Bonded for ten thousand dollars to haul anything," said Junior. "Doesn't have to be cars. I think he went an' picked up some paintings for Otis Sistrunk back when Otis thought 'bout going into the art business."

"Reckon Otis still has all them paintings?" Claxton smiled.

"Every last one of them," said Junior with a laugh. "Josiah Falls just ain't exactly the center of the art world after all." Claxton and Junior went on talking about Otis Sistrunk's collection of oil paintings that hung in the back room of his furniture shop and pretty much forgot I was there for a while. That was okay. I had a lot to think about.

Chapter Fifteen

"All those with business with this court draw near and listen," began Woodrow Silas. "Case docket number, 24154, Josiah Falls and the state of Mississippi versus Carter Monroe the Third. All rise…" Everyone stood up in the courtroom. Claxton was in the middle of the defense table dressed in his beige suit with Carter Monroe in a white shirt and tie on his left and Junior wearing his usual dark blue suit on his right. George McCluskey stood at the prosecutor's table on the left by himself. He wore an expensive looking vest under his suit coat with a gold watch chain hanging out of the pocket. Judge Harlan Clary came in through the back door to the courtroom and walked up to the desk.

"The honorable Judge Harlan Clary presiding," said Woodrow without even a backward glance to see if he was there. Clary sat down and banged his gavel down one time.

"This court is now in session," said Woodrow. "Y'all can be seated."

"Does the state wish to file any motions?" asked Clary.

"Not at this time, your honor," said McCluskey as he stood and then sat again.

"The defense?" asked Clary.

"Not at this time, your honor," said Claxton.

"Very well," said Clary. "George, you can go on an' make your opening remarks."

"Thank you, your honor," said McCluskey as he stood and walked slowly to the center of the room. He turned and faced the jury. "Gentlemen of the jury, today…you are going to hear a lot of witnesses give their opinions on what they *think* may have happened, but what you must do and I emphasize…*must do*…is set into your minds only the facts that will be presented in this case. The state will set before you the evidence, and it is very compelling evidence. The state will also demonstrate that not only was there opportunity to commit this most heinous of crimes, but there was also substantial motivation behind the commission of these crimes. When the state completes it's case, I think you will be left with no other possible conclusion than to decide that the defendant in this case, Carter Monroe the third...who sits here before you today...is guilty of the crimes of first degree murder in the deaths of Minister Evan Washburne and that of Odessa Hendricks. Furthermore, you will also find the accused guilty of aggravated arson in the burning down of the Baptist Church of God of Josiah Falls." McCluskey paused for a very long moment as if to let the jury consider the charges. "Gentlemen, these crimes...if I can even dignify these *acts* as crimes...were committed with a degree of malice that can only be atoned for by death itself. Imagine if you can, finding yourself locked inside a burning church with no possibility of escape, waiting for a certain death at either the flames, smoke, or heat while the murderer casually concealed the evidence and walked away with no more thought about those he condemned to a horrifying death than an insect he might crush under his shoe." McCluskey folded his hands behind his back and lowered his head as he waited for his words to settle in. "Gentlemen, the defense is going to regale you all with some fanciful tales. They are going to *suggest* that a number of things might be possible, but you must not let yourselves be deceived by this. The facts of the case are irrefutable, and the man who perpetrated these acts sits before you now. Thank you." McCluskey returned to his table and sat down. There was some scattered applause from the audience.

"'Nough of that now," said Judge Clary with a smack of his gavel on the round little piece of wood on top of his desk. "I'm as impressed with Mister McCluskey's colorful use of Webster's dictionary as the next fella, but this ain't no show to clap an holler at." The audience laughed a bit and then quieted. I had to admit, George McCluskey was a powerful speaker. I only understood about every third word he said, but I was impressed. Even more, I wondered what Claxton was going to do to top that.

"Claxton," said Judge Clary. Claxton stood slowly from his chair and slowly walked around behind Carter to the empty space between the two tables.

"Thank you, your honor," said Claxton. He smiled broadly and shook his head slowly from side to side. "To hear the prosecution's opening remarks, you would almost wonder if there is even a need for a trial at all. To be certain, a terrible crime was committed, and someone ought to be punished for that crime. But...let's all hold on just a minute here and make certain that we know just *who* that really is. The prosecution is going to enter some things into evidence for you to look at, and Mister McCluskey is going to build up a lot of *circumstantial* evidence, but gentlemen of the jury, there is a world of difference between real evidence and *circumstantial* evidence." He walked over in front of the jury. "You may be wondering to yourselves right now...just what is the difference? Well, let me tell you. 'Spose you walked out one mornin' and found a truck parked in the side of your barn." Claxton looked over at Herb Westmoreland in the jury box. "Could even have been your barn, Herb." There was some laughter in the courtroom, but it quickly stopped. "You might have noticed that truck belonged to your neighbor, Rollie Anderson, settin' right over yonder behind you." There was some more laughter. "Well, sir, on first thought, you might be tempted to think that ole Rollie might have come in a little late and plain missed his garage by...say...a quarter mile. It was a *fact* that his car was parked in the wall of your barn, but the *truth* was that a twister was what went and put it there. And, *that*...gentlemen, is the difference. Nobody saw that car land in that barn wall even though it was sure enough settin' there for everyone to see." Claxton took a step back and moved down the jury box a few steps. "What y'all have to keep in mind here is what is really a *fact*, and what is really *known* 'bout that fact. For you to convict Carter Monroe for these crimes, there can be no doubt in your minds. Not even the slightest little thought that...just maybe...he didn't do it. That is what we know of as a reasonable doubt. If there is even the smallest doubt in your mind, then, gentlemen, you have no choice but to acquit Carter Monroe of these charges. Gentlemen, I think when you have heard all the evidence in this case, you will have more than just a *reasonable* doubt, and you will return a verdict of not guilty. Thank you." Claxton turned, nodded to the judge and then returned to his seat. If I had been worried about Claxton being a little rusty after so long out of the lawyer business, I wasn't anymore. I think everyone watching was starting to get ready for a real heavyweight boxin' match. I settled back onto the bench. I looked around the courtroom and saw a few unfamiliar faces in the back righthand corner. One had a pad and was writing faster than I thought a hand could even move. The other one took me a bit to figure. He kept glancin' up and then back down. Then I got the idea he was drawin' pictures. I figured then that they had to be from the paper in Fayette.

"Your honor," said McCluskey rising from his table. "The state would like to call Mrs. Addie Washburne to the stand." I watched the door open on the side of the courtroom, and Addie Washburne walked inside. She was still dressed in black, with a black hat and veil, black gloves, and a black pocket book. Woodrow Silas closed the door and followed her to the witness stand beside the judge's desk.

"Do you swear to tell the truth, the whole truth, and nothin' but the truth, so help you God?" said Woodrow as she placed her left hand on a Bible and raised her right hand.

"I do," she said quietly and then sat down in the chair next to the judge in the little wooden box that was raised up a little from the floor.

"Mrs. Washburne, I have only a very few questions for you," McCluskey began. "Can you identify the set of keys that I have here in my hand?" He set the keys onto the wooden rail in front of her after holding them up for the jury and audience to see. Addie Washburne looked at them briefly.

"Yes," she said softly. "Those are Evan's keys to the church."

"How can you be certain of that?" asked McCluskey.

"The key ring with the 'EW' on it," she answered. "I gave that key ring to Evan on his birthday after we were married."

"So 'EW' is Evan Washburne," said McCluskey. "Can you tell me what each of these keys unlocks?"

"Yes," she nodded. "The long key on the end...that unlocks...it unlocked..." She stopped for a moment. "I'm sorry." She dabbed at her eyes with a black handkerchief.

"That's quite alright," said McCluskey. "Take your time."

"It unlocked the front doors of the church," she said finally. "The one next to it, yes...that shorter one, was to Evan's office upstairs. The third was to the church cash'n records box, and the little fourth one..." She smiled for the first time. "Well, Evan used to joke that it must be the key to the Pearly Gates cause it didn't seem to unlock nothin' here on earth."

"And the last key?" asked McCluskey. "What lock does that unlock?"

"That one unlocks the little tool shed out by the cemetery," she said.

"Your honor," McCluskey said deliberately. "I would like to enter this set of keys into evidence as state's exhibit 'A', positively identified as the church keys belonging to the late Minister of the Baptist Church of God, Evan Washburne."

"Will the defense challenge or so stipulate?" asked Judge Clary.

"The defense agrees that those are the keys belongin' to Minister Evan Washburne," said Claxton as he briefly stood and sat back down.

"Thank you, counselor," said McCluskey with a nod to the defense table. "Your honor, the state would also like to admit into evidence a five gallon gas can found in the tool shed and positively identified by the state arson investigation unit as having been the same gasoline used to start the fire."

"I have those reports before me," Clary nodded. "Does the defense challenge?"

"Your honor," said Claxton as he rose from the table again. "The defense would like to draw attention to the statement in the arson report that says that the gasoline in the gas can was the *same* as that used to start the fire...but it does not say that the gasoline used in the fire must have *come* from that can."

"Come now, your honor," said McCluskey.

"Now hold your horses, George," said Clary. "Claxton has a point there. I read the report, and it don't say the gas can was used for *sure*. It just says it *could* have been used."

"May we then admit this gas can as the most likely instrument used to start the fire?" asked McCluskey with a sideways glance at Claxton.

"I think the defense could stipulate the gas can as *circumstantial* evidence I 'spose," said Claxton. It was then that I started to understand where Claxton was going with his case. Everyone knew the gas can was the one that was used. Nothing else in town would have used that kind of gasoline and oil mixture, but there was no absolute *proof* it had been used.

"Your honor," McCluskey began. "I don't know if you have had the pleasure of listening to the arguments of my esteemed colleague, Claxton Delaney, in court before, but I most certainly have. I may assure you that he is renowned in state court for the large number of rabbits that he has pulled out of his hat. I for one should like to know just how *many* rabbits the state might expect to see today?" There was a general chorus or laughter from all around. Even Claxton had a smile on his face.

"George," Clary smiled. "I will rule on the gas can shortly." He turned his head and looked at Claxton. "Claxton, there goin' to be a bunch of rabbits here today?"

"No more'n I need, your honor," said Claxton with another smile.

"Claxton," said Clary. "Does the defense know of any other machine in Josiah Falls that needs that same ...*exact even*...mixture of gasoline and oil?"

"Not to my knowledge, your honor," said Claxton, "but that doesn't mean there *isn't* one, and it doesn't mean someone couldn't have mixed some gasoline and oil just to set this fire."

"Your honor, perhaps I might add a bit of clarification," McCluskey said. "Mrs. Washburne, do you recognize the gas can that I hold here in my hand?"

"Yes," she nodded. "That looks like the one that we used to fill up the old church generator."

"Do you recall when the generator was last used?" McCluskey asked.

"Sometime 'bout February or March," she said slowly. "Power went out early Sunday mornin', and Evan started up the generator for services that day."

"I see," said McCluskey, "did Evan need any fuel that day? Or was the generator already filled?"

"He used the gas can to fill it up," she said. "Used it all as I recollect."

"So the gas can was empty?" McCluskey asked. "Do you know if it was re-filled?"

"It was…and it was," she said. "Carter Monroe took it that next day and refilled it. Ought to be a receipt in the box for it."

"And was the fuel in that can used for anything else before the fire?" asked McCluskey.

"Not so far as I know," she answered.

"So something happened to the fuel that was in this gas can," said McCluskey. "Perhaps there is reasonable suspicion that the fuel in the can ended up in the church?" He paused for a moment. "Should we enter the gas can or the rabbit as exhibit 'B', your honor?" asked McCluskey.

"The court accepts the gas can into evidence," said Clary. "The defense motion is overruled."

"An exception, your honor" said Claxton immediately. "We can only *assume* the gas in that can was used in the fire. There is no proof it was actually used for that purpose. It could have been used to burn brush, leaves, or anything else."

"Your exception is noted," said Clary with a nod as he wrote something down on a pad in front of him. The gas can had been admitted into evidence, but Claxton had served notice to McCluskey that he was in for a brawl all the way, and he'd had his say on the evidence anyway.

"You may continue, George," said Clary.

"Thank you, your honor," said McCluskey with his composure obviously still intact. If he had been flustered at all by Claxton's tactics, he didn't show it, and he had played to the jury and audience just about as well as Claxton had.

"Mrs. Washburne," said McCluskey as he paced in front of the jury. "You mentioned a cash box a moment ago. Is that by chance the cash box on the desk over there?"

"Yes, sir," she said. "That is the box that belongs to the church."

"Thank you," said McCluskey. "Your honor, the state would like to admit into evidence the fireproof cash box as state's exhibit 'C'...now *positively* identified as the one belonging to the Baptist Church of God of Josiah Falls, unless the defense has something to say on the issue?"

"The defense is willin' to stipulate that this box is the same one," said Claxton with a wave of his hand. He then leaned over to Junior who quickly shook his head and then made some notes. Claxton flipped through a few pages of notes himself, and I thought maybe he hadn't expected something that had just happened.

"The cash box is admitted as evidence," said Clary.

"Thank you, your honor," said McCluskey. "Mrs. Washburne, are you familiar with the contents of the cash box?"

"Evan kept the church's receipts and a little money in it," she said.

"And was there by any chance a ledger of accounts in the box?" asked McCluskey.

"Yes, I had forgotten," she said. "Evan was very careful to keep records of the church's spendin'."

"Was your husband the only one who handled the money and the bookkeeping?" asked McCluskey.

"Mostly," she answered slowly. "Carter helped balance the books out each month an' sometimes paid some of the bills if Evan wasn't 'round to do it."

"By Carter...do you mean the defendant in this case?" asked McCluskey. "Carter Monroe the third?"

"Course I do," she smiled. "Don't know of no other Carter 'round here."

"Thank you," said McCluskey. "Did Mr. Monroe have occasion recently to have access to the cash box?"

"Well, Evan was gone 'bout the middle o' May for a spell. Carter might a paid some bills 'bout then," she said. "Probably balanced the books sometime in June."

"Your honor," said Claxton as he slowly stood. "Is there some relevance to this cash box that, perhaps, the state's prosecutor might like to share with us?"

"I was wonderin' that myself, Claxton," said Clary with a nod. "How 'bout it George? You got a rabbit o' your own in that box?"

"No rabbits, your honor," McCluskey smiled. "The contents of the box will have some relevance, but not from this witness. I am just trying to establish the box as evidence and how it was used."

"Very well," said Clary. "You may proceed, but do let us know what we were talkin' 'bout here before we get done."

"Yes, your honor," said McCluskey. "I have no other questions for this witness at this time, but I would like to reserve the right to recall this witness at a later time for any rebuttal that might require it...and to place the same reservation on all other witnesses that may be called."

"It's alright by me, George," said Clary. "What's good for the goose...Claxton, you can also recall anybody you want." Claxton nodded.

"Your witness, counselor," said McCluskey with a wave of his hand to Claxton. Claxton stood and seemed thoughtful for a moment.

"Addie," he began with a smile. "How long has Carter Monroe..." he paused and motioned to the man beside him, "been known to you?"

"Since I was a little girl, I reckon," she answered.

"And how long has Carter been the cemetery caretaker?" he asked.

"Cain't say exactly," she said. "Was a long time before Evan became minister here, though."

"In all the time that you knew Carter," Claxton began, "did you ever hear any cross words between he and Evan?"

"Never did," she shook her head.

"They ever disagree 'bout anything? Anything at all?" Claxton asked.

"They was like bread and butter together," she shook her head. "Evan done his work and Carter done his."

"So, could Carter have had a grudge against Evan?" asked Claxton. "Enough of one to want to kill him?"

"Objection," said McCluskey as he got to his feet. "That question calls for a conclusion on the part of the witness. Unless the witness was constantly in the presence of both men, she could not know that answer positively."

"Sustained," said Clary. "That was right impressive, George."

"I'll rephrase, your honor," said Claxton with a smile.

"To *your knowledge*...did Carter bear any grudge against your husband," asked Claxton.

"Didn't know of nothin' if there was," she said.

"Did you know of any differences between Carter and Odessa Hendricks?" he continued.

"Sakes no," she shook her head. "Don't even recollect them even talkin' to one 'nother more'n a handful of times."

"So, you can't think of any reason that Carter Monroe would want either, or both, of them dead?" asked Claxton.

"Cain't say as I do," she answered. Claxton nodded.

"Do you recall the evening of July Fourth," asked Claxton.

"Very well," she answered solemnly. "It was the last time I saw my husband."

"Can you tell us what you recall from that last time and after?" Claxton went on.

"Well, it was right hot that night," she said. "I reckon it was the heat kinda got to me, and I took sick. I'm also expectin'. Mighta been that too, so I went on home early to get in outa the sun."

"Have you been wantin' a child?" asked Claxton with a smile.

"Mercy, you know I have," she said with a nod of her head.

"When did you first think you might be pregnant?" asked Claxton with another amiable smile.

"'Bout the time I come to see you," she answered. "I run across Bertie over at the market, and she looked at me real close just one time and asked me if I was. Well, I said that I thought *maybe*, but told her I didn't know for sure. She just said that a woman could always tell when another was carryin'."

"Do you think that's true?" asked Claxton.

"Hard not to know if'n its somebody you knows well," she answered. Claxton nodded and walked away a bit.

"Back to that night...did Evan take you home when you took sick?" Claxton asked.

"He was havin' a good time," she said with a deep sigh. "Didn't want him leavin' on my account. Folks liked talkin' to him. Oh, he wanted to see me home, but it was just a half a block. I didn't see no need."

"And what did you do the rest of that evening?" asked Claxton.

"Drank me some water and cooled off some and went on to bed," she answered. "I reckon I slept some. Next thing I knowed, the church was on fire and folks was runnin' ever where."

"Was it Evan's habit to be at the church late at night?" asked Claxton.

"Not *real* late...like that night," she said. "But he did sometimes meet with folks after they got off work, or maybe if they had somethin' real private to talk 'bout. Some folks just ain't comfortable like, other folks knowin' their business and such."

"Did Odessa Hendricks have somethin' real private to talk 'bout with Evan?" asked Claxton.

"I reckon so," she answered. "She found God this past spring. Had her a lot of catchin' up to do on the Lord. Sure am glad she did...seein' it was her time and all."

"I see," Claxton nodded. "And was there anything else goin' on with Odessa this spring?"

"Just the usual, I reckon," she shrugged.

"Were the two of you still close friends this spring?" asked Claxton.

"Couldn't be no closer," Addie Washburne said from behind her veil. "We was always close…just like sisters."

"Was she seein' anyone special that last couple months or so?" asked Claxton.

"Nobody regular," she answered. "Wasn't like her to miss a Saturday night out dancin' somewheres, but I reckon she was just havin' fun."

"As close as you were, I'm sure that you knew that she was also pregnant," said Claxton. There was a murmur through the courtroom, but it was quickly hushed up by Woodrow Silas's upraised hand and look around.

"She never said so," she answered.

"That wasn't my question," said Claxton. "I asked if you *knew*. Just a moment ago, you said another woman would know if she knew the other well enough. You and Odessa were like sisters… closer even." Claxton paused and waited. She didn't answer.

"Objection please, your honor, what's the relevance of this line of questioning?" asked McCluskey.

"I am just trying to establish if the witness knew that her very close, lifelong friend was pregnant, your honor," said Claxton not waiting for the judge.

"Man's on trial for his life here, George," said Clary. "I'll give Claxton some room to maneuver long as he gets to the point. Overruled," He looked at Claxton. "Now get on to the point before I look foolish."

"Yes, your honor," said Claxton as he walked back over near the witness stand.

"The witness will answer the question," said Clary in a kindly voice.

"I'll repeat the question," said Claxton.

"Ain't no need for that. I done heard what you asked," said Addie Washburne. "I knew she was pregnant. She didn't have to say nothin'. Wasn't somethin' we talked 'bout, though. I think she was right ashamed of it."

"You mean by being unmarried and all," said Claxton with a nod.

"She weren't raised in no barn," she said. "She knowed better than that…gett'n herself in trouble like that."

"So, you wouldn't know who the father was," said Claxton.

"No," she answered simply. "She never said nothin' 'bout the baby at all."

"Did you ask?" asked Claxton.

"No," she answered. "I wanted *her* to say."

"Your honor…the point?" asked McCluskey impatiently.

"If'n you don't mind, Claxton," said Clary. "You got us all mighty interested. Now tell us what you got us interested 'bout."

"The point is, your honor, that Odessa Hendricks was carrying some man's child," said Claxton. "He may, or may not, have known 'bout the child, but clearly they had an intimate relationship, so I imagine he knew something 'bout *that*. Now, here she is spending her nights meeting with another man, and I am not suggesting anything improper at all in doing so, but the father of her child might not see it that way. Jealousy can drive a man to do things…sometimes even murder."

"Your honor," said McCluskey with a shake of his head. "Unless the defense can supply…this *jealous father* of the child…I do not see any relevance here."

"I think you're reachin' a bit here, Claxton," said Clary. "I understand what your get'n at, but you'll need some hard proof before you go down thata' way again."

"Yes, your honor," said Claxton. He and McCluskey exchanged a glance that I didn't quite follow. Once again, McCluskey had won the argument, but Claxton had put something new in everybody's mind. I figured folks in that courtroom were thinkin' about Dyle then. More than one jealous husband or boyfriend had come lookin' for him before.

"I have no further questions at this time," said Claxton.

"The witness is excused," said Judge Clary with a smile and a nod to Addie Washburne. "Now you run along home and get some rest."

"Yes, sir," she said as she rose from the chair. Woodrow Silas offered her a hand and helped her down from the two steps to the floor. A moment later she disappeared out the side door.

"Now, it bein' eleven thirty," said Judge Clary. "This court will take a recess for everyone to go get somethin' to eat. Court will resume at one o'clock." Judge Clary stood along with everyone else, and the courtroom slowly began to empty out. As they were leaving, Junior and Claxton were still at the table talking with Carter. I didn't wait on them because I knew that they were going to stay here at the courthouse in one of the meeting rooms to eat lunch and talk more about the case. I ended up walking back home with Bertie to eat something at the house since every eatin' place in town was packed. We talked about the trial like everyone else was probably doing and trying to guess what might come up next. When we finished eating, we walked back up to the courthouse. I'd already decided that I was going to get myself a seat over by the reporters. I was real curious to know what that one fella was sketchin' all the time. Woodrow didn't open the doors 'till five minutes 'till one, and I had to slip betwixt and between a lot of folks to get where I was going, but I got there right where I wanted behind those two folding seats with the 'Reserved' signs sitting on them. A few minutes later, the two fellas from the paper showed up and started getting out their writing tablets and sketchin' stuff.

"What paper you fellas do your writin' for?" I asked when they finally got settled down.

"*Clarion-Ledger* in Jackson," answered the writer. He was an older man about Claxton's age I figured. The artist fella looked like he was just out of school.

"Mind if I peek in on what you're drawin?" I asked.

"I don't mind," the young man answered. He gave me a wink over his shoulder and then flipped quickly through the courthouse scenes he had sketched so far.

"That's right good," I said. "Wish I could draw like that."

"Just takes lots of practice," he said. "An' a few years of schoolin' from teachers that know how." I nodded. I figured there was a little more there than just hard work. I settled back into my seat a little.

"What brings you fellas out to Josiah Falls for a little ole trial?" I asked towards the reporter.

"Little?" the reporter almost laughed. "Why, don't you know who's arguing the case? That's Claxton Delaney and George McCluskey, the two most famous lawyers the state's ever had. They haven't been at each other in more than ten years. I saw it myself at the state supreme court."

"Claxton's a famous lawyer?" I asked. I knew he'd been a lawyer, but there'd never been much talk about what he'd done in Jackson.

"Sure is, son," the man nodded. "We got a tip from McCluskey that he was coming here for this case. He owed us one. Said we wouldn't regret making the trip. He was right about that."

"Real famous?" I asked again.

"Its like Abe Lincoln and Stephen Douglas or Dan'l Webster and Henry Clay," said the reporter. I just shook my head; I'd heard of Lincoln, of course, but I didn't know what he meant. The younger man smiled.

"Suppose Davy Crocket and Dan'l Boone were getting together for a shootin' match," the artist fella said. "Do you think you'd be there up front to watch it?"

"Would I?" I said. "You bet."

"Well, that's what you've got right here," the reporter said. "When we put this story out on the wire tomorrow, you won't be able to get a seat in here. Every reporter in the state will be here."

"Reckon maybe I ought to sleep here tonight then," I said.

"Just grab on my coattail tomorrow," the reporter laughed. "We'll come through the side door over there before it gets started. What's your name, son?"

"Nathan," I answered.

"Well, Nathan," he said, "looks like we're about to get started. If you ever thought about being a lawyer, you'll never learn more about it than you will right now." I stood up with everyone else when the judge came back in and called the court to order. Woodrow Silas went over the rules again for anyone new that might have come in for the first time. The artist fella started sketchin' Woodrow this time with Judge Clary there in the background.

"George, you can call your next witness," said Clary as he settled his black robe and leaned back in his tall chair.

"The state calls Dwight Bishop to the stand," said George McCluskey. Woodrow Silas opened the side door and made a motion with his hand, and Dwight Bishop came through the door in a suit and tie that probably nobody in town knew he owned. Woodrow swore him in, and Bishop took his place on the stand.

"Mr. Bishop," McCluskey began. "Do you know the defendant in this case, Carter Monroe?"

"I do," said Bishop with a nod in Carter's direction.

"Did you and Mr. Monroe have an altercation on the evening of July Fourth?" asked McCluskey.

"If that means we had us some words," said Bishop, "then I reckon we did."

"Could you tell the court what that might have been about?" asked McCluskey.

"Well," Bishop said with a nervous scratch of his ear. "Might be a bit foggy on some of the details. I had me a little more to drink than I ought."

"That's all right," said McCluskey. "It was the Fourth. A lot of people did. Just tell us what you do recall."

"All right," said Bishop. "I reckon I hollered something 'cross the street at Carter 'bout Dyle Courtland. I was wonderin' if he might have put ole Dyle underground."

"You mean the late Dyle Courtland who was found shot to death earlier this spring?" asked McCluskey.

"There ain't been but one Dyle," said Bishop. "Don't reckon Josiah Falls could'a held two of 'em." There was a roar of laughter at that. McCluskey waited for it to die down. Dwight seemed to become a little less nervous.

"Why would you think that Carter Monroe might have had something to do with the death of Dyle Courtland?" asked McCluskey.

"Well, sir," Bishop began, "we had us some church burnin's early this spring. Two colored churches was burned to the ground. I heard Carter Monroe say right out here on this street in front of the courthouse that it didn't take no college man to figure out who done it, specially after he was heard braggin' 'bout it, accordin' to some, and that if the law wasn't goin' to do nothin' 'bout it then maybe somebody ought to do it for 'em. Wasn't but a week before somebody done just that."

"Your honor," said Claxton getting to his feet. "Carter Monroe is not on trial for the murder of Dyle Courtland. No one, in fact, has even been charged in his death."

"I'll uphold that objection," said Clary. "George, you need to be right careful where you step there."

"Your honor, I am simply laying the foundation for the disagreement between Mr. Bishop and Mr. Monroe," said McCluskey. "I am making no accusation against Mr. Monroe in that instance."

"All right, I'll let you continue, but careful like," said Clary. He then turned to the jury box. "This here is for y'all. The death of Dyle Courtland don't have nothin' to do with this trial here today. You take from what you hear as you like, but don't let that have no part of it."

"Thank you, your honor," said McCluskey as he continued. "Now, Mr. Bishop, how did you take what he said?"

"Your honor," said Claxton on his feet again. "Mr. McCluskey is asking the witness to testify to somethin' that can only be speculation."

"I withdraw the question, your honor," said McCluskey. "No further questions." McCluskey sat down.

"Thank you for sustainin' that objection, George," said Judge Clary. "Saved me the trouble. Your witness, Claxton."

"Only a few questions, Dwight," said Claxton as he walked near the witness stand. "Did you then...or at any other time...hear Carter Monroe mention the late Dyle Courtland by name when he said that 'somethin' ought to be done'?"

"Well...ever'body *knew* who he meant," said Bishop with his hands spread out in front of him.

"How would everyone know that?" asked Claxton.

"'Cause Dyle liked settin' fires from the time he was a kid," said Bishop. "He never much liked the coloreds, and when he got to drinkin'...well, you never knew just what he was apt to do."

"I see," Claxton nodded. "Is it possible that Dyle Courtland might have been braggin' 'bout something that somebody else actually did?" Bishop was silent for a moment. "Did Dyle have a tendency to want to *look* a little bigger'n he really was?"

"He did," Bishop sighed. "Anybody that knowed him well would know that. Dyle had him a mouth that wasn't always wired to his head."

"Your honor," said Claxton, "the defense would like to enter into evidence exhibit...what are we up to now, Harlan?"

"Ought to be 'D' by my count," said Clary.

"...Exhibit 'D'," said Claxton. He handed a piece of paper to the Judge. "That, your honor, is a receipt from Churchill's All Nighter. The address is at the top, and you will note that it is in Natchez."

"Your honor," McCluskey said as he stood. "If I might?"

"Sorry, George," said Claxton. "We just came on this yesterday." He took the paper from Clary and handed it to McCluskey. McCluskey studied it for a moment and handed it back.

"This receipt has two times entered on it," said Claxton. "Handwritten by the waitress. The first says 'Time in and ten thirty P.M.' and the second is 'Time out and three forty-five A.M.' This receipt was found in the personal effects of Dyle Courtland and is dated on the very same night that the second church was burned. That church was on fire at midnight that night."

"Can that receipt be verified?" said McCluskey as he stood.

"I can call Owen Mercer to the stand," said Claxton. "He can verify that the receipt was found in Dyle Courtland's wallet at the time of his death, and I can even call the waitress to the stand if you like." McCluskey shook his head and waved his hand.

"So ole Dyle was just blowin' smoke," said Bishop with an amazed look on his face. "I really thought he done it."

"I guess that's what he wanted," said Claxton with a smile. "No further questions." Claxton turned and sat down.

"Re-direct, your honor," said McCluskey as he jumped up. "Mr. Bishop, you were not aware of Mr. Courtland's innocence in regard to the church burning. Would you have any reason to believe...did you in fact hear anyone say that they knew of the late Mr. Courtland's whereabouts on that evening?" Claxton rolled a pencil between his fingers but otherwise looked undisturbed.

"Cain't say that I recall it," said Bishop after a moment.

"So there's no reason to believe that Mr. Monroe did not still hold the *same* opinion in regard to the church burning?" McCluskey continued.

"'Spose not," said Bishop. Junior looked like he was ready to stand up, but Claxton shook his head and touched him on the sleeve of his coat.

"No further questions," said McCluskey.

"Claxton, anything else for the witness?" asked Clary.

"No, your honor," said Claxton.

"The witness is excused," said Clary. "George?"

"The state calls Mr. Bostick Drury to the stand," said McCluskey. Woodrow ushered Bubba Drury into the courtroom and to the stand.

"Mr. Drury," McCluskey began with a glance at his papers. "Are you acquainted with the defendant, Mr. Carter Monroe?"

"I am," said Bubba. "That's him right over there." He nodded toward the defense table.

"Were you among those that heard Mr. Monroe make comments about the church burnings?" asked McCluskey.

"I was there," said Bubba. "He said he figured he knew who was behind the burnin's and that somebody ought to do somethin' 'bout it right quick." I noticed Carter lean over and whisper something to Claxton. Junior shuffled through some papers and pointed at something. Carter nodded.

"Your honor, I am somehow failin' to find the connection between some words spoken by the defendant and the proceedings here today," said Claxton.

"Where you headed with these witnesses, George?" asked Clary.

"Your honor," McCluskey started, "the state is trying to establish that the defendant said that some action needed to be taken in retribution for the burning down of the churches, and there was, in fact, a murder of a man thought to be behind them as well as possibly a burning down of a white church. The timing of the remarks form a cause and effect relationship in regard to the burning of the church."

"I'll allow this," said Clary. "Go on, George."

"Mr. Drury," said McCluskey. "Would you consider Mr. Monroe to be a man of his word?"

"I reckon so," said Bubba. "Generally says what he means and means what he says."

"So if he said he was going to do something," McCluskey said slowly, "you would tend to believe him."

"I would," Bubba nodded.

"Thank you," said McCluskey. "No further questions." McCluskey returned to his chair.

"Bostick. That your real name, Bubba?" said Claxton with a grin as he approached the witness stand.

"I'd ask you to keep it to yourself," said Bubba, "but I reckon it's too late for that. Looks like everybody done knows it now. And I'd 'preciate it if you'd all just forget 'bout it, too."

"Goin' to be hard, but I'll try," said Claxton with a smile. "Now, Bubba, would you consider yourself to be a man of *your* word?"

"I think so," Bubba nodded.

"So when you told me not too long ago that you were set to kill me," said Claxton, "then by all rights I ought to be dead by now."

"Aw, now I was just mad," said Bubba. "I didn't mean nothin' by it. You know that."

"I do, Bubba. I surely *do* know that," said Claxton. "So when you say somethin' like 'I'll kill you, or I hope you get run down by a train, drown in the river', or somethin' like that…it's just anger talkin'…not somethin' you'd really do or want?"

"Everybody says stuff like that," said Bubba defensively.

"Maybe even Carter Monroe?" asked Claxton. Bubba was silent a moment. He looked at Carter across the courtroom.

"I reckon he gets his dander up just like the rest of us," said Bubba. "But, it don't mean he didn't follow through on it."

"No, that's right," said Claxton with a nod. "Sometimes folks go on and do just *exactly* what they say." Claxton folded his hands behind his back. "Bubba, do you recall makin' a trip out to Vicksburg some time back?"

"I go up there regular," said Bubba. "Got a man that sharpens up my blades and gets my cuttin' tools good'n clean."

"Do you recall havin' a flat tire there on one trip?" asked Claxton.

"Couple trips ago," Bubba nodded. "Set me back a few dollars."

"Can you tell the court what happened?" asked Claxton.

"Well, I come out from Johnstone's machine shop," Bubba began, "got in my car and was set to leave…then I felt that flip-flop of the tire. Sure enough it was settin' on the rim just 'bout. Had me a slice in the sidewall."

"Did you run into anyone you knew after you came up with that flat tire?" asked Claxton. "Maybe somebody here in the courtroom today?" Bubba was quiet for a long minute.

"I was no more'n out of my car lookin' at the tire when Carter Monroe drove up in his truck," said Bubba with a nod.

"My jack ain't no account, so Carter got his out and we set to workin' on the tire. Well, sir, when we seen the split in the sidewall…there wasn't no way to patch it, so I run over to the auto place 'cross the way and bought me another. Carter'n me put on the new one, and then I headed out."

"What time would that have been?" asked Claxton.

"Reckon it was about lunch time," said Bubba. "Fella at the auto place was just startin' on his sandwich when I come in."

"So it was somewhere 'round twelve, or one o'clock?" asked Claxton.

"Twelve-thirty," said Bubba a moment later.

"And what time did you get done puttin' on the new tire?" asked Claxton.

"Well, fella at the parts place dickered with me on price, and we looked at a few tires," said Bubba carefully. "Musta been after one before we put the car back down on the ground."

"One o'clock then," Claxton nodded.

"And how long did it take you to get back to Josiah Falls that day?" asked Claxton.

"'Bout an hour or so," said Bubba. "Like always…"

"Are you sure 'bout that?" said Claxton.

"Well, no that couldn't a been," said Bubba. "Bridge was out for a spell now wasn't it? I had to take the long way back 'round town. Probably put me another hour and a half on that new tire. I 'member thinkin' that they maybe didn't repair that bridge just so's I'd use up my new tire on the way out."

"So you didn't get back to Josiah Falls until late afternoon? Maybe three thirty to four o'clock?" Claxton nodded.

"Be 'bout right," said Bubba.

"Was Carter Monroe right behind you when you left Vicksburg?" asked Claxton.

"Naw. He had feed to pick up an' some new fertilizer he was goin' to try out," said Bubba.

"And you didn't notice him passin' by you on the way back to Josiah Falls," said Claxton.

"Shux, Carter's old pickup don't do forty when it's loaded and goin' downhill all the way," said Bubba. "He couldn't a got back before six."

"So, what's the earliest time that Carter Monroe could have got back to town and then hiked up to the falls and shot Dyle Courtland?" asked Claxton.

"I dunno. Maybe seven o'clock? Could be a little later?" said Bubba with a shake of his head.

"That's close enough, Bubba," said Claxton. "Your honor, I'd like to admit into evidence the coroner's report on the death of Dyle Courtland. The coroner set the time of death at between eleven a.m. and five p.m. on the day the defendant has just been shown to have been in Vicksburg."

"He couldn't a killed Dyle," said Bubba absently.

"No," said Claxton with a nod of his head. "So maybe Carter was just lettin' off some steam that day?"

"Maybe he was at that," said Bubba just above a whisper. "I reckon we all done said some things we'd like to call back."

"No more questions, Bubba," said Claxton. "And Bubba...I'll be needin' a trim when this is over."

"I'm always a little light on Thursday mornin'," said Bubba.

"George?" asked Clary.

"No redirect your honor," said McCluskey. He took a few steps out in front of his table. "Your honor, the testimony of these witnesses is more to describe the character of the defendant. As it has been pointed out, the defendant is not on trial for...nor accused...in the death of the late Mr. Dyle Courtland. The state would like to call a number of witnesses who were on the street at that time and heard the same statements," said McCluskey.

"That won't be necessary," said Claxton. "The defense is willing to concede that what Dwight Bishop heard and testified to is substantially correct...provided that we can now agree that Dyle Courtland was innocent at least of burning down a church and Carter Monroe is innocent in his death."

"I think we can agree on that. Thank you, Mr. Delaney," said McCluskey cordially. "Your honor, the state will forego calling more witnesses to testify in that area, and would like to now call Sheriff Owen Mercer to the stand. Owen Mercer came through the door with his shiniest sheriff's badge on the pocket of his short sleeve shirt. Woodrow Silas motioned for him in the direction of the witness stand.

"Darn it Woodrow," said Mercer with a shake of his head, "think I ought to know where I'm goin' by now." Silas grinned at him and then swore him in.

"How long have you been the sheriff of Josiah Falls?" asked McCluskey

"Goin' on seven years," Mercer answered.

"And in that time you have probably investigated your share of crimes," said McCluskey.

"A few," said Mercer.

"Assault, burglary, vandalism, drunk and disorderly," McCluskey went on.

"That last sort of dropped off when Dyle passed on," said Mercer, "but we've had all of those."

"And this spring and summer…you've been investigating three homicides," said McCluskey.

"Yes, sir," said Mercer. McCluskey nodded and paced slowly in front of the jury.

"The court has heard some of the details of those murders," McCluskey began, "but now I would like you to tell us about the evidence. Can you recount what happened the day that you met the defendant, Carter Monroe, at the tool shed once the area had been re-opened following the arson investitgation."

"Yes, sir," said Mercer. "That mornin'…the one you're talkin' 'bout…was the day I had just got done takin' down the crime tape and the signs keepin' people away from the church area." He paused for a moment and then went on. "The arson investigators were done with everything, so they said it was okay for cleanup to get started on the place. Carter had just come by to get started on the cemetery grounds, so I went over to the shed to say hey and let him know it was all right to work anywhere he liked. I was also goin' to see 'bout getting the key to the lock box. Well, sir, we stepped on into the tool shed…"

"Did he unlock the shed or was it already unlocked?" asked McCluskey before Mercer could go on.

"Carter unlocked the shed while I was standin' right there," said Mercer.

"And did you note what he unlocked the shed with, Mr. Mercer?"

"Keys?" asked Mercer.

"Yes, I think we gathered that," McCluskey smiled. "Whose keys were they?"

"Oh, those were Carter's keys," said Mercer. "He keeps 'em on one of them clips on his belt, but it's long 'nough for 'em to ride in his pocket."

"So, Mr. Monroe unlocked the shed, using his own keys, and then what happened?" asked McCluskey.

"Well, we went on in like I said," said Mercer. "First thing, I noticed was the smell of gasoline…real strong. Carter smelt it, too. Shed had been shut up quite a spell I reckon. Found out it was the gas can that's kept in there, but the lid was settin' only half on it, like it was screwed back on with the threads cross-threaded. You know what I mean there?"

"Yes," said McCluskey. "The cap was not put back on properly, so it only turned once and did not seal. Is that correct?"

"'Bout it," Mercer nodded.

"What did you do then?" asked McCluskey.

"Carter picked up the can and screwed the lid back down tight and proper like it ought to be," said Mercer.

"Did you notice anything else in the shed?" asked McCluskey.

"Yes, sir," Mercer nodded again. "Minister Evan Washburne's keys was layin' right there on the little shelf-table inside the door. Me'n Carter talked 'bout them keys a minute there, but well, sir, there just wasn't nothin' else I could do but arrest him."

"And why was that?" asked McCluskey. "Why did you have no choice?"

"It was the *keys*," Mercer shook his head, "there weren't but two of them that could open the shed."

"So if one of the keys was inside the shed," McCluskey nodded, "then the other must have been used to lock them inside the shed. Was there any sign that the lock had been tampered with? Any way the keys could have gotten in there another way?"

"No sir," said Mercer. "Me'n Carter looked that place over top to bottom and checked the lock, door, and hinges. No other way to open it."

"Could the lock have been picked, perhaps?" asked McCluskey as he walked in front of the jury box.

"Thought 'bout that, too," said Mercer. "Next day, I walked out there with Harvey Walker. Harvey's sort a handy with locks. He went to work on it just like a burglar might, but he couldn't get it to budge. Harvey figured if anybody had found a way, they'd a messed it up inside, but it still turns just fine."

"So you came to the only conclusion possible," said McCluskey as he walked back to the witness stand. "You came to the inescapable conclusion that only Carter Monroe's keys could have locked the keys belonging to Evan Washburne inside the tool shed. Is that correct?"

"Yes, sir," said Mercer with a glance at Carter.

"Are any other copies of any of those keys on either key ring known?" asked McCluskey.

"No, sir," Mercer shook his head. "If there are any, I've never seen them."

"Thank you, sheriff," said McCluskey. "Your witness..." McCluskey turned and went back to his desk looking like he had just landed a thirty-pound bass, and from what I had just heard there I thought that maybe he had. Claxton got to his feet and seemed to be thinking hard about something.

"Owen, when you entered the shed, did you see the keys right off?" asked Claxton deliberately.

"Probably walked right past 'em," said Mercer.

"But you *didn't* see them at the moment the door opened," said Claxton. "How long was it before you saw them there?"

"Don't know exactly…maybe two or three minutes," said Mercer. "We fiddled 'round with the can 'bout that long I reckon."

"Is it possible that the keys were *not* there when you entered the shed?" asked Claxton. "Maybe you didn't see them because they weren't there?"

"Well, now," said Mercer. "Hadn't thought of that. You sayin' somebody walked up right after Carter opened up the door and we walked inside, and then put 'em there…and just…walked off?"

"I'm not sayin' anything," said Claxton. "I'm just askin' if that's possible. Could someone have done just like you said?"

"I just don't know, Claxton," Mercer shook his head. "Sure would take some brass. 'Spose one or the other of us had seen 'em do it or heard them keys rattle when they was set down. Might as well have put their ownselves in jail for us, but I reckon anything is possible. Sure don't seem likely, though."

"But it is *possible*," Claxton added.

"Yes, sir, it could have happened like that," said Mercer.

"Is it also possible that there could be another set of keys to the church and shed?" asked Claxton.

"I've heard that there was at one time," Mercer nodded. "Nobody's seen 'em in quite a spell. Probably not since before the war I reckon."

"Do you know anything else 'bout those keys?" asked Claxton.

"Reckon you ought to ask one of the church elders," said Mercer. "I always heard that they belonged to the elder deacon up 'till they disappeared, that is."

"Thank you, Owen," said Claxton. "Your honor, is it sufficiently well known Josiah Falls folklore that this third set of keys did *actually* exist? I can call several of the elders of the church who will testify that they either saw or used those keys as late as 1938."

"I think I'd like to hear that testimony," said McCluskey. "Just to make it official."

"All right, Woodrow, swear me in," said Judge Clary. "I was probably the last deacon here that actually saw and used 'em. I passed 'em on to the next deacon when I took over the bench full time back in 1935."

"That won't be necessary, your honor," McCluskey smiled and shook his head. "The state is more than prepared to take *your* word on the issue of the existence of the keys."

"Thank you, George," said Clary. "Would have been sort of a problem havin' to run another judge up here an all. Probably would have had to recuse myself as judge. Maybe even call for a mistrial."

"The state will stipulate that Mr. Mercer's testimony can be substantiated by a sufficient number of town residents as to make it a known fact," said McCluskey after a moment's thought.

"Much as I'd like to have you on the stand, Harlan," Claxton smiled, "the defense is content with you sittin' where you are." Claxton walked back over near the jury box. "So, tell me, Owen, how did Carter seem to you there in the tool shed?"

"Like usual I reckon," said Mercer.

"He didn't seem nervous? He didn't seem like a man who had just burned down a church...murdered two people...and somehow carelessly left all the evidence on display for you to find it?" asked Claxton.

"Objection, your honor," said McCluskey. "How is the witness to know how a man would *seem* after he had done all these things?"

"Your honor," said Claxton. "Owen Mercer is an experienced officer of the law who has learned to notice the way people *act*."

"I will uphold that objection," said Clary. "We've all seen men who were guilty act as though they had come from a church social...and innocent men nervous as a schoolboy askin' a girl to a dance."

"One last question," said Claxton as he turned back to Owen Mercer. "*How* did Carter lift the gas can?"

"By the handle I reckon," said Mercer. "Not sure what you mean exactly."

"Have you ever lifted something that you thought might be very heavy but it wasn't?" asked Claxton.

"Sure. I went to pick up my toolbox once. Usually weighs near on thirty pounds, but I forgot I had cleaned it out a week before. Just 'bout tossed it through the window of my house," said Mercer.

"Did something similar happen when Carter lifted up the gas can?" asked Claxton.

"He fell back a step when he picked it up, Claxton," said Mercer. "Like he was expectin' it to be full an there weren't but a few drops left in it..." There was a look of growing realization on Owen Mercer's face. Carter Monroe had been *expecting* a heavy gas can. If he'd emptied it in the church, he would have known it. I was only ten, but I'd done the same thing Owen Mercer had done. I reckoned just about everybody had at least once. It was like expecting a step on the stairs, except you were already on the floor, and just about jarring your backbone to pieces when you stepped down again.

"Thank you, Owen. No further questions, your honor," said Claxton.

"Re-direct, your honor," said McCluskey striding quickly from his desk. "Sheriff Mercer, could the defendant have been simply *pretending* that he was surprised the gas can was empty?"

"I don't rightly know anything right now," said Mercer with a shake of his head as he rubbed his neck. "I reckon that's   possible."
"Do you really think someone could have sneaked up to the shed and placed those keys inside on the table without *either* of you seeing or hearing?" asked McCluskey.

"Shed's only six feet square," said Mercer. "Don't think we could have been two feet from the table. I can't see as somebody could have done that very easy."

"Thank you, sheriff," said McCluskey.

"Re-direct, your honor," said Claxton rising from the table and walking out front again. "Owen, how long from the time you found the keys until either of you looked outside the shed?"

"Could have been a couple of minutes," said Mercer.

"Long enough for someone to have placed those keys there and slipped away across the cemetery?" asked Claxton.

"Wouldn't take a half-minute to get clear of the cemetery from the shed," said Mercer with another shake of his head. "Could just slip 'round behind and cut between the minister's house and Norm Abernathy's house. Just have to be quiet as a cat and have the nerve of a cat burglar."

"But it *is* possible," said Claxton as he walked back to his table. "No further questions."

"You boys done with me now?" asked Mercer. "Startin' to feel like a blame tennis ball goin' back and forth."

"You can step down, Owen," said Judge Clary. "Possible you might be re-called before this is all over, so stick around close as you can each day 'till were done."

"I've still got Gerald and Ted with me," said Owen. "Less'n the bank gets robbed, I'll be here." He stepped down and out the door.

"George," said Clary. "I've been lookin' over your witness list and what you've been presenting. We passed on some of your witnesses. Anyone else you want to call today?"

"Your honor," said George McCluskey, "the prosecution rests."

"Fine work today, George," said Clary. "Fine work on both sides. As it's goin' on four o'clock, I think I will adjourn the trial 'till ten a.m. tomorrow morning. This court stands in recess." Judge Clary banged down his gavel and stood. Everyone stood with him. He left the courtroom and everyone started talking all at once.

"Thanks for lettin' me look on," I said to the fellas from the paper. "I gotta catch up to Claxton an see if he's coming home to supper tonight or not." Before either could speak a word, I was gone into the crowd and working my way to the doors. I knew it would be a spell before they came out, so I figured my best chance would be to find him once everyone else headed for home.

As it turned out, it was the better part of an hour before Claxton, Junior, Carter, Owen, and Ted came out of the courthouse. Everyone outside had mostly gone home except for a few folks who apparently had nothing else to do but sit on the courthouse steps. I followed along as they headed over to the jail. Claxton wasn't' going to be home any time soon and told me to go on home and he'd see me later.

"Bertie," I said while we were eating supper. "Do you reckon Claxton was really a famous lawyer?"

"Cain't really say," she said after a moment. "Didn't really know lawyers was famous."

"Reporter at the trial today said he was," I said. "Why do you reckon Claxton don't talk 'bout it none?"

"Guess he just likes bein' private 'bout it here," she said. "Don't reckon he'd like folks chatterin' 'bout some lawyerin' he done a bunch a years ago. Claxton's just regular folks like you'n me an everyone else. He don't want to be treated no different. You got that?"

"I 'spect I'd have me a big ole sign out in the front yard if'n I was famous for somethin'," I said. Bertie laughed at that.

"'Spose you went an' become a famous ballplayer like Babe Ruth," she said after a moment. "An' ever time you so much as put a foot out o' your house there was a bunch a folks wantin' to holler at you or stickin' a paper under your nose wantin' you to sign your name on it, just so's they could say the met you."

"Could get mighty tiresome I reckon," I said. "Claxton is kinda quiet like most o' the time. I don't reckon he'd care for that at all." We finished eating and I went on to bed. If Claxton looked in on me, I was already asleep and didn't know it, but I'm pretty sure he did because that's just the way he was. There was something real comforting in knowing that about him.

Chapter Sixteen

The reporter fella had done called it just like Babe Ruth had pointed at the outfield stands and called his home run right before he hit it there. The courthouse was swarmed over early the next morning with reporters from all over runnin' up and down the steps. One fella said that he'd drove through the night from Atlanta to get there, and another one had come down on the 'red eye', whatever that was, from Nashville. Owen, Ted, Gerald, and Woodrow, too, had their hands full just trying to sort 'em all out and get 'Press' tags around their necks. I ran across the reporter and the artist fella I'd met the day before. They had already staked out a good spot near the side entrance that probably nobody else knew was the way the press was going to get inside.

"Morning, Nathan," said the reporter.

"Mornin'," I said. "Turned out just like you figured. I counted me car tags from seven states." The reporter nodded.

"So you're Claxton's boy are you?" he asked.

"Reckon I am," I said. "Course, I ain't seen 'em this past week no more'n anybody else. I 'spose they was up half the night talkin' 'bout today."

"I imagine they were," said the reporter. "McCluskey was tough yesterday. I think he's got a strong case. Just between you and me, I don't think *anybody* could get Monroe off the hook for this."

"I reckon Claxton will give it a go," I said.

"It'll be a show anyway," he said. "Better grab on. It's going to get crowded." I got hold of the reporter's jacket and sure enough when Woodrow came to the side door, he brought a bunch with him. The door opened and in we went. The reporter, with me on his tail, got through right off and made a beeline to the chairs on the right. I saw right away that there were a lot more folding chairs set up on the floor and there was just about no empty space left over. There was a rope tied across that separated the press row chairs from the rest of the gallery. I wasn't with the press, but I didn't figure Woodrow would chase me off no matter where I sat. I looked around and saw the young artist off to the other side.

"He ain't drawin' with you today?" I asked.

"Getting a better angle to see the defense table today," he explained. "I want to see the jury myself. I can usually figure out the verdict just by the way they walk out of the courtroom." I nodded and sat back as everyone else started filing inside. They were coming in pretty orderly, so I figured Woodrow was only lettin' 'em in a few at a time. By the time it was over, just about every chair was taken and there were a lot of folks standing around the back and the sides. Claxton, Junior, and Carter came in the side door with Woodrow and George McCluskey came in right behind them.

"All rise!" Woodrow bellowed across the room and it immediately got quiet as everyone got up. "The honorable Judge Harlan Clary." Judge Clary walked in from the back and up to his desk. He banged the gavel on the table once. "This court is now in session. Y'all can sit down...if you got a chair."

"Well, George...Claxton," said Clary. "Seems we've got quite a big turnout today. Woodrow? All the windows open? Gonna be hot today."

"All open, your honor," he answered. "Opened up the doors to pull some air, too." Clary nodded. At that moment Carter's wife, Luwuana, slowly walked inside. Everyone turned to look as she walked slowly towards the front. I saw that she didn't have her cane with her today. There were no empty chairs down there, but George McCluskey had an empty one at his table. Without a word, he folded it up and walked over behind the defense table and set it up again.

"Right kindly of you, sir," she said softly as she very slowly sat down with his help.

"Not at all," said McCluskey with a smile and started to return to his table.

"I'm beholdin' to you, Mr. McCluskey, sir," said Carter Monroe. McCluskey only nodded back to him. A minute later, the courtroom was settled back in again.

"All right, Claxton. I hear you got a little change for us."

"Yes, your honor," said Claxton as he rose from the desk and walked out in front of the table. "I had requested the military service records for Carter Monroe, and I was expecting them to be sent here by special courier today."

"There a problem get'n those records?" asked Clary. "I can see 'bout that directly if there is."

"No, your honor, the records are here," Claxton shook his head and smiled. "But I've had a request by the courier that he testify on them here today."

"No problem for me," said Clary. "George? The state have any problem with that?"

"No, your honor," said McCluskey. "I've grown accustomed to certain…shall we say, *usual* irregularties in Mr. Delaney's cases." There was a low rumble of laughter from the gallery and a large one from the press corps on hand.

"Go on ahead then, Claxton," said Clary.

"Thank you, your honor," said Claxton. "Woodrow, there should be a gentleman outside with the records. I don't think you can miss him." Woodrow Silas opened the door.

"Think I found him," said Woodrow as he turned back around. He stepped aside and a young man in a dress army uniform with a lieutenant's bars walked briskly inside, turned sharply on one toe, and approached the judge. He made another sharp turn and faced the defense table at rigid attention.

"The defense calls Lieutenant Rutherford Armbrister to the stand," said Claxton.

"Sir!" said Armbrister and saluted.

"At ease, Lieutenant," said Claxton with a smile and then returned the salute. "I'm not a captain anymore, lieutenant, but thank you anyhow."

"You don't really ever stop wearing the uniform, sir," the young officer said.

"Do you swear that the testimony you give will be the truth, the whole truth, and nothing but the truth, so help you God?" asked Woodrow Silas as Armbrister placed his hand on the Bible and lifted his right hand.

"Sir, yes, sir," he answered sharply.

"You may take the stand," said Woodrow. Armbrister moved around the side and up the two steps in one bounce and sat down.

"Lieutenant Armbrister," Claxton began, "are those the military records for Carter Monroe the third?" He pointed to the large folder that he now held in one hand.

"Yes, sir," said Armbrister.

"That sure seems like a lot of papers there," said Claxton. "Sure that's just for *one* soldier?"

"It is a lot of papers, sir," said Armbrister. "And, yes, sir, for just one soldier, sir."

"Do you perhaps have a *summary* of Carter Monroe's service in there?" asked Claxton. "Take 'bout a whole day to read through that whole stack."

"I do. Yes, sir," answered Armbrister.

"Your honor," said McCluskey rising from his desk. "I don't think a recounting of Mr. Monroe's war record, even in summation, has any relevance here. A good many men here in this room right now, the defense counsel himself included, have served…many with distinction. The state is willing to concede that Mr. Monroe served his country and that his service can be made a part of the court records without any reading."

"Claxton?" asked Clary with a nod in his direction.

"Your honor," said Claxton. "I have no intention of slowin' down the wheels of justice, but at the same time, I'd hate to have those very same wheels greased with the blood of the accused without a fair say here in this court. I think the court and the jury need to have a full accountin' of a man's character if they are to sit and pass judgment on him. The prosecution thought it was important enough yesterday to establish the character of the accused that half the town was 'bout to be called to testify to that."

"I'd like to hear what this young man's come all the way here from Washington to say myself," said Clary. "George, you're out of order on this one. We're gonna sit an' listen."

"Thank you, your honor," said Claxton. "Lieutenant?"

"Yes, sir," said Armbrister. He opened the cover of the folder. "Carter Monroe the third...age twenty-two, enlisted in the United States Army on eighteen October 1917 and was part of the American Expeditionary Force under General Pershing. Private Monroe saw action in combat on six occasions during 1918 as part of the 371st Infantry fighting with a French division in France. Awards and commendations were the Purple Heart, silver, and bronze stars. Promotions to corporal and sergeant. Sergeant Monroe returned home in January 1919 and remained in the army where he advanced to the rank of Master Sergeant at the time of his retirement at the end of 1937. Master Sergeant Monroe continued his service in the reserves until recalled to active duty on ten January 1942. He reported to Ft. Bragg, North Carolina and was placed in charge of training new recruits. On one May 1942, Master Sergeant Monroe was sent to the European Theater of operations where he saw combat in Sicily, Italy, Normandy, France, and Germany. Commendations: the Purple Heart, awarded four times, the silver star with oak leaf cluster, the bronze star, awarded three times, and the Distinguished Service Medal. Master Sergeant Monroe left Germany on eighteen January 1946 and was placed on detached service until eighteen October 1947 at which time he formally retired from the United States Army after thirty years of service, age fifty-two."

"I would say that is an impressive service record by anyone's measurin' stick," said Claxton.

"Yes, sir," said Armbrister.

"Of course, this record could have been delivered to us by courier," Claxton began, "So, tell me, Lieutenant, why did you feel the *need* to bring this personally and testify here today?"

"I requested the duty, sir," said Armbrister. "There is an open inquiry in Washington concerning Master Sergeant Monroe, sir. And, sir, as you know, the army takes care of it's own, sir."

"An inquiry?" said Claxton. "That sounds official to me? Carter Monroe in trouble with the army, too?"

"It *is* official, sir," said Armbrister. He smiled for the very first time. "However, Master Sergeant Monroe is not in trouble with the army, sir. Quite to the contrary, there is new evidence concerning Master Sergeant Monroe's service relating to combat action outside Berlin on two April 1945 taken from the personal papers of Colonel Jeremiah Armbrister that were discovered to also contain a formal report directed to the commanding General Omar Bradley. That report was never filed since Colonel Armbrister was killed in action the following week."

"Was Colonel Armbrister any relation to you, Lieutenant?" asked Claxton.

"My father, sir," said Armbrister with a sharp nod.

"And what were the contents of that report?" asked Claxton. Armbrister opened another folder inside the folder.

"It reads," Armbrister began, "…under great personal hazard and risk of life and limb, and well beyond the call of all reasonable service, Master Sergeant Carter Monroe did under heavy fire on the field carry back to safety no fewer than sixteen wounded American riflemen and one officer of the rank of major as well as five wounded enemy soldiers, despite being hit twice by enemy fire and sustaining shrapnel wounds from a grenade. It is my recommendation that Master Sergeant Monroe be recognized with the highest of honors this army can bestow." Armbrister paused a moment. "Signed, Colonel Jeremiah Armbrister, commanding." Armbrister closed the folder and then closed the outer folder.

"No further questions, your honor," said Claxton.

"George?" asked Clary.

"The state has no questions for Lieutenant Armbrister," said McCluskey.

"You are excused, sir," said Clary. "Thank you for comin' on out here today."

"My privilege, sir," said Armbrister. He stood and came rapidly down the two steps to the wooden floor of the courthouse and walked quickly towards the side door, but stopped when he got there. He turned back towards the defense table. "Master Sergeant. would you do me the honor?"

Carter looked at Junior and then at Claxton. Claxton gave him a nod. Carter got up from his seat, came to attention, and saluted.

"The Colonel was a fine man, Lieutenant," said Carter as he finished the salute. Armbrister returned the salute.

"Good luck, Master Sergeant," said Armbrister. He put his hat back on, turned, and disappeared out the door.

"Masterful?" whispered the reporter as he wrote quickly. "I don't know how he did it, but he got Monroe's whole service record out there to the jury and McCluskey couldn't challenge a word of it! Who's he putting on the stand next? Harry Truman?"

"Sounded like it was just bein' lucky," I said. Who coulda figured that there was somethin' like that to come out?

"Don't you believe it, son," said the reporter. "Luck's what's left over when you plan smart, and Claxton plans…*everything*. He used some army connections of his to get this done. Claxton knew Carter had a solid gold war record and got the army to tell the story for him. You're seeing a master at work here, son." The reporter just shook his head and smiled. McCluskey made a gesture of a magician pulling a rabbit out of his magic hat. Clary laughed silently back at him and shook his head. I was beginning to wonder if Claxton might just *be* the smartest man in the world. Still, I figured Claxton was a might short of gett'n Carter out of trouble. A war hero could still burn down a church and kill folks.

"Your next witness, Claxton?" asked Clary.

"Your honor," Claxton sighed. "The defense would like to call Mr. Riley Shimmerhorn to the stand." Every head in the room turned like they were on swivels to see if he was going to come walkin' into the room next. "But, unfortunately, Riley can't seem to be located." Claxton paused and walked down in front of the jury. "Just for a minute there, you were wonderin' if ole Riley was goin' to come through that door over yonder, and you were wonderin' if he was goin' to have somethin' to say 'bout that third set of keys."

"Your honor," said McCluskey getting to his feet. "The defense is now trying to testify for a witness who *isn't* even here. If I'm going to try a case against a town *full* of rabbits, I'd at least like to *see* the rabbits first."

"That objection is sustained," said Clary. "Claxton, you'll have a chance to say all that in your closing remarks, so I ain't going to tell the jury to forget what you just said…cause they ain't likely to anyhow, but you need to try and get your evidence from witnesses that *are* on the stand."

"Yes, your honor," said Claxton. "In the absence of Riley Shimmerhorn, the defense re-calls Sheriff Owen Mercer to the stand."

"Woodrow, get Owen back in here," said Clary. A moment later Owen Mercer was back in the courtroom.

"Once sworn…still sworn," said Clary as he walked up to the stand. "Let's get at it."

"Owen," said Claxton. "Did you have occasion to go up to the cabin up above Josiah falls belongin' to Riley Shimmerhorn?"

"You know I did," said Mercer tiredly. Even I could see that the trial and the past week had begun to wear on him.

"Now the court does to," said Claxton with a smile. "Can you tell the court what you found there?"

"This here cabin where Riley lives," Mercer began, "sets off the stream feedin' into the falls by not more'n a few hundred paces. When I got there, the door was unlocked. The padlock he usually keeps on it was gone. I think it was found, but I didn't see another anywhere, so that was probably it. Inside, the place was tore up like a twister had gone through ever last drawer and place in it. Some of the floorboards was even pried up; the mattress was split down the middle with a butcher knife I reckon, and that knife was stickin' blade point down in the middle of the table. There was some blood on the knife, on the table, on the mattress, an' on some of the floor boards. I even found some on the back of the door."

"What is your *expert* opinion on what you saw there?" asked Claxton.

"Looked like it coulda been robbery…maybe just vandalism as I don't think Riley had nothin' anybody'd want," said Mercer.

"What did you make of the blood?" asked Claxton.

"It tested out human," said Mercer. "Kit said it was type 'O' if that's important."

"Where do think the blood came from?" asked Claxton.

"Well, Claxton," said Mercer, "I did me a little detective work there an' I think I know the answer to that. If you start over at the mattress, there's a little line of blood. Then there's drips on the floor over to the table, an' then there's the knife stuck in the table. Now if you was to handle a knife like that one…" Claxton put up his hand for a moment and went to the defense table, opened a box and came back with a big long knife. I could tell it was the one that had been up there at Riley's cabin.

"Is this the knife?" asked Claxton.

"That's the one," said Mercer.

"Your honor, defense exhibit 'E'," said Claxton. He held it up towards McCluskey but he only waved back that he didn't need to see it up close. Claxton then handed the knife to Mercer. "Go on with what you were sayin' there."

"All right, with a knife like this one," said Mercer, "it'd be too long to cut with it like this…" He held the knife in an underhand grip. "If I was goin' to cut through a mattress I'd hold it like this…" He moved the knife to be handle up in his hand and blade downward. "Now, I figure the fella that was cuttin' through the mattress figured there might be something inside, so he's cuttin' down with one hand an' holdin' the mattress down with the other. 'Bout near the bottom, the knife hits somethin' hard, an' the fella's hand…this here knife ain't no Bowie knife…ain't got no hilt on it to stop your hand from slippin', so it slips kinda sudden down onto the blade and cuts his palm. Blood runs down the blade, an' also sprays a little line onto the mattress like so…" He carefully moved his hand down onto the blade and indicated the direction of the blood. "I figure the fella got a little ticked cuttin' himself, an' come over to the table and stuck that knife down into the top of it. Hand musta been right sore 'cause the tip was in the table just enough buried to make it stand upright 'cause when I touched it, it come right up. After that, I 'spose he must have wrapped it up to stop the bleedin'. Left a spot on the door on the way out is all."

"Certainly a very colorful tale," said McCluskey as he got to his feet, "but, your honor, isn't this straying into pure speculation?"

"Owen, you *know* what you're sayin' to be a fact?" asked Clary. "All this stuff 'bout holdin' the knife, an' the blood an' such? That somethin' you think or somethin' you done proved?"

"Got it straight from the Jackson homicide fellas," said Owen. "I told 'em what I saw there an' they asked me a bunch a questions 'bout the knife an' the blood trail. Had to go back up there an' put a tape measure an' everything onto it. But, truth is, Harlan, I seen my share of knife fights an' I know what they can do. Don't take but a little cut, an' this un' shoulda been plumb smartin'."

"I'll let the testimony stand as expert," said Clary after a moment's thought. "Good 'nough for you George?"

"I'll wait and see where this leads, your honor," said McCluskey. "But, the state is content, for the moment, with Sheriff Mercer's *interpretation* of the events at the cabin."

"Was there anything else, Owen?" asked Claxton.

"Just one thing," said Mercer. "There was a sewed up piece in the end of the mattress…sewed up on top and bottom, but big 'nough you could put your hand in between where the beddin' was pushed back. I think Riley mighta been hidin' somethin' in there an' whoever cut open the mattress mighta found it." He looked over at McCluskey. "Course that's just my *opinion*, Mr. McCluskey."

"Was there any sign of Riley or anything else you can add?" asked Claxton.

"Didn't look like Riley, or anyone else, had been there in quite a spell," said Mercer.

"One last question," said Claxton. "Could that little hidin' place in the mattress have been big enough to put a ring with a handful of keys?"

"I reckon it was," said Mercer.

"Thank you, Owen," said Claxton. "No further questions."

"Your witness, George," said Clary.

"Thank you, your honor," said McCluskey. "Let's put this business to rest shall we? Did you, in fact, find any keys in the cabin, sheriff?"

"No, sir," said Mercer.

"Did you find anything that indicated that there *might have been* keys there?" asked McCluskey.

"No sir," said Mercer as he lifted one finger to stop McCluskey from going quickly on, "an' that's what's real puzzlin' now ain't it?"

"What do you mean 'puzzling'?" McCluskey asked cautiously.

"I didn't find *any* keys at all," said Mercer. "Not a one. Not even Riley's spare keys. He always kept one on him, one inside a board on the outside of the cabin, and one he *said* he kept hid somewhere inside. I checked for the one outside an' it was gone, and there wasn't one inside either. Maybe that inside spare was on that ring of church keys."

"The church keys that Riley Shimmerhorn *allegedly* once had?" asked McCluskey. "The same *alleged* keys that have not been seen in more than a *decade*...by *anyone*?" McCluskey stopped and sighed. "Isn't it just as likely that those keys no longer exist at all? Isn't it just as possible that Riley Shimmerhorn lost his spare keys? And isn't it very possible that Riley Shimmerhorn is an eccentric old man who has maybe lost possession of his senses entirely and caused all the damage you saw in his cabin himself?"

"Now, I don't know 'bout them keys, an' Riley might not be right in the head like you say. You're a right smart fella an' I ain't nothin' but a backwoods country sheriff...an' you might be right as rain 'bout all that you said 'bout the keys, but Riley wouldn't a cut himself like a danged fool with his own knife," Mercer snorted. "He handles a knife like you handle them fancy words comin' out o' your mouth, Mr. McCluskey, an' that's the gosh danged gospel on that." For the first time, George McCluskey seemed to have no response.

"No further questions," he said finally with a shrug.

"All right, Owen," said Clary. "You can get you're dander back on down. You're excused." Judge Clary looked around the courtroom and focused on Luwuana Carter for just a second. She was sittin' there lookin' like she was 'bout to fall off that chair. "I think everybody here could use a break. The court is goin' to adjourn for lunch an' be back at one o'clock, same as yesterday. Woodrow, can I borrow you a minute, please." Woodrow Silas came over to the judge's desk. I saw him nod a few times. Clary banged down his gavel and people started to file out.

"How you callin' it now?" I asked the reporter.

"I think you still got a set of keys locked in a shed and only one key to put 'em there," said the reporter nodding his head. "But, Carter Monroe was standing with one foot in the grave and one foot on a banana peel this morning. I'd say he's standing on both feet upright beside it now, but it wouldn't take but a shove to put him in it." I saw Woodrow Silas come over and help Carter's wife up out of her chair. She looked like she was hurtin' something awful from settin' there all mornin', but she just smiled and went off with him through that little side door. Lunchtime went just about like the day before except there were even more folks in town today.

Chapter Seventeen

The court came back into session at one o'clock on the dot, and Claxton was still talkin' with Junior and Carter when the judge came back in and sat down. When Luwuana Monroe came back into the courtroom, there was a big padded chair brought from the judge's office for her to sit in, and I figured it was a might more comfortable than that hardbacked foldin' chair.

So far, I couldn't tell if Owen Mercer's testifying had been good or bad for either side, but the army fella's had sure changed some folks ideas 'bout Carter while they were lookin' on. I noticed right away how most of the men that had gone off to fight in the war stood up real respectful when Carter went out and came back in. A couple of them, black an' white, gave him salutes of their own. Claxton had told me once that there was something different 'bout men that go off to war and fight together. There's a glue that you can't see that makes 'em stick together, and it don't matter where they come from or even what color. Maybe that Lieutenant Armbrister said it just right, 'Army takes care of it's own,' he said. I didn't completely understand it, but I could see that Claxton did, and so did Carter, and some others too.

"The defense calls Garson Ashe to the stand," said Claxton. Heads turned as Ashe made his way across from the open door to the witness stand. Woodrow started to swear him in.

"Garson," said Clary. "It true you been fishin' this whole last week?"

"I just got back this mornin'," said Ashe. "Found me that summons on my door."

"Since neither the prosecution or the defense has had a chance to interview the witness," Clary began, "do either of you want to hold off on this testimony?"

"The prosecution has no objection to the witness," said McCluskey. Claxton did not answer right away.

"He's your witness, Claxton," said Clary. "You want him up here, yet?"

"Yes, your honor," said Claxton after a moment. "Go ahead and swear him in." I could tell that Claxton wanted him on the stand, but at the same time he wasn't just exactly sure.

"You can say 'I affirm' if you like," said Woodrow. Ashe looked at the Bible on the edge of the stand.

"Think I'd like to put my hand on that book right there," he said quietly. I saw Claxton and Junior exchange a glance. The man on the stand *looked* sure enough like Garson Ashe, but he didn't *act* like him.

"Do you solemnly swear that the testimony you shall give shall be the truth, the whole truth, and nothing but the truth, so help you God?" asked Woodrow.

"The Lord as my witness, I swear it," said Ashe. Claxton stood slowly. I thought he looked a little uncertain for the first time in the trial, but maybe he was just thinking. McCluskey was watching him more closely than the witness now.

"I reckon those fish must have kept you right busy out there on the river to keep you away a whole week," said Claxton with a smile.

"Best catch I've had in a spell," said Ashe. "Sold a lot of 'em up in Vicksburg and some more down in Natchez."

"You come by fishin' kind of natural?" asked Claxton.

"My daddy and granddaddy was fishermen," said Ashe. "Cain't rightly remember not fishin'."

"Seems like your granddaddy was right handy with stone, too," said Claxton.

"Yep,' said Ashe. "He done some stone work on this here courthouse and done that marble carvin' an' writin' out where we come in."

"Didn't he do some of the fancy headstone monuments here in town an' at some of the private cemeteries 'round Josiah Falls?" asked Claxton.

"He did," said Ashe.

"You know," Claxton began slowly, "when I saw that headstone at Evan Washburne's grave the next mornin' after he was buried, I was thinkin' it looked a whole lot like the fancy stone work your granddaddy used to do. Did you ever work with him on those headstones he made?"

"A time or two when I was a boy," said Ashe. Claxton just nodded and paced over towards the jury box.

"Why do you 'spose somebody would have put that stone up?" asked Claxton.

"I reckon it was put up by somebody that was payin' their respects," said Ashe with a look 'round the courtroom. "Ain't no harm in that is there?"

"Not at all," said Claxton. "No harm in puttin' up a fine stone like that, but it just got me wonderin' why nobody would own up to it. Got me to wonderin' if maybe someone had a little bit of a guilty conscience. You know how sometimes a body wants to say he's sorry for something he's done, an' it's just plum too late? Maybe this stone was somebody's way of saying that."

"Hadn't figured that," said Ashe.

"Relevance again, your honor?" asked McCluskey. "Is there some connection between the witness, the headstone, and the case?"

"How 'bout it Claxton?" asked Clary. "Sounds like lots of if'n an' could be'n right now."

"Just pursuin' a local mystery, your honor," said Claxton. "One that involves the victim an' might be tryin' to tell us somethin' 'bout what happened."

"All right," said Clary. "You can go on, but let's make sure we get there."

"Yes, your honor," said Claxton as he turned back to Ashe. "Garson...I did a little checkin' 'round to see who might of bought a stone like that. Harshburghers didn't make or sell anything like it. I even called out to Fayette an' everyplace I could think of. Know what?"

"What's that, Claxton?" asked Ashe.

"*Nobody* would claim it," said Claxton. "Now that got me to thinkin' again. That piece of marble was right expensive an' 'bout the size for two markers. Started wonderin' who might have one that he didn't have a need for. You know anybody like that, Garson?" Ashe glanced around the courtroom.

"It was my daddy an' momma's stone," said Ashe. "Was supposed to be theirs, but they got washed away in that flood an' never was found. Just thought it was fittin' for a man like Evan Washburne." A murmur ran through the courtroom.

"So you carved an' put up that stone yourself," said Claxton once it passed. "Why didn't you just come out an' say so?"

"It was somethin' personal 'tween me an' the minister," said Ashe.

"That's just what I was wonderin'," said Claxton. "Was there maybe a little guilt in puttin' up that stone?"

"Got me a lota guilt 'bout a lotta things," said Ashe. "But, not 'bout puttin' up the headstone. I done right by that."

Claxton nodded and walked back towards the defense table, and then turned towards the witness box.

"Garson," Claxton began slowly. "We've heard here in this court that Evan Washburne was a man without an enemy in the world. Nobody could have harbored a grudge against him. But, that's not exactly true, now is it? Would it be fair to say that you had a number of run-ins with the late Minister Evan Washburne?" I saw right off what Claxton was tryin' to get, an' I think everybody in the courtroom did, too.

"Reckon we had some words a time or two," said Ashe with a nod.

"Did any of those 'words' turn angry?" asked Claxton.

"You know they did," said Ashe. "You was there once."

"And how did Evan Washburne respond?" asked Claxton.

"Well, I reckon he got his dander up at least once...that time you got in between us," said Ashe. Claxton was about to say something, but Ashe went on talking. "He was a hard man to rile. Wasn't just 'cause he was a man of God, though."

"How's that?" asked Claxton.

"Evan...Minister Washburne, he didn't just *say* them words from the Book," said Ashe. "He *lived* them words he preached. I come there that night of the Fourth, spoilin' for another go out him. I was full of fightin' an' such, but Claxton, he turned all that away an' opened my eyes to the light again."

"So, you had a *good* talk with Evan that night?" asked Claxton. "Did that happen to change later on?"

"It did," said Ashe. "I went on up to the church a little later on an' caught up with him coming out of the church."

"Go on," said Claxton, but I could tell he was not sure what was going to happen. "You said this talk was different." George McCluskey shifted in his seat like he wanted to get up and object to something but couldn't quite figure out what to object to.

"It was kind of private like," said Ashe looking around the room. "Do I have to say? Ain't talkin' to your minister protected and such?"

"If you mean a confession of sins," said Clary, "then yes. But we're you making a confession, Garson?"

"No, sir," said Ashe. "Not just then."

"Then you need to tell us 'bout that other part then," said Clary.

"Well, sir," said Ashe. "I been away from the Lord a long time. Reckon you all know that. Minister Washburne had done give me a heap o' things to think on, so I made up my mind that I ought to see to it right then."

"You decided to have it out with him?" asked Claxton with a nod.

"Asked him if he might baptise me in the Water," said Ashe. "Let me start getting' back in God's way again."

"That was what you were talking about with Evan Washburne on the steps outside the church?" asked Claxton.

"Yes, sir," said Ashe. "We went in directly and done it. He listened to my confessions after that."

"How long were you in the church?" asked Claxton with a shake of his head.

"Only 'bout fifteen minutes," said Ashe. "Oh, I didn't but touch on *all* my sins. Shux, we woulda took all night going down that list, but I admitted to the bigguns." There was a low rumble of laughter again. To my surprise, Ashe smiled. Then he was all serious again. "He mighta lost his life that night, but he saved my soul, Claxton. I'll be forever beholden to him for that." Claxton took a step back. Whatever he had thought Ashe might say hadn't happened. George McCluskey sat there looking like a man that had just dodged a bullet headin' for his noggin. Claxton didn't show much one way or the other, but it was clear enough that he didn't get what he was hopin' for.

"No further questions," said Claxton. "Thank you for tellin' us about that. George, your witness."

"I can't think of a single thing for this witness, your honor," said McCluskey.

"All right, Claxton, you're up again," said Clary. Claxton gave a nod and plunged back in.

"The defense calls Carter Monroe to the stand," said Claxton. Carter stood and moved with the same quick sharpness that the lieutenant had when he went up to the witness stand. I understood that ramrod straight spine of his now. Thirty years of marchin' doesn't just go away. He placed his hand on the Bible and raised his right hand. Woodrow Silas swore him in.

"Carter," said Claxton with a deep sigh before he started. "I could have called a hundred folks up here...maybe everbody in town to tell us 'bout your character. They would have said that you worked hard, kept to yourself mostly, and didn't much bother anybody, but folks 'round here know all that. Now, they know a lot more 'bout you than that. They know you didn't kill Dyle Courtland, an' they know that you'd help a neighbor with a flat tire when he needed a hand, an' they know that you'd risk your life to save another's...even if that man wore a different uniform than yours...or his skin was of a different color. What the court and the jury wants to hear from you now is what you know 'bout the Fourth of July."

"I was out there on the street with my grill," said Carter. "Had me some barbecue chicken on it, some ribs, an' steaks. Lot o' folks come by for a bite."

"It was right tasty," said Judge Clary. "Go on."

"Thank you, your honor," said Carter. "Got me some special seasonin' that I puts in the sauce. I'll writes it down for you later."

"'Preciate that," said Clary. There was a mild current of laughter across the room at that. "Reckon we'll talk 'bout the cookin' later."

"Yes, sir. Well, night pushed on," Carter continued. "You done heard what mister Dwight had to say. Wasn't nothin' but the drink doin' the talkin' though. He didn't mean nothin' by it. I seen mister Evan late that night. He was headin' by the church. I was cleanin' up 'bout then, an' most folks was headin' for home. Once my grill got cooled off, I loaded up and headed for my house. I wasn't tired or nothin', so I worked on me a piece of fence that needed mendin' an' tended some stock before I went up to the house. Next day I heard 'bout the church an' what happened to mister Evan and Odessa. Awful thing that."

"Yes, it was," said Claxton. "What did you think 'bout all that?"

"Couldn't believe it," said Carter with a shake of his head. "Take a *strong* hate for a body to do somethin' like that. Now somebody shootin' Dyle, that there was just cowardly, shootin' a man that ain't got no gun, an' ain't got no chance to defend hisself. Just shootin' 'em down like you'd put down a mad dog. Be like shootin' a man wavin' a white flag after he done give up the fightin'. I cain't see that, but leastwise, I hear he didn't suffer none, but the other...I don't have no word for that. Burnin' 'em up *alive* an' *knowin'* they's in there. Now, mister Claxton, sir, I seen death, an' I seen a lot of it in the army, but those men like Colonel Armbrister, my boy, all them other boys...they was men gone to do a job. This kinda killin' cain't have nothin' but hate drivin' it."

"Could you do something like that?" asked Claxton. "Even if you *had* to do it? Even if you were ordered to do it?"

"No, sir," Carter shook his head. "Ain't nothin' nobody could do to me or mine that I could do that back to 'em. Wouldn't have no way to answer to the Lord on the Judgment for somethin' like that. An' mister Evan, why, Claxton, there weren't no kinder fella ever lived, an' all of y'alls knows that. I'd a walked through that fire my ownself to fetch him if I could'a."

"I believe that," said Claxton. "I surely do, Carter." Claxton walked back towards the defense table. "No further questions." I'd heard what Carter said clear enough. All he'd said was that he didn't do it. They didn't try to say somebody'd seen him someplace else and didn't offer any proof at all, but I could see on some faces in the jury box that how he said what he said touched something there. I didn't know if it was enough, but it was sure enough there. I wondered if Mr. McCluskey had seen the same thing because he was up on his feet like a cat jumpin' off a hot tin roof. He didn't want that good feelin' 'bout Carter to simmer too long in that jury box.

"Mr. Monroe," McCluskey began. "Can anyone verify that you returned to your home and were there at the time of the fire?"

"No, sir," said Carter. "Not a soul seen me. Only saw my livestock, an' I don't reckon they can testify."

"Perhaps your wife saw you?" McCluskey suggested. He glanced at Luwuana Monroe.

"No, sir," said Carter. "She'd been feelin' poorly, an' I didn't want to wake her. Sleep comes mighty hard for her these days, an' it's the Lord's own blessin' when it does." Carter looked out at his wife as did McCluskey. Her fingers were all swollen and twisted, and I reckon they must have been right painful.

"My mother suffered with the same rheumatoid arthritis," said McCluskey with a sigh. "It can be quite painful to have and to watch."

"The Lord only give us what we can handle," said Carter. "Luwuana don't complain 'bout it none. She just tries to be thankful on what she is blessed with."

"Let's talk about that. You've had a lot of misfortune in your life," said McCluskey. "All of your children passed before you. Your father was killed. You served in two World Wars, and your wife is seriously afflicted. Two black churches were burned this spring in what were probably racially motivated attacks. It could make a man bitter. Are you bitter, Mr. Monroe?"

"There was times I thought hard on that, Mr. McCluskey, sir," said Carter with a nod. "I questioned the Lord in my heart even though I knows that ain't right. Wanted to know why he took all my children, my daddy, an' why he took so many of them young boys in the wars that had so much life ahead of 'em. Couldn't see how no lovin' God could do such as that."

"So you *are* bitter," said McCluskey with a nod.

"I was," said Carter. "Then one day, I seen the light on it. The Lord don't take nothin' from us that he don't give us somethin' back an' sometimes more'n we had before. I near got back all the land my daddy lost in the Depression. My boy, me an' Luwuana is raisin' his youngun's with his wife,

188

an' see Mr. McCluskey I ain't *lost* a family…I just been *given* another. Now them churches, they was get'n old an' rickety an' wasn't being kept up like they ought. Now they's buildin' new ones that's bigger'n better than what was there. It says in the Bible that the Lord, he giveth and he taketh away. We just got to be respectful o' *both* them. Took me a spell to get right with the Lord on it, but I be there now."

"But you still feel anger sometimes," said McCluskey.

"I do," said Carter with a smile. "An' sometimes I run my mouth a bit more'n I'd like. Luwuana give me a scoldin' for it sometimes, an' I get over bein' mad real quick. But, bein' mad…cain't do much 'bout that, but you ought not *do* nothin' when you feels that way."

"That sounds like good advice. It's too bad we can't all follow it," said McCluskey as he walked away from the stand in front of the judge. He didn't look like he was get'n back from Carter what he had been lookin' for, so he started movin' on to something else. "Let's talk about the cash box for a moment. It's been said here in this court that you sometimes paid bills and helped the minister settle the books each month. Is that true?"

"Yes, sir," said Carter. "Mister Evan had him a lot to do. Some in town an' some out, so I helped out what I could."

"Was there a lot of bookkeeping to be done?" asked McCluskey. "After all, it was a small church."

"Oh, there was a lot of figurin' to do," said Carter. "That's why mister Evan ask me to help out. Numbers always come easy to me, an' come in handy in the army, too. Seems like we was always countin' somethin'."

"So if you were to buy some tools for ten dollars at five percent sales tax and paid for it with sixteen dollars and forty cents…" McCluskey started.

"I'd have me five dollar and ninety cents left in my pocket," Carter finished for him. I couldn't tell if McCluskey was surprised or not, but he kept on going.

"That would be correct," said McCluskey. "I figured that out on paper at lunch today. That's very impressive."

"Just numbers," said Carter with a shrug.

"It's not likely then that you would make a mistake. Say, possibly miscount the church's money?" asked McCluskey. "Perhaps make a mistake in balancing the receipts against the cash in the cash box? Perhaps write down the wrong numbers in the ledger?"

"Ain't perfect," said Carter. "No more'n what God made me, but I be real careful with the church's money. Treat it just like it was my own. Mister Evan and them does a lot o' good with it, and mister Evan always wanted to make sure them books was right 'case any o' the members wanted to look at 'em. Better a ounce of preventin' than a heapful of curin' he was always sayin'."

"Do you recall when the church ledger was last balanced?" asked McCluskey.

"Be 'bout June second," said Carter immediately.

"Would you mind checking over the cash box and books for us now?" asked McCluskey.

"Reckon I can do that," Carter answered. McCluskey retrieved the cash box and set it in front of Carter. It was already unlocked. I saw Junior and Claxton whispering back and forth. It didn't look like they knew what McCluskey was up to, but I figured that it was 'bout to come out o' that box up there. Carter made a quick count of the cash, and I could hear the coins dropping back into the box in the silence of the courtroom. He picked up the top drawer and set it on the railing, and then began counting some more cash that was underneath. We all waited while Carter opened up the ledger book and began checking against the receipts, markin' and enterin' as he went along. It seemed like a long time, but when I checked the clock on the wall, it hadn't been but four minutes before he was done. Carter put the pencil back in the box.

"Ain't right," Carter said with a shake of his head. "Cash is short for May an' June both."

"There's money missing?" asked McCluskey.

"Ten dollars from May an' ten from June," said Carter. "Books was balanced for May havin' eighteen dollar an' seventy-seven cents in cash an' eighty-one dollar an' twenty-three cents in receipts. Got each one checked off, but now there ain't but eight dollar an' seventy-seven cents." He picked up the dollars and showed them. "These here bills is brand new an' all crisp, but there ain't none stickin' together. Same for the June money. Mister Evan got him two hundred dollar from the bank at the end of April. They come in two of them wrappers with a hundred one dollar bills each. You seen them before?"

"The bills are pre-counted at the bank or from the Federal Reserve Bank," McCluskey nodded. "I think most businessmen here in town have seen those. Go on."

"Yes, sir," said Carter. "Mister Evan usually get just ones for payin' small bills and the charity and such, but I cain't figure where that money coulda gone."

"Were the books balanced for June?" asked McCluskey.

"Looks like mister Evan was workin' on it," said Carter. "Got him a question mark here at the end. We was figurin' on balancin' the books right after the Fourth."

"Who has access to the cash box?" asked McCluskey.

"Mister Evan an' me had the keys," said Carter shaking his head. "Cain't figure he used the May money 'cause he had plenty o' the June money on top. He was right careful to put in a receipt even if he filled it out hisself."

"So you can't explain the missing money at all?" McCluskey nodded.

"No sir," said Carter. "I cain't explain it."

"I believe you mentioned that you were re-buying all the land that had once belonged to your father," said McCluskey.

"That's right," said Carter. "Been puttin' my army pension money, my jobs, and my farmin' money into it."

"Did you perhaps add some church money to it as well?" asked McCluskey.

"Sayin' I stole money from the church? Stole it from mister Evan?" asked Carter his eyes wide with surprise.

"Maybe you didn't think about it as *stealing*," said McCluskey. "Maybe you thought about it as a loan, or you were just borrowing it for a while intending to put it back before it was noticed as gone, and then maybe Minister

Washburne noticed the missing money noted by his mark there in the ledger showing he knew something was wrong. Possibly, he confronted you about it. Maybe the night of the Fourth?" McCluskey paused for just a moment. "You were frightened. There could be charges filed. That could mean scandal, jail maybe. You went to the church, picked up his keys from the table near the door where he almost always set them, locked him and Odessa inside after you doused the church with gasoline from the can in the shed, and then went back to the shed and locked up the gas can, but you forgot that you laid the keys down inside and didn't see them in the dark when you locked the shed and left. Isn't that what really happened, Mr. Monroe?"

"It ain't," said Carter shaking his head. "I didn't do no such a thing!"

"Then how did the keys get in the shed if you didn't put them there?" McCluskey demanded forcefully. "You had the only key that would open it. It was there in your pocket where you always kept it. Nobody else could have had it."

"I don't rightly know," said Carter staring down at the floor.

"No more questions, your honor," said McCluskey. He walked back to his table like a boxer who'd just knocked out the other fella in a prizefight. It sure didn't look good for Carter. Listenin' to McCluskey, I could see that most everybody was noddin' his head in agreement.

"Your honor," said Claxton. "I'd like to ask a few moments to examine some evidence that has not been admitted yet."

"I'll allow that," said Clary. "The court will recess for thirty minutes." Clary banged down his gavel. Claxton spoke with Junior for about a minute and then was out the door in a hurry. Everyone was watchin' him hustle on out, but nobody more'n McCluskey. Five minutes turned into ten, and then Claxton was comin' back inside the door with Owen Mercer.

"Your honor," said Claxton. "I'd like to call Owen Mercer back to the stand to testify about some evidence."

"All right everbody," said Clary. "I reckon the recess was ten minutes not thirty, so let's simmer on down." Clary waited for the gallery to come to some kind of order. "Claxton, you finished with Carter?"

"I am, your honor," Claxton nodded.

"Carter, you can step down," said Clary. Carter looked at the judge and then at Claxton as if he wasn't sure that was a smart thing. "Go on ahead. You can be recalled if'n there's a need."

"Yes, your honor," said Carter as he slowly walked back to the defense table. Luwuana reached out and caught his hand with her twisted fingers and held it a second. Neither of them said a word. Then she let go. Junior gave him a pat on the arm as he sat down, and he quickly leaned across to Junior to ask what was goin' on.

"All right, Owen. I think you're get'n good at this now," said Clary. "Once sworn…still sworn." Mercer sat down in the witness stand.

"Your honor," said Claxton. "I'd like to submit defense exhibit 'F', a wallet found on the late Dyle Courtland at the time of his death. A receipt from that wallet was admitted previously, but now I'd like to admit the wallet and all the contents." Claxton walked over to Owen Mercer and handed him the wallet.

"Owen," said Claxton. "Can you identify this wallet?"

"It's Dyle's wallet just like you said," said Mercer. "Got his license an' huntin' permits in here."

"What else has it got?" asked Claxton.

"There's ten dollars in it," said Mercer. Claxton then handed him something else. "And this here is five more dollars that was found in Dyle's pocket."

"What do you notice 'bout these bills right off?" asked Claxton.

"All one dollar bills," answered Mercer with a second glance at them.

"What else?" asked Claxton.

"Had to count 'em three times to get it right," Mercer said. "Bills is sharp 'nough to cut with, like they was just issued."

Claxton walked the bills over to McCluskey and let him examine them. Then he took them to the judge.

"Your honor," said Claxton. "Might we compare these bills with the ones in the cash box?" Woodrow Silas retrieved the cash box, and the judge, Claxton, McCluskey, and Owen Mercer started looking at them all. They had their heads down on the table while they laid out the bills. They finally broke up and went back to the trial.

"Owen, we just now looked at the bills," said Claxton. "Is there one more similarity to them?"

"Sure is," said Mercer. "Those fifteen bills of Dyle's have consecutive serial numbers, an' they match up with the money in the cash box."

"Would you be led to believe then that this money, found on Dyle Courtland, must have come from the cash box of the church?" asked Claxton.

"Cain't see it any other way," said Mercer.

"So, someone took the bills from the cash box and gave them to Dyle," said Claxton. "It would look then like Carter Monroe did not have the church money after all. Dyle didn't own any property, didn't farm any land, so I wonder just how that money came to be on him?"

"He's good," said the reporter in front of me. "Not so sure he couldn't get Judas off with time served."

"George," said Clary. "Got any questions?"

"Plenty," sighed McCluskey, "but not for this witness."

"You're excused again, Owen, but…" said Clary.

"I know. I'll stay close by," said Mercer as he stepped down.

"Now, let's take the rest of that recess," said Clary. "Everybody back at three o'clock."

Chapter Eighteen

"Norm," Claxton began slowly as the afternoon session got underway. Norm Abernathy looked 'bout as comfortable on the witness stand as a fish floppin' on the bank wishin' he was back in the water. "How long have you lived at your present address?"

"My whole life," said Norm Abernathy. "I was born there. I inherited the place when my folks passed on."

"Do you recall the night of the church fire on the Fourth?" asked Claxston.

"I do," answered Abernathy. "Sound of a piece of the roof fallin' woke me up. My whole bedroom was lit up almost like it was daytime."

"You were 'bout the first one there, is that right?" asked Claxton.

"Think I was," Abernathy nodded. "Ran down the way an' set off the alarm. Then right quick there was some others. Then you was there an' we were puttin' water down on the place as best we could."

"When you're at home, where would you be most apt to be found?" asked Claxston.

"Kitchen," he chuckled as he gave his rather round stomach a pat. "Settin' room in the evenin', an' bedroom for sleepin'."

"And where do those rooms all face?" asked Claxton.

"That's the back of the house," said Abernathy. "Settin' room looks out most directly at the edge of the church cemetery. Kitchen window points at the back of the church, an' the bedroom window looks out at the back of the church, too."

"Can you see the side of the church from there?" asked Claxton.

"Might be able," said Abernathy. "Can't say I been ponderin' it much."

"That's all right," said Claxton with a shake of his head. "Let's go back to the night of the fire."

"Hate to think 'bout it myself," said Abernathy.

"I know, but just a few questions," said Claxton. ""Bout the time I was turning on the water all the way from the hydrant, Owen Mercer went runnin' up to the church doors to try an' open 'em up."

"Damn brave thing don't ya think?" Abernathy smiled. "Ain't never seen nothin' like that."

"It was," said Claxton. "But I've been wonderin' all this time…why did he do it?"

"There was folks inside there," said Abernathy. "You'd done the same if you'd known."

"Well, that's just it, Norm," said Claxton. "I didn't know, an' it was middle of the night. I wouldn't have thought 'bout there bein' anybody there at that hour. Why'd Owen think there was somebody in there?"

"Well, there *could'a* been somebody in there," said Abernathy with a sideways look at the judge. He seemed like he was nervous now. "There could'a been and turns out that there was."

"No," Claxton shook his head. "Owen Mercer went up those steps like a man who *knew* there was someone in there, threw himself at those doors an' didn't stop 'til he broke the hinges. You know what I think, Norm?"

"What's that Claxton?" said Abernathy cautiously.

"I think you told him there was somebody in there," said Claxton. "I think you were trying to save somebody's life, Norm. That's what I think."

"Maybe with all the hollerin' an'…an' it was all confused out there," Abernathy began. "Maybe somebody said, 'There someone in there?' an' Owen heard "There's someone in there, an' off he went." Claxton waited for a moment.

"You recall when we were talkin' that day I was lookin' the church grounds over? I asked if you could see the church door," said Claxton.

"I recollect that," said Abernathy.

"You said that you didn't see anybody 'round the door," said Claxton. "Seems like the only door you could see from your house is that little side door that just plain don't open. Only other doors are in the front. If we all know that door don't open, why didn't you say, somethin' like 'Don't know Claxton, I can't see the front doors of the church from back here'?" Abernathy looked 'bout the color of milk right then, but he said nothing.

"Norm, do you know somethin' 'bout that little side door that nobody else does? Do we need to call Owen back in here an' see if he can say who was close enough that he might have heard that there was somebody in the church? Somebody who was right up on the front of that firehose with him?" asked Claxton. Abernathy was silent. "'Spect he'll be madder'n a wet hen, but I'll call him back. Your honor..."

"Don't have to do that," Abernathy sighed and shook his head. "I just didn't want no trouble's all. I promised, an' Claxton, I don't feel right 'bout it either way. Been eatin' at me night'n day, but I cain't see how it helps nobody now."

"Goin' to have to just say it an' let us decide that, Norm," said Claxton. "I've known you a long time. Now get it off your chest. You been shoulder'n it long 'nough now."

"It's 'bout them keys," Norm said quietly. "Riley *had* 'em all these years. After he quit bein' deacon an' moved up into them woods. Well, folks just kinda forgot 'bout 'em. I know I did, an' then the war come on, an' lot o' the church men was off to it. Well, one night, reckon it was back in forty-two, I was up late, had me a bout of indigestion. So I was starin' out the back just bein' miserable an' here comes Riley up to that side door. Well, I'm scratchin' my head tryin' to figure out what he's up to, an' well, sir, he up an' *opens* it right up. Yep, that door that ain't ever been open since nobody can recall. I come on out of the house an' walked over there and went on inside. Ole Riley's up there in the front down on his knees prayin'. I kept back a spell, still tryin' to be respectful an' all. Finally, he gets up an' comes back my way. Then he sees me an' just about runs off, but there ain't no place to run an' he comes back. I asked him what he was up to at dern near two o'clock in the mornin' an he said that he wasn't doin' nothin' but spendin' some time in the church with God. He said he'd been comin' down there once a week for a long time. He wasn't harmin' nobody, an' wasn't doin' nothin', so I told 'em, shux, I *promised* 'em that I'd keep quiet 'bout it. An' I have for all these years. Ever once in a while I'd see 'em comin' or goin'. I'd wave an' he'd wave back if he saw me. Then that night, I seen those flames, an' I said to myself, 'Norm, Riley's done lit him a candle or somethin' an' caught the place up.' It was 'bout the time he would be there. Then I ran out, an' you know the rest."

"Did you see Riley that night?" asked Claxton.

"No, sir," Abernathy shook his head. "Hadn't seen him for a few weeks before that, but that ain't unusual. I didn't see 'em ever time he come an' gone. He's like tryin' to spot a possum that don't want to be seen."

"Did Riley have a key that's not on the other rings?" asked Claxton.

"No, they's all three just alike," said Abernathy with a sigh. "But you're wonderin' 'bout that side door ain't you? Riley's only one I ever saw get it open. It's that littlest key on the ring, not the one we always thought it was. You know, the one Evan Washburne always was jokin' 'bout on Sundays. Lock's got a trick to it, too. I don't know what, though." He looked down for a minute. "I didn't have no idea all this would come of it. I was just tryin' to help ole Riley stay right with God."

"I know you didn't," said Claxton. "I don't think anybody thought somethin' like this could happen. Do you think anyone else could have seen Riley goin' in an' out like you did?"

"Hadn't thought 'bout it," said Abernathy. "Hard to see that side door from the street 'cause it sets back quite aways. Riley was always there when it was dark, an' there ain't no lightin' over there. The minister's house sets on the other side o' mine, course. You thinkin' Evan mighta seen 'em?"

"I was hopin' you might know," said Claxton with a shrug.

"We was right neighborly," said Abernathy, "but I don't recollect him ever talkin' 'bout anything wrong at the church, an' I sure don't recollect him mentionin' Riley. Sorry, Claxton, don't think so."

"That's all right, Norm," said Claxton. "You've been real helpful in helpin' us sort things out here. No further questions, your honor."

"George, your witness," said Clary. McCluskey sat at his table looking through papers. "George, you need some time?"

"No, your honor," said McCluskey as he looked up finally.

"You got any questions for Norm here?" asked Clary.

"No, your honor," said McCluskey. "No questions for this witness."

"Claxton, you got anybody else to call?" asked Clary.

"No, your honor. I wish there was," said Claxton. "I know the court still has some questions, but I don't think they're gonna be answered." It occurred to me right then that the trial was done, and from where I sat, it wasn't no more'n a coin toss if Carter was goin' to get off or not. I wasn't sure if the jury even knew what they thought. Either way, I'd heard a lot of things in that courtroom, an' one way or another most folks was tryin' to do the right thing. Everybody but me, that was.

"Claxton," I said as I stood up from behind the reporter. Claxton turned around.

"I'm a might busy right now, Nathan," Claxton smiled. There was some laughter across the courtroom. "Can it keep a bit?"

"I don't reckon it can," I said. "I got me some things to say, an' I reckon you, Mr. McCluskey, an' Judge Clary ought to be knowin' it."

"Do you know something 'bout what's goin' on here, Nathan?" asked Clary.

"Yes, sir," I said. The courtroom seemed to get 'bout twenty degrees hotter 'bout then an' I could feel ever eye in the place borin' a hole in me.

"Claxton...George, you got anything to say on this?" Clary asked.

"I'd generally prefer not to have children testify, your honor," said McCluskey, "but if he has some evidence to share then maybe we should hear it."

"Reckon he can testify now or when we get home, Harlan," said Claxton. Just 'bout everyone laughed at that.

"Might be good to know who your testifyin' *for*, son," said Clary. "You talkin' for the state or the defense?"

"Reckon I'm just tellin' the truth, sir," I said. "Before all this I didn't know the truth took up sides." Clary rubbed his chin with one hand for a minute.

"That sets okay with me, Nathan," said Clary. "An' your right, when it's done right, truth don't take sides." He looked at me for a whole minute and then out at the courtroom. "Might be something we *all* need to remember. You come on up here an' have a seat. Claxton, you an' George can sit back. I'll ask what needs to be asked, but you can jump in whenever you like." I walked up to the witness stand.

"All right, Nathan," said Woodrow Silas. "You know what it means when you put your hand on this here Bible and say 'I do'?"

"Means I promise to tell the truth," I said. I put my hand on the Bible and raised my other one.

"Do you solemnly swear to tell the truth, the whole truth, and nothin' but the truth, so help you God?" he asked.

"I do," I said barely above a whisper.

"You speak right on up," said Woodrow with almost the same whisper. "You doin' the right thing. That's all that matters now."

"Yes, sir," I said.

"All right, Nathan," said Clary. "Sounds like you got somethin' powerful to tell 'bout. Start right there at the beginnin'."

"Well, sir," I began. "I was out there at the falls that first day that school was out this spring, an' I took me a ride out over it an' was on my way back up to do 'er again when I heard some voices off a little way. I couldn't make 'em out. You know how that canyon echoes a might?"

"I know just what you're talkin' 'bout," Clary nodded patiently. "I used to shout across it when I was a boy."

"Couldn't tell who it was," I said, "but I'm 'bout certain that there was two of 'em, an' they was jawin' back an forth.

They sounded kinda upset like on one but the other mighta been yellin' an' laughin' at the same time. I decided I ought to go on an' get clear o' that, so I done headed up that lower trail a piece. Then I heard it."

"What did you hear, Nathan?" asked Clary.

"Rifle shot, a huntin' rifle it was," I said. "Now I know there ain't 'sposed to be no huntin' up there, but weren't no question it was a shot."

"An' your sure it was a rifle shot?" asked Clary. "Couldn't be no handgun, no shotgun, nor such?"

"No sir," I shook my head. "I been huntin' with Claxton an' heard both of them, an' I seen Sheriff Mercer shootin' targets with his .38 an' that big ole .45 of his. That there sound come from a .22 rifle."

"How many shots in all?" asked Clary with a nod.

"Just one," I said. "Come from right over there by the falls where that jawin' come from."

"An' what time was that?" asked Clary.

"Didn't have no watch on me," I answered. "I reckon I didn't get out to the falls 'till after two o'clock. Probably two-thirty to three o'clock when I heard it. It might just help that coroner fella know when Dyle was killed."

"Your honor," said McCluskey. "That shot could have meant a lot of things. There's no way to know if it was the one that killed Dyle Courtland."

"Could have been somebody else out there shootin'," said Clary.

"Wasn't but a few minutes before I heard somebody runnin' down the trail behind me," I said. "I lit out for home."

"Did you see who was runnin'?" asked Clary.

"No, sir," I shook my head. "Wish I'd had a peek, but no, sir, I didn't see nobody. I can run right fast when I have to."

"Is that everything?" asked Clary.

"Wish it was, judge," I said. "Well, that night I got to thinkin' on that rifle shot, an' that runnin' down the trail. I couldn't sleep so's I went back on out there."

"I'd have heard the floor squeak if you'd gone past," said Claxton.

"Yes, sir," I said. "That's why I went on out the window an' swung down from that big ole maple tree out front. Reckon you'll be sawin' that limb back a might."

"I'll be sharpin' up that saw when we get home," said Claxton. "Goin' to take you a spell to cut through it."

"Yes, sir," I said.

"What came next?" asked Clary.

"I got me the lantern out o' the garage and went back out in the woods," I continued. "Cut over on that middle trail that comes out just under the falls…you know that one?"

"I do," said Clary. "Been on it once or twice with the missus. So you were out there after midnight on that little ole trail. Musta been kinda scary."

"Yes, sir. Wasn't carryin' on like no girl, but I think the hairs on the back a my neck was walkin' 'bout as much as I was."

"I imagine so," said Clary. "Trail clear enough to walk down?"

"Tolerable I 'spect. Folks don't use it much," I said. "So I was walkin' down it kind a slow, an' that's where I seen him layin' dead in the trail."

"You saw Dyle Courtland layin' there," said Clary.

"Yes, sir," I said. "I went up close 'nough to make sure it was a dead body, but I didn't know it was Dyle right then. He was kinda…kinda…et up a bit."

"So you saw there was a dead body," said Clary. "What did you do then?"

"Well, I had to have me a talk with myself 'bout goin' up close enough to see," I said. "When I did get the light on 'em, I had me another talk 'bout keepin' my supper down."

"I 'spect a lot of folks older'n you would a high-tailed it out a there before that," said Clary.

"Was too late to run then," I said. "Didn't figure it to get no worse than that." Clary smiled but didn't laugh.

"What did you do once you knew what was there?" asked Clary.

"There was some coins layin' there in the dirt. I picked 'em up an' I went back on down the trail to go home," I said. "Didn't figure there was nothin' I could do 'bout Dyle."

"Were you goin' to tell 'bout what you found?" asked Clary.

"Knew I had to," I said. "Figured I catch it for bein' out there, but I was set to do it anyway, but then I run right smack into Riley."

"Riley Shimmerhorn?" asked Clary.

"Yes, sir," I answered. "It was him that told me it was Dyle layin' back there. Like I said…Dyle was et up a bit, an' I didn't rightly know it was him."

"Did Riley shoot him?" asked Clary. "He say anything like that? Even accidental like?"

"Course not," I said and shook my head. "Riley couldn't shoot nobody. Oh, he knew Dyle was layin' out there, an' even said he'd get a shovel and help bury 'em if'n I wanted to. You know…just to be Christian like. He didn't know that it wasn't legal to just up an' bury a fella that'd been shot in the woods. 'Bout that time I got me an idea that maybe I could get outa some trouble. I asked him if he'd help me out an' come on into town an' tell the sheriff 'bout Dyle. He was right skittish 'bout it. Was worried somebody might wonder if he'd done it, so's I give him one of the coins I found back up there an' he thought on it, an' then said he'd do it so's I wouldn't get in no trouble. 'Spect I got me all the trouble I'm ever gonna be needin' right now anyway."

"Cain't say 'bout that," said Clary, "but we know Riley was there next mornin' to find Owen Mercer and tell him 'bout Dyle."

"Your honor," said McCluskey, "I think that all this helps to do is establish the time of death of Dyle Courtland, and possibly that he was killed by one person acting alone. I'm not sure it tells us anything about this case, however."

"Anything else, Nathan?" Clary asked.

"Just one thing," I shrugged. "Don't know how it figures in, but that coin I done give to Riley? It weren't no ordinary coin. It was a 1874 double eagle twenty-dollar gold piece. It's down the street over in Mr. Bardwells' jewelry store right now."

"Are you certain it's the same coin?" asked McCluskey.

"Couldn't be no other," I nodded. "Mr. Bardwell bought it off Bernie Chesterfield that sells coins, an' stamps, cards'n such, and they say it's real rare."

"Then perhaps Riley Shimmerhorn knew the same thing and sold it to Mr. Chesterfield," said McCluskey.

"Thought 'bout that, but don't see how," I said. "I done me some more askin' an' found out from Mr. Bardwell that the coin was sent to Bernie Chesterfield by special delivery after he got him a call, so's he didn't know who it was. He bought the coin an' sent the money back the way it come. Well, I was up yonder at the falls again after it was all right to be up there again, an' I went on up to Riley's cabin. It was all tore into, an' the knife an' all was just like Sheriff Mercer said. I got me to thinkin' that maybe somebody went back out there lookin' for that coin an' didn't find it where they figured. Then maybe they got to figurin' that Riley come on it an' took it. Somebody sure enough took that coin from Riley an' maybe that somebody killed Dyle, too, an' maybe got hold o' Riley's keys an' killed the minister and Odessa. I told Claxton 'bout Riley's cabin, an' you know the rest."

"Certainly an exciting tale there," said McCluskey with a raised eyebrow. "Let's also consider the imagination of a young boy, out in the dark, maybe a little scared…"

"I was scared *plenty*," I said. There was laughter again in the courthouse.

"Exactly that, Nathan," said McCluskey with a smile. "Sometimes, a person gets scared, and they don't remember things just the way they happened."

"I reckon I was just as scared," came a voice from the back of the courtroom. "But I recollect it was just like Nathan says it was." Everyone turned to see who was talking. It was Willie.

"Come on down here, son," said Clary. "Was this boy with you *all* this time?"

"Shux, Willie, you done it now," I said as he walked down the aisle between the chairs. "Now we're both gonna get in trouble."

"Reckon I can help you saw on that limb now," said Willie with a grin. He looked over at McCluskey. "I was more scared'n Nathan, but if he's lyin' I'll be tellin' the same one."

"You were there at the falls?" asked McCluskey.

"There an' again that night," Willie nodded. "Nathan come by my house that night, an' I was up worryin' 'bout the same thing. I jumped down out my window...ain't high like Nathan's, an' we went out there to have a look see. Then later I went up there to the cabin with Nathan an' it was just like he said it was."

"That it now?" Clary asked. Willie and I looked at each other.

"Spect it is," I said.

"Then you can step down," said Clary. "I'm glad you boys owned up. Just don't be so long in doin' it next time. Might be better if you don't *need* a next time."

"Yes, sir," I said as I got up and jumped down from the stand.

"All right," Clary sighed. "Has anybody else got anything else they'd like to talk 'bout here today? Anybody know 'bout this coin business?" Everyone in the room looked around.

"Junior had him an idea," I called back down as I was sitting back down behind the reporter.

"Junior?" asked Clary.

"Yes, your honor?" asked Junior as he stood up.

"Let's put that college book learnin' to use," said Clary. "What's Nathan get'n at?"

"I think he's talking about the special delivery," said Junior. "He asked about it at dinner. He was wanting to know who might have delivered something valuable to another town. I said that Cliff Masters might do something like that. He brought back some very...expensive...paintings to town once as I seem to recall."

"Ugly-as-sin..." Del Hardaway coughed and everyone in the courthouse roared in laughter. "Sorry, your honor."

205

"Cliff, are you out there somewhere?" asked Clary as he looked around the courtroom.

"I'm here," said a tall, thin, graying man with a long beard.

"What you know 'bout all this?" asked Clary.

"Didn't know I knew nothing," said Masters, "but I *did* run a little package out to Bernie Chesterfield in Fayette, an' I brought back a' envelope just like you heard."

"Cliff, you could sure ease up this headache I got startin' right now," said Clary, "if you could tell us who sent this coin up the road an' who got the envelope when you got back."

"Wish I could, Harlan," said Masters. "I got that package just settin' inside my tow truck early one mornin'. It had some typed up directions to call Bernie over in Fayette and tell him there was a coin for sale he might be interested in. The note said to ask for four hundred dollars but take no less'n two hundred. Bernie offered two twenty five for it, so I carted it up there and brought back the money after he looked it over."

"And who did you give the money to?" asked McCluskey.

"I didn't get a chance," said Masters. "I set that envelope down right next to my cash register on the counter and went in back to set down my lunch. I reckon somebody was watchin' for me, 'cause that envelope was gone when I came back out 'bout a minute later. I looked 'round to see if maybe it'd fell off. I even walked out the door. Didn't see nobody anywhere. I reckon whoever picked it up was the one that give me the coin 'cause I never had anybody come callin' for the money."

"Right slippery fella," said Clary. "Reckon we should have had Cliff sworn in. George, Claxton are you okay with takin' what he said without an oath."

"Under the circumstances, the state has no objections, your honor," said McCluskey.

"No objections, your honor," said Claxton.

"This is for the jury," said Clary. "You are to take what Cliff Masters just said just like he would have said it if he was sittin' right up here in this chair next to me." Clary turned back to the court.

"I think if I was to sit on the bench for 'nother hundred years I'd not hear 'nother case like this one," said Clary. "Claxton, you got anything else?"

"The defense rests, your honor," said Claxton.

"Think you boys can wrap up in an hour?" asked Clary. "I want the jury to hear the closin' arguments right together."

"The state will be brief, your honor," said McCluskey. He looked at Claxton.

"I'll leave my hat on the table, your honor," said Claxton.

"All right, closing arguments, then," said Clary. "George, whenever you're ready to start. Claxton headed back to his table.

"Thank you, your honor," said McCluskey as he walked out in front of the jury box. "You gentlemen are charged today with the task of deciding what the *truth* in this case is. As one witness very candidly reminded us, 'the truth doesn't take sides', and that is what you have to determine here today. What exactly is the truth? You have been presented with a lot of facts, a lot of opinions, and a lot of evidence. Some of that evidence has seemed to be contradictory at times, but that is the nature of a trial. We don't always know which pieces of evidence are important and which ones are not. Sometimes there is evidence that we don't even know is there, and sometimes there is evidence that isn't really evidence at all. What I want you to do now is step back from your close examination of the case and give thought to what is actually known in this case. There were two victims whose murders call out to you for justice. There is an empty gas can, which, in all probability, was used to start the fire. We have the keys to the church found locked inside a shed with only one *proven and known* key that could have locked them there, and we know who the owner of those keys is. The critical elements that are required to convict the defendant are all present here. The defendant had opportunity in that he cannot be proven to be elsewhere other than by his own testimony. Secondly, there was motive, retaliation for the burning down of two black churches, or possibly to conceal the theft of church money from a cash box that, again, only the defendant and the victim had access to. And third…there is the evidence, a gas can familiar to the defendant, in a shed that he commonly used, and locked with keys that only he has been proven to possess. Let me emphasize the word…*proven*. You have heard much testimony about a third set of keys to the church. Even if those keys did, and perhaps do still exist, there is no *proof* that they were used in the commission of this crime." McCluskey paused for a long minute. "When I was a much younger attorney, a very wise attorney, that I often met in the courtroom, once said that the answer we are seeking is almost always the simplest one." He gave Claxton a long glance, and I thought that I knew right where he had heard that bit of advice. "Gentlemen, I think that is precisely the case we have here today. As complicated as the defense would like you to believe this all is, the simplest answer is right before you. The defendant, Carter Monroe, did, in fact, pour gasoline over the interior of the Baptist Church of God, and that he did with premeditation and malice take the keys that could have allowed the victims to escape a terrible death, and then locked them within the church. I think when you go to your deliberations that you will return the only verdict that is simplest and most possible, guilty of arson, guilty of the murder of Evan Washburne, guilty of the murder of Odessa Hendricks. Thank you." McCluskey gave a nod to the judge and made his way back to his table. Claxton rose and they passed on the way between the tables. If there was a look between them, I didn't see it, but I'd bet that there was.

"Gentlemen of the jury," Claxton began as he walked in front of them. "It sounds kind'a odd to hear that doesn't it? We think of ourselves as the citizens of Josiah Falls. We are neighbors, friends, and relatives, but the word *jury* has a special meaning for us. It's that job that you hope never falls on you. It doesn't matter if the crime is murder or spittin' on the sidewalk, it's hard to sit there and know that somebody else's life is restin' in the palm of your hands. The decision you make today can give life or take it away. An' that decision *should* be hard. It *must* be hard. It makes us think…what if it was me sittin' over there waitin' for my friends to decide over me? But for the grace of God, could sit anyone of us, but today the defendant is Carter Monroe. His biggest crime? He can't prove where he was at one o'clock in the mornin' on July the fifth. How many of you could prove that? I don't reckon I could. How many of you knew that Evan Washburne left the church keys there on that little table inside the doors? Probably most of us. But now your thinkin' who else had a set of keys to the church an' could have locked those keys up in the tool shed? The answer? Could have been any one of us. That's right. Any one of us. Anyone could have gone up there to Riley's cabin an' taken them, an' maybe just to do just what was done. We know that he had them not but a short spell before the fire. All they would have needed to do was see Riley open that door once, maybe just sneakin' away one night, to know that he had them. Now 'bout the evidence in the shed. How many gas cans do you think Carter Monroe's screwed on an' off in his lifetime? Do you think he couldn't figure out the cap wasn't on when it didn't turn but one time? How many times you figure he's done work with his hands before first light in the mornin' or after dark late at night? Carter Monroe could assemble a carbine rifle in the dark. And, why would he put evidence that could only point right at him where it could be so very easily found? If it was *you*, what would you have done with those keys? Would you have buried them? Maybe dropped them down a well? Maybe tossed 'em into the Mississippi? Carter Monroe's a *military* man, was one most of his adult life. The military has a *way* of doin' things. It's like marchin'. You put one foot out in front of the other. You do it any other way, you're apt to trip an' fall on your face an' every man behind you will walk up your back and down the other side. Everything is thought out. I'll grant…there was a lot of things *thought* out in the comittin' of this crime…except for the most important ones…what to do with the evidence? There's only two reasons those keys would be in that shed. Either the person that put them there was too scared to know it…you all heard what Carter did while he was busy bein' shot at over there in Europe, an' it don't sound like he scares easy at all….or somebody put those keys there thinkin' that it would point away from them an' right at Carter." Claxton walked back and forth once and then stopped. "Do you recall when all this started? I said that all you had to walk away to that jury room with was just one, single...solitary...reasonable doubt. Unless you can say in your mind, and live with your conscience clear for the rest of your days, that you have no doubt whatsoever, then the only verdict that you can even think about returnin' is one of not guilty on all counts. Let me remind you all that no one was seen comin' or goin' from the church, an' there are no eye witnesses. There's no finger prints anywhere that shouldn't by right be there and no proven motive for comittin' these crimes. In my way of thinkin' that's more'n just *reasonable* doubt...that is a great big ole mountain o' doubt. So, gentlemen of the jury, what you are goin' to have to do is look at the man you've known over there for a lot of years, some of you your whole lives, an' weigh him against this crime. Mr. McCluskey was right when he said that the simplest answer is almost always the right one. Now I know that everyone here wants to see justice done, and everyone here thinks someone ought to be brought to task for doin' this, but we need to make sure that we bring the *guilty* to answer for what was done. If we don't do that, then we don't do justice. If you don't find Carter Monroe innocent, then justice hasn't been done. I thank you." Claxton walked slowly back to his table and sat down.

"Can you call it?" I asked to the reporter.

"Looks like a jury that just doesn't know what to think," he said. "Can't say I do either."

"Then I reckon that's it then," I said. "If you don't know, you can't say that you do."

"Maybe you're right, Nathan," said the reporter with a shake of his head. "That does just about define 'reasonable doubt' I reckon."

"All right," said Clary. "I'd like to thank Mr. George McCluskey for tryin' this case for the state and Mr. Claxton Delaney for tryin' this case for the defense. Junior Preston, you done just fine your first time out. I don't know 'bout anybody else, but I think both sides was represented as well as could be done. Now, first thing's first. Mr. Foreman of the jury?"

"Yes, your honor?" said Reuban James.

"I'm goin' to send y'all off to talk this out," said Clary. "You can have five minutes or five weeks. It don't make no difference to the court. You want to see any of the evidence, you just poke your head out the door to Woodrow an' he'll get it for you. You want to have some testimony read back, we got it all written down right here. He'll get you that, too. Eat when you want and sleep when you want. But here's the thing…all twelve of you got to come to one decision. It's all one way or all the other. Don't come back in three hours and tell me you can't get together. You keep talkin' it out until you do. If there's a problem that Woodrow can't handle for you, then you send word to me. Got any questions?"

"No, your honor," said James. "Think we know what we got to do now."

"All right then," said Clary. "Woodrow, take 'em on out." I watched Woodrow Silas lead the jury out of the box and past the judge, then out the door.

"Y'all know as much as I do 'bout when they'll be back," said Clary. "This court stands adjourned until the jury comes back with a verdict. Now just to let you all know, I don't think we'll read it today as it's now get'n late, an' won't be before ten o'clock tomorrow mornin' at the earliest 'cause I'm sleepin' late an' don't none of you wake me up." Clary got up and left out the back of the courtroom to his office. I walked down towards the front. Owen was getting ready to collect Carter and get him back to the jail.

"Counselor," I heard George McCluskey saying. "It's been a pleasure, sir."

"Thank you, George," said Claxton. "Don't think you've missed a beat, maybe better than ever."

"Think this will give you the itch to get back into law?" asked McCluskey with a rare smile on his face.

"Don't think so, George," Claxton shook his head.

"I'm afraid you're not going to stay a secret here much longer," said McCluskey. "For myself, I've missed our run-in's, and I hope you change your mind."

"I 'preciate you sayin' that, George," said Claxton.

"And don't go too hard on him," said McCluskey when he spotted me nearby. "We were boys once."

"I'll take that under advisement, counselor," Claxton smiled. I wasn't sure what that meant exactly, but I thought maybe I *might* get off with a lighter sentence than I had first reckoned.

Chapter Nineteen

"I'd a spoke up sooner if I'd known right off there was somethin' to it," I said once we had gotten home.

"I know that," said Claxton. "I wish you'd have trusted me to tell me a little sooner, but I'm proud that you stood up an' told the truth when you did."

"I didn't want Willie get'n in trouble is all," I said. "Didn't want to get in trouble myself, an' it didn't seem like nobody was get'n hurt by it."

"Sometimes it's like that," said Claxton. "You take that little step 'cross the line from what's true to what's not…it's still *mostly* true for a while. Pretty soon, you can't see the line behind you anymore, an' you don't know the difference."

"Seems easier to go on as go back," I said. "But it don't do nothin' but get deeper when you goes on."

"You made a man's decision today," said Claxton. "I know that for certain. If you'd not spoke up, nobody'd known, an' that's what it's 'bout…doin' the right thing, an' the good thing 'bout it is you can start anytime you want."

"Do you reckon Carter will get off?" I asked.

"I don't know, Nathan," Claxton shook his head. "A jury will tend to latch onto one thing during a trial. In this here trial, I think they latched onto those keys. Those keys were the one thing that was solid. You could pick them up an' look at them. Riley's keys, now those keys never turned up in all this, so the jury can't see 'em. The jury is the one that's got to decide if those keys are *real enough* to be evidence. Courtroom is a funny place, it ain't always, an' most times it's not, 'bout what you an' everybody *know*. It's 'bout what you can *prove*. Those two things don't always show up together."

"I think I understand what you're saying there," I nodded. "All them objections an' stuff was 'bout that."

"That's right," said Claxton. "We both *knew* things that we wanted to say, we just couldn't always prove them. My job was to catch him doin' it, an' his job was to catch me doin' it. An' the judge was supposed to catch both of us. Now it's up to the jury."

The evening passed and we went on to bed at a regular time for the first time in what had seemed like a long time. Folks in town tried to go 'bout their business like usual, but they were all keepin' one eye on the courthouse. The reporters were scattered 'round the courthouse and the eatin' places in town. They were watchin' the courthouse for any signs that the jury was back as well. The morning turned into afternoon, and by three o'clock there was still no word. I heard folks sayin' how it meant Carter was guilty while others said that them not rushin' back in meant he wasn't. I heard some of the reporters talkin' 'bout there maybe bein' a hung jury. First time I'd heard that they might hang the jury if they didn't come up with a decision. I asked Claxton 'bout that right away. He just laughed and said that it just meant the jury couldn't agree, and that there might have to be a new trial. Claxton said that he'd waited as much as a week for a jury to come back once. George McCluskey was sittin' there with Claxton most of the day at either the courthouse or 'cross the street get'n coffee. It was hard for me to see how they could go at each other so much in the courtroom, but seem more like fishin' buddies after it was over. I asked 'bout that. Claxton just said that nothin' that happened in that room was ever personal.

George McCluskey said that all that was important was seein' that justice was done. He said he didn't want to see an innocent man go to jail any more'n he wanted to see a guilty one go free. Much as I wanted to ask him if he thought Carter was guilty or not, I somehow didn't. I didn't think he'd answer that one anyway. A couple minutes after four, there was a stirrin' up on the steps of the courthouse. One of the reporters was wavin' back and forth.

"Jury's back!" he hollered. That done it. Everybody came runnin' from all over. The only ones that didn't get in a big hurry was Claxton and George McCluskey. I jumped up, excited an' ready to run.

"Don't reckon they'll start without us, Nathan," said Claxton as they began walkin' up the steps from the shady bench where they'd been sittin' for the last half hour. I slipped inside with everyone else and stood in the back since there was no way to get any closer or find a seat by then. It was a few more minutes before I saw Claxton and George McCluskey walk in through the side door. A minute or so later, Woodrow brought in the jury. They filed by in two lines and sat down up in the jury box six in front and six in the back. Judge Clary walked in and sat down.

"All right," said Clary. "Court will come to order." He banged the gavel down hard a couple of times. "It's my understandin' from Woodrow that y'all got yourself a verdict. That right, Reuben?"

"That's right, your honor," answered James.

"The defendant will rise," said Clary. Carter, Junior, and Claxton all stood up. "The foreman will read the verdict."

"On the count of aggravated arson," said James, "the jury finds the defendant…not guilty. On the two charges of murder in the first degree, the jury finds the defendant not guilty." The courtroom erupted in cheers, yells, and general confusion. I saw Judge Clary just sittin' there. He didn't bother bangin' his gavel 'cause nobody would have heard him anyway. After a couple of minutes, he did get everyone to quiet down.

"Mr. Foreman, jury," said Clary. "Thank you, and you are dismissed. Owen, you can let Carter go on home when he sees fit. George, I'll go ahead an' ask you if the state will be filin' an appeal."

"No your, honor," said McCluskey. "Based on the evidence available, I don't think the state will want to retry at the appellate level." He walked across to the defense table and shook Claxton's hand. Then he shook Junior's hand. I was a little surprised, but he even shook Carter's hand, too. The courtroom gradually broke up, an' folks started goin' on their way. The reporters went 'bout get'n the rest of their stories for their papers. The two lawyers and Judge Clary made a few remarks to them all as a group and then said that was all they had to say. Owen Mercer had a bunch of questions about investigatin' the case, and he told them all that the three homicides would remain open for as long as he was sheriff there. Carter Monroe went on and became a downright celebrity, though. Everyone wanted to know 'bout his wartime service an' all the facts behind what Washington was investigatin' there. One reporter had done checked, and said that the committee was tryin' to decide if he was goin' to get the Medal of Honor. That by itself just 'bout set the whole town on its ear.

Little by little, Josiah Falls got back to what passed for normal those days. The baseball season went on and ended, and pretty soon Willie an' me were back in school. The events of that summer slowly faded in folks memories, and after a while folks stopped whisperin' an' pointin' when Carter come in to town. Nobody ever fessed up to the church burnings or the murders that summer. By the end of the year, the Baptist Church had been rebuilt enough to hold services there again, and Claxton went back to his regular job of treatin' patients for whatever ailed them. He took on a few legal jobs from time to time like he had before, but after the trial he made it clear that he wasn't goin' back to arguing big-time criminal cases. Eventually, the calls comin' in from all over the state started to ease up and finally stopped. As for Riley Shimmerhorn, well, he turned up in a New Orleans hospital after wakin' up from a coma in January of the next year. He'd been found in his fishin' boat with the back of his head 'bout busted in when he was just 'bout to float out into the Gulf of Mexico. He didn't recollect much of anything, an' didn't know who'd clobbered him over the head, but he did say that he'd had the keys to the church until somebody had come up from behind him an' give him that big ole headache that lasted near on seven months. He didn't remember the coin at all…even when he saw it again up close, an' he didn't remember Dyle Courtland bein' dead out there in the woods either. Claxton said that he might not recall some things ever again, but then again…they might come back one day. By the next spring, Riley was up an' around again, an' livin' back in his cabin, but he if he ever recalled who else he might have seen in the woods that hot afternoon in 1950, he never mentioned it. He didn't make any more secret visits to the church either. The new minister who visited each Sunday just up an' gave him a key to the place an' told him to come on anytime he had a mind to.

Chapter Twenty

I pulled up outside the Baptist Church of Josiah Falls and parked there on the street. The church looked a lot like it had from before the fire, although it had taken a lot to fix up those big oak doors again. The old tool shed was gone now. It had been torn down and replaced with a new pre-fabricated building. I could still see the courthouse down the street from where I sat, and it still looked like it had during that hot eventful summer of 1950. Main Street still had some of the old places, but many of them had closed and shut their doors for good. The only thing that had kept the town alive at all had been the farm of Carter Monroe. Most of the people who had stayed in Josiah Falls either worked at the farm, or worked in some business that supported it. The farm had grown to almost ten thousand acres and supported everything from some dairy cattle to chickens aside from the regular produce. A little piece of the land had even yielded a dozen oil wells and was now a part of the Monroe Oil Company. Carter Monroe passed on in 1983. His grandson accepted his Distinguished Service Medal and Medal of Honor in 1993 after a German survivor of his heroics was located and testified to it before a Congressional committee.

Behind the church cemetery, I could see the minister's house where Evan Washburne and his wife had lived more than a half century ago, and I could see a little piece of Norm Abernathy's place where one night Norm had been up late and seen Riley Shimmerhorn sneaking into the Baptist church. On the drive into town, I had driven down Maynard Street and seen Willie's old house. Willie and I had gone off to Vietnam in 1963. He was the sergeant in company 'A' and I was the sergeant of company 'B'. He was killed in action in 1965, and there had been a folded flag tucked in the corner of the front window of the house for years after that. The house was closed up now, and Willie's folks had long since passed on. He had a brother someplace, but I'd lost track of him a long time ago.

"What you thinkin' 'bout Chief?" said the young detective next to me.

"Just rememberin' things," I said. "Let's go on in."

We walked up through the cemetery. I saw the graves of Dyle Courtland, Evan Washburne, and Odessa Hendricks as I passed by. There were a lot more names out there that I recalled as well. We came up past the back of the old minister's house and rounded the corner to the front porch. I rang the bell once and gave the door a few knocks. I heard someone moving around after that and waited. An ancient woman arrived at the door and peered out the screen at us.

"Can I help you?" she said in a cracking voice.

"I was hoping we could visit with you for a few minutes if you don't mind," I said. "My name is Delaney and this is detective Reardon."

"One my great-gran'chillin in trouble o' somethin'?" she asked.

"Nothing like that," I shook my head. "Just wanted to catch up with you on some old times. See I used to live here a long time ago."

"I see," she nodded. "Well, come on in." We followed her inside and sat down on the old sofa in the front room while she sat down in the rocker a few feet away.

"I don't know if you remember me," I said, "but maybe you'll remember this." I stretched out my hand and dropped an 1874 double eagle gold piece into hers. She stared at it but said nothing.

"It took me a long time to trace down that coin," I said after a few minutes as she looked it over in silence. "I bought it from old Simon Bardwell after I asked him to hold it for me until I had the money. Took me three years of workin' all kinds of jobs to save up for it, and I've had it all these years. I started doing some research on it, but I never found out much. Then one day a few months ago, I ran across a picture from an auction magazine. It had a picture of a hand of playin' cards. A pair of black aces an' eights it was. And there in the picture was an 1874 double eagle gold piece. That was the Dead Man's Hand that Wild Bill Hickok was playin' when he was shot in the back of the head by Jack McCall an' killed way back in 1876. An' that gold piece was on the table there at Nuttal and Mann's saloon in Deadwood. Well, somebody kept those cards and that gold piece an' it got sold a few times. The last time was to a man named Leonard Carson. Well, I tracked Mr. Carson down and found that he had lived in Josiah Falls for a little while and then moved on. He left behind a couple of things when he left. One of them was a poker hand with a gold piece. The other was a daughter named Addie." I glanced over at the wall and saw the playing cards still up there in the frame where they had been sixty years earlier. There was a small round spot where the paper was not quite as faded, and I knew that was where the gold piece had once been mounted.

"Reckon I never figured to see that ole coin of daddy's again," she shook her head and smiled sadly for the first time.

"Don't guess you did," I said. "Seems like it just kept turnin' up that summer of 1950. I went back to the old case an' I had the DNA run on everything again. Couldn't do that sort of thing back then, or maybe Owen Mercer would have solved this case. Anyway, I found some old-timers down in Natchez that said that Odessa was seein' Dyle Courtland that spring. It was her that he was havin' dinner with down there in Natchez the night one of the churches were burned. It was his baby she was carryin' when she died in the fire."

"Dyle?" she said with a shake of her head. "That cain't be. She was seein' *Evan* all the time. Never once saw her with Dyle."

"It is," I said. "The DNA was a match, no mistake on that. There were also some other things the old-timers in Natchez remembered. Odessa wasn't the only girl he took there that spring. Folks down there recalled another girl who always seemed to be wearing a hat or something and trying not to be seen, but she was and a few of them even had a name. Dyle called her Addie." I waited for a minute to see if she had anything to say. "I also found some medical records on Evan Washburne from a doctor he'd seen in Jackson, and they confirmed something else that another doctor I talked to said as well. It seems that Evan had a bad case of the mumps when he was twenty-four. Both doctors said that it probably made him sterile. Nobody could guarantee it then, but it was likely. I imagine he would have been real surprised to have found out he was going to be a daddy. Course, he wasn't was he?"

"Dyle just couldn't keep from runnin' his mouth," the old woman shook her head. "Then he was wantin' money, or else he was goin' to tell Evan."

"He was blackmailing you," I finished for her. "He was going to tell Evan about the two of you." She nodded.

"I gave him money," she said. "Twice...I did, but he kept on wantin' more, so I took that gold piece up there. I knew it was worth a lot an' I thought it would keep him quiet." She shook her head slowly. "He just laughed at me an' said it'd do for a start, but I didn't have nothin' else, an' I couldn't just keep takin' from the church. We started yellin' back an' forth, an' then I saw his gun just sittin' there."

"And you shot him," I said. She nodded.

"I just done it," she said. "Didn't think 'bout it none."

"I figured that," I said. "But why burn down the church? Why Evan and Odessa?"

"Because I thought they was..." she began. "I knew she was pregnant an' all an' she was seein' Evan regular all the time. I just knew it was his baby." She pounded her thigh with a bony fist. "She was just scared wasn't she? Dyle wasn't goin' to be no daddy, an' she was lookin' for help. Then later he was dead. Whyn't she just ask me for help?" There were tears running down her face now. "I was her friend. Why was she tryin' to hide it from *me*?"

"I think she knew about you and Dyle," I said. "Maybe she thought you were going to leave Evan for Dyle because he could give you a baby and Evan never could. Everyone knew how important a baby was to you."

"That wasn't it at all," she shook her head tearfully. "I wouldn't have *ever* left Evan. What happened with Dyle...I done it *for* Evan. It was wrong an' I knew it, but I tole Evan that I just *had* to have a child, an' he just couldn't, an' then I couldn't take it *back*. It was eatin' him up from the inside. I seen it ever time he looked at me. Then he was gone for a spell up to Jackson, so I thought I could make it right for him. He would have been a *good* daddy. I didn't even want Dyle to know, but he saw me gett'n some pills an' figured it out."

"How'd Carter get mixed up in it?" I asked.

"I didn't want nothin' to happen to Carter," she said. "You got to believe that. I just tossed down them keys when I was tryin' to get the cap back on that blamed can. Locked up and run off." Wasn't 'till next day, I seen that I had Riley's keys an' I'd left Evan's in the shed. I never figured anyone'd think Carter coulda done somethin' like that. I wanted to say somethin'. I was hopin' an' prayin' that Claxton would get him off. The Lord was listenin' I reckon." I looked at the coin in her hand and saw the long deep scar in her palm.

"Is that why you started wearing gloves all the time?" I asked. "You cut your hand up at Riley's cabin?"

"My hand was hurtin' from where I'd banged Riley upside the head with a piece a wood. Knife slipped when I hit them keys in the mattress…or maybe it was that coin," she said. "Both of 'em was in there." She shook her head. "That blame coin…just no get'n away from it is there?" She was silent for a moment. "I done killed my friend an' my husband. I reckon you'll be lockin' me up for it." She stared at the floor silently for a very long time as if she was recalling all of those events from that long ago summer. "Said your name was Delaney, did you?" she asked finally.

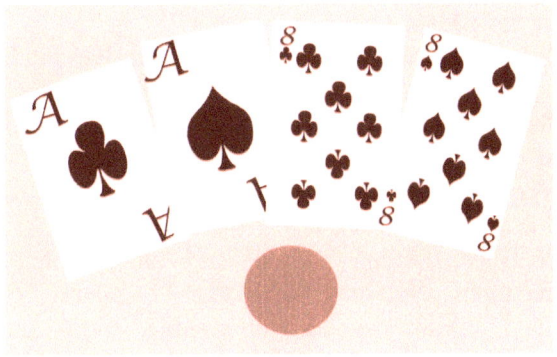

"I ate cookies over at that table in yonder back in 1950 while Claxton was talkin' to you right here in this room," I said. "Even saw that frame with the poker hand, but I didn't even know what I was seein' until years later when I ran into the picture of it with the coin next to the cards."

"You must be Claxton's boy, Nathan," she shook her head again. I nodded and stood up.

"We'll be on our way now," I said.

"I done murdered…done it three times," she said. "Ain't you goin' to do nothin' 'bout it?"

"I did," I answered. "I always thought I'd solve this case, and I must have had twenty suspects over the years, but you were never one of them until I saw that picture in the paper.

Then I figured that Norm Abernathy wasn't the only one that saw Riley going into the church one night; then, I knew. I was still wondering what I would do when I got here, but I was thinking about what Claxton would have said, and it kind of came to me what I should do. I brought that coin home to you, so you could put it with the poker hand. They never caused any trouble 'til they got split up. I figured that coin was just trying to get back to where it belonged. Ought to go to your grandchildren. And, it's time for you to let go of what you've been thinkin' about Evan and Odessa all these years. The law can't punish you any more than you already have been." I looked around. "You never moved an inch from this place. It's been your prison, in a way, looking out over that cemetery. It's over now. Make your peace with it."

"Ma'am," said Reardon. "We'll see ourselves out."

"Is Mama okay?" said a small man dressed in black as he hurriedly approached the house. "I saw the government tag on your car over there."

"Everything's fine. Just paying a social call," I explained. "I used to live here in Josiah Falls a long time ago." I saw the concern leave the man's face, and for the first time I recognized him. "You must be Minister Washburne."

"I am," Washburne said with a smile. "Going on twenty years now. Took over when Minister Ashe passed on. Should I know you, sir?"

"I don't suppose so," I said. "I left town when you were probably just a kid still. Nathan DeLaney." I put out my hand and he shook it.

"Evan Washburne, Jr." the man said with an eerily familiar smile. I squinted closely at the man. He was now about sixty I thought, and I was surprised by how *unlike* Dyle Courtland he looked. In my mind's eye I aged the Minister Evan Washburne that died when he was thirty, and this was very much the face I would have come up with. There were a lot of things on my mind at the moment, but I said none of them. I supposed that Addie Washburne would have known just exactly what was on my mind just then.

"I was talking about some old times with your mother," I said. "She might just need someone to talk to just now." I paused for a moment. "The Lord does move in mysterious ways, doesn't He, Minister?"

"That he does, Mr. DeLaney," said Washburne. We left without another word and walked back out across the cemetery. I stopped for a moment along the way at a tall marble marker that said simply enough, 'Claxton Delaney' across the top, and asked Claxton if he was good with it.

"Did I do it right, Claxton?" I asked. "Did we see justice done?" He didn't say, but I thought he might just be right as rain with the way it turned out. As we passed by and I looked back on Josiah Falls Cemetery for what I figured to be the last time, I hoped that all the rest of the ghosts out there would finally make their peace as well. At least I'd made mine. I thought back a bit on an old backwoods country lawyer and the things he taught me that helped me become a man. It took me sixty years, but I finally got to the end of that summer of 1950 and turned that last page in time.

The town and characters of Josiah Falls, Mississippi are works of fiction. Any similarity to any person living or dead is completely unintentional.